BRUTAL PROMISE

A DARK MAFIA ROMANCE

VOLKOV BRATVA SERIES

ZOE BETH GELLER

KINKY INK PUBLISHING, LLC

BRUTAL PROMISE

Copyright © 2023 Zoe Beth Geller
Kinky Ink Publishing
All rights reserved.
Cover Design Shephard Designs

INTRODUCTION

I hope you enjoy this book as much as I did. It is mafia lite-ish with a morally grey character who defends his new acquaintance. This combines many mafia tropes and all the smaller mafia elements we've come to love.
This contains
Touch her and you …
Never let her go
Possessive alpha
Wounded MMC
Beast
FMC who brings light
Suspense & Mystery
Spicy Scenes
and so much more!

XO,
Zoe

ACKNOWLEDGMENTS

Special thanks to edited by Sherri Shackelford and my ARC Proofreaders Maureen Riley, Jeanne Jabour.

CHAPTER 1

DMITRY

The view of the New York City skyline never grows old as we prepare to land at JFK airport. The commercial overseas flight is jam-packed with families. Men and women who are on business trips work on their computers. The only positive on the trip is an attractive flight attendant who kept my cocktails coming. She spoke English and Russian, so we flirted in both languages. There's something about my brooding nature that attracts women to me. I prefer to stick to myself. However, she's a pretty Russian. I'm sure she'd be happy with a quick fuck and wouldn't complain when I left her after I'd finished with her. I remind myself that I'm here to help a friend.

The flight from London is always long. The business class seat gives me more legroom than the standard seat, but it's not like the family jet I've become accustomed to. Nikolay is using it this week. My left leg hurts like a son of a bitch, and the vodka eases the pain. It's stiff from sitting, so I adjust my seat. When my butt goes numb, I get up and walk in the aisle. I need to keep my blood flowing. It's a reminder of a drug deal that went sideways with the Italians. They were bent on flipping my car and didn't care if I burned alive.

One trigger-happy motherfucker is all it took to be a thorn in my side. It's another reason I'm not partial to the Cosa Nostra because their fighting spills blood in the streets. I'm not trusting, and it's what keeps me alive. I have rules I live by. Is it a superstition or a deeply held belief? I never leave a loose end that could come back and bite me in the ass. My world is dark, and I embrace it as it's all I've ever known. It's the world I share with my brothers.

If Nikolay were traveling with me, we'd have used the jet. This is not an official business trip for the family but a social call to a friend who needs me. It's a predominant skill set I have—hacking. I developed it living in the underworld. I can't escape the family business, nor do I want to. I want to weed out unsavory men in the brotherhood, and it seems my friend has a thief to catch.

As the plane taxis to the gate, I pop my earbuds out. They come in handy to discourage conversations with strangers, especially the female passenger sitting next to me, who kept talking. I wasn't interested and ignored her to watch a mafia movie on my phone.

This trip is as close to a vacation as I'll ever get unless it's a honeymoon. And I don't see that happening. Seeing my oldest brother getting married recently was a shock. But it's his responsibility to carry on the family name and produce the next Bratva King. I have no wish for brats to feed. If I did find a woman, I wouldn't want to share her breasts with a little urchin.

I'm stifled at home, living in my mostly landlocked country, where every day looks like the last. I'm sure this is why I dream of visiting the beaches of Bali, maybe even floating on a surfboard. I'm tired of traveling only for business. Going somewhere where no one knows me or my past would be nice, even if it's only for a few days. I'd have to go that far for my name not to be recognized once my father's or Nikolay's name is mentioned in the affluent circles. We have legitimate international businesses. To the world, we're the face of the corporation, not the mafia.

I unclip my seatbelt and take my phone off airplane mode while waiting for other first-class passengers to move ahead. I grab my luggage from the overhead compartment and shove my phone in my back pocket. I've been traveling for over twelve hours and long to take a hot shower to get the dust off. It made sense to fly out of London after I met with Nikolay.

My older brother is the new don, and my younger brother, Roman, is holding down the fort in Russia. Our Bratva merged with one of my father's oldest friends, and it will be interesting to see how it plays out. Expansion usually comes at a price. Growing pains, like those I had growing so fast in my teen years, are not a myth. My teeth hurt, remembering how uncomfortable it was growing an inch taller within one week.

Once I'm off the plane, I walk through the jetway to the terminal, breathing in the cold crisp air, refreshing compared to the stale, stagnant canned shit on the plane. I'm excited to be there again and want to enjoy the city's nightlife.

I wonder what Kirill is up to. We can only discuss so much over our phones without encryption, but I'm not trusting of it. I like complicated systems bouncing our cells around the world. The toys government agents have today are more sophisticated than anyone can imagine. The criminal units who fare the best are those that go old school, getting in and out like a snake in the grass. They quietly strike their target and operate alone. They never leave a witness behind.

If a deal goes south, I cut loose ends. When I was called upon to lead soldiers in turf wars, they knew I wasn't a forgiving man. The small things always trip up men in my line of work. I don't fancy living in a prison cell. I prefer to do what must be done to make sure nothing comes back on me or my family.

My family is beautiful, but it can be brutal. We're all brothers in the Bratva. The only difference is what level you live on. We keep things compartmentalized to insulate ourselves from lower ranks who aren't used to being tortured and might give us up, but they can't if they don't know our name and have no details to spill.

I walk for what feels like forever. My leg aches, and I'm thinking about my father and why he ever entered into a deal with his friend Igor. He would still be alive if it were not for some fucked up political shit with Russian oil companies. I know all about the importance of friendships. That's why I'm here to help Kirill.

We met at Princeton and soon realized we were from connected families. As a result, we became friends immediately and had a few years to fuck around being typical college kids. We were known for our clubbing in New York City. I met his family, and we made the most of spring breaks when we took road trips that consisted of family obligations and partying, especially in Miami Beach. Maybe I need my soul cleansed. It wouldn't be the first time I've found myself to be a blight on humanity.

Besides, nothing could erase the brutal nights we spilled blood on New Jersey streets, learning how to be enforcers. Maybe it's why I prefer the solitude of the computer world, creating programs and hacking others. To say we learn on the street at a young age is an understatement. I chuckle as I stroll through the airport terminal toward the exit.

On the other side of security, I see Kirill and give him a rare smile.

"Brother," he says, and we hug each other.

He starts talking in Russian. In my grandparents' days, we'd stand out as peculiar foreigners speaking Russian at an airport. Today, it's a cosmopolitan world, and we blend in like everyone else. We're just two men speaking one language while others around us talk to each other.

"You have to see our new club tonight." Kirill's voice is filled with pride.

I listen to him tell me all about their newest club in the city and about the hot chicks just begging to be picked up and fucked. He tells me the girls today aren't into getting married. Isn't that great?

"That's too good to be true," I reply.

Women always want something. I don't anticipate living long enough to commit to a woman. Kids? Forget it. They are all liabilities, and I love my home, where everything is in order.

I'm married to the Bratva. I will only marry to fulfill an obligation to the family if I'm ordered to. In my world, marriages are usually arranged for financial gains such as money, territories, or allying with an enemy.

Because I'm in the company of the largest producer in Europe, my eyes scan our surroundings, looking for breaches in security or anything out of the ordinary on the way to the parking garage. Call it a gift. All I know is that it's saved my life more than once. Just because I'm not home where I'm a moving target doesn't mean I'm safe. There is wisdom behind the phrase, sleep with one eye open.

Looking at the women around us, I see a huge difference between Americans and Russians. American women wear what looks like pajamas or workout clothes in public. I'm not inspired or enticed to fuck any of them.

Volgograd isn't the biggest city in Russia, but most people want to live their lives unnoticed. There are those trying to climb the echelon and make enough money to buy designer outfits and obtain an apartment in a Russian city. Getting an apartment that's not shared requires bribes or favors from elected officials.

Kirill follows the chirp of his car alarm and pops the trunk of his black Charger. My luggage makes a thick *thunk* in the trunk before we sink into the custom leather seats.

"Nice car. They pay you too much. I can't have this back home without having a bullseye on my back," I say, half-joking.

"New York City has its rats and dons, too," he replies with a smirk as he puts a cigarette in his mouth, puts the car in reverse, revs the engine, and heads down the exit ramp going way too fast.

The noise of the squealing tires echoes off the cement walls. I can tell he had the muffler modified, and from the engine's sound, it's also tricked out. It's a beautiful car, but beauty can be a brutal downfall.

Kirill pays the parking fee, and we exit the airport.

Kirill's past is complicated, as his parents were in an arranged marriage. His mother is the daughter of the Italian Don, Santino Moretti. He chose to work for the Russians because his dad is a brigadier in the bratva and serves as a liaison to the Italians in New York City. This created an alliance with the Italians over twenty years ago. Still, the relationship is strained by disagreements over who controls the ports and gets what percentage of the profits. Screw arranged marriages. The only way out of one is death.

I notice Kirill now has tattoo sleeves on both arms.

"Nice tats," I say in English, ignoring the dirty looks from onlookers in traffic who are annoyed with the noise of the car and his crazy driving. If only they knew I've killed for similar looks.

"Thanks, I see you have more yourself. Was that for a lover or to commemorate a mission? Tell me the truth," he coaxes me as he pushes the gas, and we lurch forward.

He laughs. I chuckle. He's still an asshole.

"Something like that."

I leave it open. I don't like talking about myself. I can't let anyone into my inner circle. I can be an asshole too, and it's cost me a few relationships. My only girlfriend died because I got into a beef with an Italian, and all my money couldn't save her. I blame myself for not protecting her. If I can't commit to anyone, I can't risk disappointing a lover again. I would rather continue this way than to live a repeat of the guilt I feel over the past. I wonder what it would be like to be married and live like my brother sometimes. Would I have committed to Lena had she lived?

I don't know. I try not to think about it because things like that are unobtainable for men like me. It doesn't exist in our world. *Beauty is Brutal* is inked under my collarbone in Cyrillic. I got the tattoo after Lena's death.

I'm cursed to wander the world alone, and I shut out other possibilities. It's better not to want what I can't have. I'm not worthy of the love of a good woman. This I know. Everyone I touch dies—first, my only girlfriend and now, my dad.

Kirill lights his cigarette with the lighter in the dashboard and puffs out a circle as he merges into the dense traffic on the highway. I fill him in on Nikolay's crazy drama in London. I mean, his fiancé is kidnapped before the wedding, for fuck's sake. How could I not save the day for my brother?

"If I had been in charge of security, that wouldn't have happened," I declare.

"I know that you are a wickedly good techno-geek." He puts the cigarette in his other hand, leans over, reaches in front of me, and pops open the glove compartment. "Open it," he says with a grin.

I bet he's had this car customized for his lifestyle. When I reach in, I touch cold metal and immediately know it's a 9mm Glock.

"What the fuck, man? I assumed I was just here for some hacker shit and downtime, not involved in the action," I complain as I cock it and check the chamber for bullets, and the gun is loaded. Satisfied, I reach back into the glove box, pull out the clip, attach it to my belt, and slide the gun into place. I conceal it with the tail of my dress shirt.

"You can't be here with me and be empty-handed."

Fuck. Like this never goes without an explanation.

"Is there a war I don't know about?"

"Nah, just everyday life." He looks in my direction and grins.

"What's up?" I ask.

I'm getting older, and with my leg the way it is, I have no love of running into unnecessary shit. It's the main reason I switched from enforcement and turned to overseeing security on our safe houses and handling our holdings. It all falls under security, and I head it.

"I'm just saying. It's my playground now, but you never know who's gonna join you in the sand pit." He shrugs. "We have an hour to kill. Tell me about what you need for the job."

I rattle off the computer I need, and he pulls a burner phone from his pocket, makes a call, rattles off in Russian, and tells me I'll have it.

"So, any chance it will warm up while I'm here?" I ask. Hockey players love the frozen ponds in Russia. I want to try warmer weather for a change.

"It's June. We might hit eighty a few times. Why? You working on a tan?"

"Mm, it would be nice to be on a beach." I don't mention Bali to him. If I ever have to disappear, it's a place where no one knows to look for me. Most people who disappear themselves return to old patterns, and it's only a matter of time before they show up at their favorite pizza place or with an old lover when the loneliness of being on the run gets to them.

We roll into Greenwich Village in the city. I haven't been here in years. Ironically, as we became educated men, our parents wanted us back home with our Ivy League degrees to make our legitimate business ventures look credible. When we were moonlighted on the streets, we knew there were plenty of contractors we could hire to do the dirty jobs for us. I polished my English while living in New Jersey, and Kirill lived the party life and made contacts.

The difference between me and contracting something out is trust and the fact I'm willing to kill to protect my own. People who join us because they need a paycheck aren't in a life of crime for the right reasons. Their loyalty is to money. My loyalty is to blood, family, and honor, my holy trinity. Most of the men we kill are traitors, and we find them by following their trail of greed and misguided decisions. Men with addictions to gambling or vodka are not uncommon, but the men who skim to feed their vices will be exposed for their weakness. You steal from us, and you pay with your life. It's the code we live and die by.

I lean back as Kirill blasts tunes from speakers that make the car vibrate. It's not like we can talk over it; he has the windows open. My hair is so short it barely moves from the wind. I see the morning sun and think this could be anywhere in the world.

My college degree is in business finance, but I learned more off the books than in class. Dad wanted me to have something he never had a chance to pursue: a legitimate path in life. Other than learning perfect English, I often wondered what the point of going to college was. There is only one path when one is born into our family.

It's nice to see Kirill. I figured we were due for a visit when he called. With Roman and Nikolay running Russia and London, I decided not to question it and take the trip. Why not? It will only be a minute in the scheme of things., but it gets me out of my routine. Our sophisticated surveillance systems are online. At times, I have to organize numerous men in many locations physically. It's enough work for two people. I needed a break.

Kirill's skill set is more brutal than mine, which is why he works with the enforcers. He's not a computer sleuth like me. I joke when I tell him his mother must have caused his anger issues. I've seen him in action, beating a target to a bloody pulp and leaving him with a head covered with hematomas and a broken jaw. We had many long weekends in Miami over long holiday weekends. His family used college to give him real-life exercises. I learned a few things from him but lacked his years of martial arts training.

He recently called me to help him in an official capacity. I have the blessing of his boss, Mikhail Pasnov. This wouldn't be the first time an outsider looking at their books and tracking digital footprints is more successful than their own men. I won't have preconceived notions of who it can't be due to family ties or loyalty within the Bratva. I don't have any family in Alexsei Sidovo's Bratva. He is rumored to be one scary motherfucker. Even by my definition, he's someone to be feared.

In my book, there is no such thing as absolute loyalty. I have few friends, so Kirill and my brothers are extremely special. I trust them, and only them. Outsiders are unknown variables and make me uncomfortable.

Kirill pulls up before a high rise, and the building screams security.

"What's this?"

"Your crash pad. It's my secret safe house, so don't let anyone follow you here. The place is equipped with upgrades."

I'm sure he doesn't mean tile and granite countertops.

I give him a sideways glance and furrow my eyebrows.

"You're not in trouble, are you?" I am not getting involved in a New York City turf war, especially if he knows a shit show is coming.

"I'm legit, bro. We have no idea who is stealing from us or why. This is why we called in someone who doesn't know our guys. We need your unbiased analysis." He tosses me a key card, and I watch him punch in his code. "It's registered under a name that's not Russian and can't be traced to me. It would take years of government over time to track this."

He leads me up a private elevator to the eleventh floor of fifteen, and my card opens the door to a lavish condo with the city's landscape below. It's breathtaking. Yes, the place is fresh with a makeover, considering these buildings were constructed over one hundred years ago.

I let out a low whistle. "This had to set you back a few pennies."

He chuckles. "I report to the don's advisor. It has its perks. It's for Mikhail if shit happens, but I use it as my private getaway to decompress because I live with my parents. I doubt you'd want to stay with me," he explains as he flips a switch that illuminates the overhead recessed lighting and the lights under the countertops.

"If Mikhail picked this place, he's got great taste. It's insane."

I leave my luggage by the door and slide out of my shoes, leaving them in the entryway before walking through the kitchen to the living room. My toes sink into the plush white carpet as I stare out the huge picture window overlooking Washington Park. The condo is pristine. Everything is white.

Ironically, more blood gets shed under the advisor's directives than the Brigadier's.

"I hope you brought some dress clothes in that garment bag because we're going to Club Sixty-Nine tonight."

Hearing Club *69* mid-swallow, I almost choke on my spit.

"What? Are you serious?"

"Oh, fuck yeah. Great name, right? My boss's daughter will be there."

"You fucking her?" I quiz him.

"Hell no, I'd be crazy to do that. She's just out of college. She's nice and fun, but I'd never touch her. I fuck other girls." He grabs a glass and fills it with tap water. "Gee, you must be hungry. Let's grab some food. You name it. I'll take you to it."

Watching him drink the tap water, I wonder if he's working tonight. Kirill is the man for the job if this girl needs protecting. He's so honorable that her daddy won't worry about her safety or anyone getting in her pants.

How was I to know how incorrect my assumptions were?

CHAPTER 2

IZZY

It's another Saturday without a date. I'm not sure which is worse, being alone on a Saturday or being without a job. What screams loser more? It's a toss-up.

I did not attend the graduation ceremony from the Fashion Institute of Technology. My roommate Alena offered to pay for my cap and gown, but I didn't want her family's blood money.

We are best friends and like matching as much as possible when we dress up to go out. We're the same height, but that's where the similarities end. She has blond hair and a fair complexion of Eastern European descent. I have the dark hair and olive complexion of a Sicilian. My hair is jet-black and shiny, like a pair of patent leather tuxedo shoes. I'm told it looks blue in the right light. Men turn their heads when we're together, no doubt, to look at her, not me.

She owns our flat and receives a monthly allowance from her father. She loves to party on the weekends and always gets the man she wants. She's that pretty. I'm convinced she could apply her makeup in the dark and still have it come out perfect. Even in five-inch heels, she can walk like a runway model, making it look easy. I'd fall like a bowling pin, so I prefer wedged heels.

She swings her narrow hips suggestively and acts like she's completely unaware of her effect on the men watching. If that's not enough, she also has huge boobs that defy gravity. I wish I had an ounce of her beauty, poise, and sophistication.

I've seen her in action too many times to count. We'll go into a crowded nightclub, and some guy will immediately surrender his bar stool so she can sit at the bar. The bartender will ask what she's drinking because some unseen admirer has offered to pay. Cocktail in hand, she'll swing around, cross her legs, and boldly stare at an attractive man across the room. And not necessarily the man who bought her the drink.

When he returns her gaze, she'll flip her hair over one shoulder like she's in a shampoo commercial and curl her index finger to suggest he join her. Without hesitation, the lucky man will make a beeline for her, smiling as if he won the lotto.

She doesn't need the assistance of a glam squad to look camera-ready. I've seen her do it using only two products—lipstick and foundation. Somehow, she uses lipstick to make a cheeky color for her high cheekbones. The rest is history.

She's confident and knows how to use her body to get what she wants from a boyfriend. They never last long, and it always ends in heartache because she has no plans for a long-term commitment.

When it comes to men, we could not be more different. I'm intimidated by most people, gorgeous men. I feel awkward and uncomfortable around them. I never assume anyone is watching me. I like working out at the gym in the building, and I'm shy.

Regarding sex, my experiences are limited to occasional hookups that typically end in disappointment. Trust me, nothing worth repeating is going on between my sheets. Passionate sex is something I read about in steamy novels. I've given up on flirting with strangers in bars because they take my number but never call. I'm beginning to think I lack sex appeal.

I subscribe to several fashion magazines to prepare for a career in fashion. Before they're delivered to the newsstands, they're delivered to my mailbox downstairs. I spend Sundays leisurely flipping the pages and studying the designs. I can't afford any high-end designer brands, but that doesn't stop me from dreaming.

Her wardrobe is so extensive that she has things hanging on racks with rollers. Alena makes everything look effortless, from her hair to her makeup to fitting in with the girls from elite boarding schools.

My attempts to compete with her look juvenile and end in disaster, like fake eyelashes. When I attempt to glue them on, I end up poking myself in the eyeball or gluing one to my cheek.

I think the men like Alena because she is approachable and can have random sex without falling in love. Even with a hookup, I always wish it were more. I've never had a serious boyfriend. At this point, I'm convinced there may not be anyone for me in the city, or anywhere else for that matter.

My mother said Daddy passed before I was born, and the lonely look in her eyes still haunts me. She was broken over losing him and didn't date anyone seriously until I was five. She was killed in a car accident when I was seven, and my Aunt Emma raised me. We already lived with her in Connecticut, so I didn't have to move. I still miss my mom, especially when my life is in the dumpster.

When college started, Alena would pull me out of my funk on days when nothing was going to plan. She knows my worst days are at the beginning of every month—when I take money from my student loan account and immediately hyperventilate. When my mood turns black, she literally talks me off the ledge.

My only family is my Aunt Emma, so I feel fortunate to have Alena in my life. She's the sister I never had and gives me a sense of family. I wish I could afford to pay more to live here, but I'm up to my eyeballs in bills. And that doesn't even begin to describe my dire situation. The reality is that I'm drowning in a tsunami of debt because nothing in New York is affordable. It's days like this when I reconsider every decision I've made up to this point and fear I made a huge mistake. I'm reaching for things I can't afford to support myself.

I met Alena at a mandatory student orientation. We were in sync from the moment I said she looked familiar. I have no clue why I said that. Maybe subconsciously, she reminded me of a childhood friend. We exchanged information, and I wasn't even sure if a cool girl like her would want to hang out with me. But she called me to grab a coffee, and we've been inseparable ever since.

When she said her family was in waste management, I was afraid to be her friend. I might be naïve, but even I knew that meant mafia. I also knew she liked me, and I wasn't going to risk spoiling our friendship by asking many stupid questions.

While I was still living in a cheap motel room, a lawyer sitting next to me on the train seemed the right person to answer some of my questions. I told him my concerns, and he said that mafia members make good friends as long as I don't piss them off.

Alena and I continued to see each other in classes, and when she heard I needed an affordable place to live, she suggested I live with her for next to nothing. Beyond the low rent, there are plenty of other perks. I've been to her house for Christmas and Thanksgiving when I couldn't afford the train fare to see my aunt in Connecticut.

Her father is a large man with a booming voice that commands everyone's attention. He's intimidating, and on the rare occasions he visits, I duck into my room to avoid him. Rumor has it he's high up the food chain in the Russian organization. I never fact-checked this information because I don't want his name in my web browser's history. Instead, I'm satisfied with whatever Alena tells me and stick to the rule of keeping my mouth shut and being loyal to them.

I need her generosity because I'll have to move home if I don't get a job in the next few weeks. This means my dreams of making it big in the big city have failed, and I'll end up working at some shitty mall in Connecticut. I doubt Alena would let me move out over my pride, but they say it goes before the fall.

We live in Greenwich Village. Talk about great luck. The only caveat to this arrangement is that I'm not allowed to invite strangers over or tell anyone she's my roommate. I initially chuckled, thinking it was a joke.

Then she showed me the gun she carries for personal protection. My jaw dropped, and I agreed to do whatever it took to keep us safe. And so began my foray into the underworld. I only use her first name, and even at that, I only use it when necessary, especially when a slip of the tongue could put her safety in jeopardy. I have no desire to meet the men who are sent to punish traitors.

She doesn't talk about her home life much. Eventually, she told me her last name was Pasnov. Her father is the right-hand man of the Russian don, Alexsei. I don't ask for last names. What's funny is that her father thinks I'm a conservative girl who will tame his daughter's wicked and wild ways. Little does he know no one will tame her.

Alena is flying through life like a Ferrari, speeding along the twists and turns of the Amalfi coast. If anything, she's changed me. She coaxed me out of my cocoon and opened my eyes to the real world.

When she's not snorting coke in the bathroom or puking in the toilette, she's showing me how to enjoy the city. It's a great place to live and party when you have money and connections.

School ended on a sour note when my internship ended in May. The company went into a hiring freeze and could not offer me a job. *Great.* Can anything go my way?

I want a day where everything goes as planned: a day of cappuccinos topped with a mountain of whipped cream and a cinnamon stick on the side, a stack of fashion magazines, and an email offering me a job with the locally based Haute couture by Ellis Grant or the New York City Ballet Company.

What could be better than designing costumes for the dancers? I imagine my boss would be the latest version of Amanda Priestly from the movie *The Devil Wears Prada*, but I have to start somewhere. I'll suck up what little pride I have left and hand out coffees and sandwiches to the most popular designer's staff if it means I can work with the best. I will do whatever it takes to get my foot in the door. I can't go back to Connecticut with my tail between my legs.

Besides, I needed a paycheck a week ago. Even if I got this job by some miracle, it would take time to get my place between the limited housing available in NYC and the exorbitant deposits required.

But here I sit, sipping a foamy drink while Alena digs through a closet overflowing with clothes. I watch her with amusement from my perch at the end of her bed. It's like watching a feral Jack Russell terrier look for their favorite toy.

She pulls armloads of dresses still clinging to hangers for life support and tosses them on the bed. Some end up on my lap, and I run my hand across the exquisite fabrics. The way she's fussing over what to wear, you'd think she was preparing to walk the red carpet at the Academy Awards.

"What are you doing?" I cajole her.

"I need the perfect dress. We're meeting some guys tonight. One of them works for my dad."

She ducks back into her closet and returns with an armful of designer stilettos. Her shoe collection is one that Imelda Marcos would envy.

"What? I'm not going," I say as my eyebrows practically join my hairline.

"Fine." She huffs. "Do you have plans tonight?" She drops the shoes and puts her hands on her hips as if I've done something wrong.

"No." Of course not. She knows I'm a homebody.

"Then you're going. Kirill has a friend with him, and it will be perfect," she explains matter-of-factly as she picks up a dress and gives it a second of attention before tossing it on the discard pile.

"*Hm*, let me guess, a friend of your dad's? No, thank you."

"Don't be such a stick in the mud. He's nice."

"I'm sure, but I don't need to know more about them."

"It's fine. You're my best friend. We've graduated, and you need to mingle. It's a new club. Everyone who's anyone will be there. You might make connections. My family knows people, and these guys know people. You need to realize the mafia has their hand in every pot, especially fashion."

Fuckity, fuck. She's right. I'm sure her father could find me a job in a New York minute, but I'd never ask. I have enough problems without getting into bed with the mafia.

Right then and there, I decided to get in bed with something other than the mob. I want tonight to be a night of debauchery. I take life too seriously, and maybe a good fuck is just what I need to turn my luck around. What would be the harm in a one-night stand? It has to be better than hooking up with my silicone appliance every night.

Why not get royally fucked by a hot man? The city is full of them. How difficult can it be to get one to take me to his place and make me come on his dick?

NYC is where the buzz on the street makes or breaks an establishment. Posting yourself on social media and getting into a club with an impossible waiting list is newsworthy. It takes status and power to open those doors. Maybe I'm going about this all wrong because Alena has a valid point. I'm not in Connecticut anymore. It's time to reap the rewards of living in NYC.

"It's new. We'll never get in," I point out, knowing full well she or her dad will make sure we get the red carpet treatment.

"Oh, pish posh." She flips her wrist in a don't-worry gesture. "We're in. Dad is a silent partner with the owners."

I should have known. This is her life. Her family name opens doors, or if necessary, her family kicks them down.

Fuck. This club will undoubtedly be full of wannabes with over-inflated tits and asses and lips. What is it about wanting to look like Jessica Rabbit? No one stops to think about the liposuction required to keep that cartoon waistline. Or how much booze and pills they need to numb themselves from the constant scrutiny of public opinion.

I'm not about to give up solid food to be that thin. I hear champagne has the least number of calories, which is why all the Alisters drink it. I make a note to drink that tonight when they bring it to the VIP table.

I do enjoy being Alena's wingman. She protects me from the snooty socialites who have no clue what it's like to work for a living. I'll never fit in, and I'm okay with it because I know what they have comes at a price.

Alena's father pressures her to make family appearances and attend social events when she's the youngest in the room. All she wants is to be carefree and live like an immortal. Hell, we only live once. She has plenty of years to do her father's bidding, in my opinion.

"Before you say you have nothing to wear, pick something. I have tons. In fact, I haven't worn half of these dresses." She dumps an armful onto my lap.

I set aside my drink and ran a hand across the textured lace fabric of the dress on top. I lift it, eyeing it with interest. It's a cream-colored minidress with lining on the inside. It's gorgeous and elegant. The price tag dangles from the designer label, and I can't resist the temptation to peek. I turn it over and gasp when I see all the zeros.

"I'm too afraid I'd ruin this, Alena. It's very expensive."

"Oh, that dress," she says upon seeing my choice. She dismisses my concerns. "I've never worn it, and if it gets ruined, I can buy another one. That color is perfect with your skin tone." She eyes the dress and then me. "You'll look amazing in it. I'm so jealous of how your skin looks tanned even in May."

"Sicilians, you can't beat the nice complexion," I say as my giggle emerges as a snort. "Are we really graduates? I feel the same, don't you?"

I hug the dress to me. It's gorgeous. If it weren't for the fact that it barely covers my thong panties, it could be used as a wedding dress.

The long sleeves will be perfect for a cool night, and it will hide the tattoo on my wrist.

"Yes, that's the fun of it. We're young and we live in a city that never sleeps. Let's stay up all night. Eventually, things will change, and one day, we'll wish we had more nights like this…" Her voice trails off as she holds a red dress up to herself looks at herself in a long mirror hanging on a wall.

"What's up? You don't sound happy."

"Oh, nothing. I mean, Dad will want me to get married soon. I have a degree, but no one expects me to use it." She tosses the red dress in the discard pile and picks up another.

"Oh, that sucks. I thought you were kidding when you mentioned it before. Isn't it archaic?"

"Yes, but it is the way," she says, borrowing a line from Obie One in *Star Wars*.

"Still, you worked hard for your degree. Don't you want your independence?"

"Ha, like Dad will allow that. He let me have four years of freedom during college, but that will be over soon," she replies matter-of-factly.

"All right, well, I have to run out and pick up some stuff for dinner. Do you need anything? I thought we'd make paninis."

"Oooh, sounds great." She drags out the "O" We're not expected at the club until ten. That's early, but I thought we'd spend time alone before we meet the guys. You know my father's men are cock blockers."

I can't stop my chuckle as it bubbles out. She's so flippant about how things work. She's got all the angles, that's for sure. Growing up in her father's shadow taught her as much, if not more than,

than any soldier under him. I wouldn't put my money on her in a street fight, but a battle with words is one she would dominate.

We discuss the ingredients needed for dinner before I grab my small purse and keys and exit through the lobby. The lobby, with its black and white checkerboard floor and walls lined with mailboxes, is secure, requiring residents to use a code to enter.

As I walk five blocks to a corner grocer, I can't shake the feeling of being watched creepily. Having Alena as a friend, I've gained more street smarts, but I still can't tell the difference between a stalker and a birdwatcher. If scary movies have taught me anything, it's that stalkers wear hoodies, not binoculars.

I tell myself I'm being suspicious and paranoid. There's no abusive or disturbed ex in my background. I'm sure Alena, who is connected, is who they want. *Shit!* What if they think I'm her?

The store is a few steps away when a customer exits, and I slide through the open door like I'm stealing third base. I feel safer under the glare of the bright fluorescent lights, but I'm still too scared to look behind me.

CHAPTER 3

IZZY

"Hi, Marco," I say as I pass the owner and make my way to the meat section.

It's an Italian deli, and everything here is sublime. Pricey—but worth it. I sent resumes out to theater companies today and hope something comes through. *Crap*, if Alena gets married, I'll need to move out. She'll rent or sell hers and will probably live in an incredible penthouse overlooking Central Park.

I'm sure she'll go to a bigger and better place, especially if her dad has money to sink into a nightclub. Even I know liquor licenses are limited and costly. I select pre-cut meats for today, grab cheese, and hear the bell on the door jingle. I see a large man in a black hoodie, his hands are shoved into his pockets. I quickly turn my back and think he won't see me if I don't look at him.

Fuck. This can't be a coincidence. Young kids wear those, not men in their forties, right? I grab a loaf of Italian bread. Done. Well, hell, mafia men on the street love joggers.

"How are you, Izzy?" Marco rings up my food.

"Great, you?"

"Good day. Supposed to rain tomorrow. We'll see." He's in his fifties and is always nice, but he's known me for years. I've heard him speak Italian, and it's such a pretty language. It makes me wish I knew one romantic language.

I'm relieved to see in the mirror behind Marco that the stranger has moved to the other side of the store. I wonder how the shopkeeper manages to do his job when the crime rate is so high. I smile at him nervously as I slide my card into the machine and breathe a sigh of relief when it beeps and "accepted" shows on the screen.

"Have plans tonight?"

"Yes, thank you, we're going to a new club. Thanks, Marco."

I take the bag filled with our dinner and nervously bump open the door when I exit. *Shit, that hurt my shoulder.*

It's in the seventies today, and the walk home is lovely as I pass the park. The trees are getting ready to bloom. I want to turn around and see if the guy is behind me, but that's too obvious. I pull out my phone, making it appear like I'm filming a video. Only it is a video to ensure my safety. I push the red record button on the screen and hold it above my head so I can see behind me. I feel like a dork.

"This is me by the park…great day for a walk," I speak loudly so that strangers walking by can hear me. But this is New York City, and no one pays attention. I notice the man in the hoodie slows his pace and ducks his head.

Fuck.

He confirms my worst nightmare. I post the video to one of my social media accounts in case I disappear in the following three blocks and send it to Alena.

I text. *This dude is following me. Do you know why?*

Dots appear, then her reply, *Fuck, I'll meet you downstairs.*

My breathing is more like a chugging freight train, heavy and laboring with terror by the time I reach the door. Oddly, we both peek at the street again, and the man is gone. Alena hugs me to her.

"Whew, that was so weird," I say, embracing the comfort of her arms. I'm shaking.

"Are you sure he was following you or…."

"I'm wondering if he wants you," I reply as we squeeze into the elevator.

Her eyes loom across the small space like flying salad plates.

"Oh, shit." Her face turns pale now that she's connecting the dots.

"There's a reason you're in a secure building near a park, with lots of pathways and traffic," I add.

"I never thought much of it. Dad picked the flat."

"Is something going on with your dad?" It's the only logical conclusion. My hand shakes as we get off on our floor, and by the time I open our door, Alena is texting her dad. I drop the food in the kitchen and head to my bedroom. I sit in front of my sewing machine, fussing with fabrics until my heart rate returns to normal.

My mind is cluttered, wandering. I'm in shock. What if I was taken? What if someone wants me to get to Alena?

When I'm anxious, working with my hands helps me stop fidgeting and transports me back to when I was seven and learned my mother wasn't coming home. It started shortly after that, the fidgeting and the heaviness in my chest. I can't dismiss the thoughts of what could have happened and those thoughts racing through my mind. Then, my mind drifts into what might happen in the future. Then it's a train ride of doomsday thoughts going to dark places.

Over the years, I've learned to stop the thoughts from getting away from me. Using my creativity is one way I escape the ugliness of the world. I want to think, in some small way, my talent makes the world more beautiful. My time is better spent being productive than rehashing the past or dwelling on misfortunes I can't control.

I might not be able to change the past, but I'm trying to control my future. Mom didn't want me to live in New York City, and my aunt protested my move. I refuse to be a slave to the past. Mom's not here, and she'd want me to pursue my dreams. She loved it when we'd play dress up, and I'd add accessories to our outfits. I wonder what she would do with her life if she were still alive.

I head to the kitchen to prepare dinner, and Alena joins me.

"Dad said no one should have a beef with me or you. But he'll investigate it. I'm not sure if he believed me." Her face is quizzical. "Why would someone want me?"

"Because your dad is someone of importance. Who knows? Could be a million reasons."

She sits in our tiny nook in the kitchen and waits for me to dig into the paninis I pressed. She has a device for making them, and they come out perfect. I don't know what she'd get as a gift for a wedding. She has everything. I'm being silly. I remember *The Godfather* and realize she'll be handed oodles of cash.

She's wearing faded skinny jeans and a white blouse that ties at her navel. Her mouth wraps around the sandwich. She takes a bite, chews, and swallows. "These are delicious, thank you." She swallows her diet soft drink and seems to have dismissed my near brush with death.

Maybe this has happened to her before. I'm afraid to ask, but if she isn't worried, maybe her dad has security on us. Perhaps I'm delusional. I shrug it off, but I can't forget the waves of panic that gripped me as I walked faster to make sure I reached the safety of our building. I'm fortunate she was home and opened the door for me. Who knows what would have happened if I had to take a minute to punch in my code?

Alena thanked me for making lunch and volunteered to clean the kitchen. I return to my room and hold the dress briefly, wishing my mother was here. I hold it before me and move in front of my full-length mirror. The long sleeves are lacy, and my skin will show through the open areas in the sleeves, which are elegant and tastefully sexy. I love the dress and can't wait to get my first assignment on creating something incredible and get paid for my labor. In the corner of my room is a free-standing rack with a man's suit and dresses I created for my senior project. Money was tight, and school kept me busy, so I didn't make many items for myself. Now, I wish I had made something with the nightclub in mind. I'm sure there's a market for affordable dresses without the high price tags.

I wonder if I'll get noticed in this dress. No man has ever given me the kind of attention Alena receives. Her male friends will carry on conversations with me, even bat their eyes at me and tell me funny stories to entertain me, but I see through it. They pass the time in a club before it gets late and then launch the sales pitch for me to return to their place. I know they want sex. I don't believe love happens in an instant. Maybe for a man, but for me, not so much. I can't say I'm not envious of how men look at Alena with hunger in their eyes. She's known most of these men for years. It's one thing the mafia offers, and ironically, it's the one thing I don't have. Family. They have stories from their youth. They know each other's faults and love each other no matter how many arguments they've had over the years.

I believe love exists. Otherwise, my mother wouldn't have been so sad without my father. I sigh as I swirl around with the dress held to me. I'll go out tonight because I love to dance and it will help me forget about this afternoon. Maybe I'll meet a mature man who makes me dizzy with desire. I'm tired of the toys in my dresser drawer, and maybe tonight, with this dress, I'll get lucky and find someone who captures my attention. Why not? What's the harm in a hookup? I'm giving myself a pass to have sex, and I hope I pick a man who knows what he's doing.

"Do you want me to do your eyes?" Alena hollers from her vanity.

"Sure, just no fake eyelashes. I don't want to look like Cleopatra."

"You're always so dra-ma-tic," she annunciates the word *dramatic* to mock me.

I'm not dramatic, just the opposite. I don't like to be the center of attention because I don't think I'm worthy of it. I like making other people look glamorous; if they want something dramatic, I'll do it. I don't have an acting bone in my body. I attended and graduated from an incredible college, hoping it would improve my odds of getting a job. With the economy the way it is, I don't feel so optimistic now that my leads are drying up.

Alena has her bills covered and doesn't need work. She says she'll be marrying some Russian soon and hopes he's not old and reeking of vodka. It's their tradition to carry out arranged marriages.

I was the center of my mother's world, so maybe I don't know what it's like to be the center of a man's affection. I've often wondered why Mom didn't bring many men around until I was older. She said she had me, and it was enough.

The coincidence of both my parents dying in car accidents makes me consider that there might be a conspiracy theory to explain it all. But my dad died before I was born, and my mom died seven years later. Besides, I'm no one special. I can't imagine why anyone would want me.

Kidnapping and killing are extreme measures, and I would assume they would only be used in dire situations. I can't imagine I'm important enough for someone to consider me a threat to them. It's not like I'm wealthy. However, I do worry about Alena. The hoodie man was tailing me to get to her or slip into our building.

I take a shower and wash my hair. After I dry off, I wrap the towel around me and wrap another around my head. It tends to be curly. I walk to Alena's room on light feet.

"Are you going to get married soon?" I observe her laying foundation and BB cream on her face. She's a perfect Russian princess with perfect skin. Where will I live if she gets married before I obtain my own apartment?

"Probably. Daddy will arrange something. Maybe it will be to the don's son if I'm so lucky." She scoffs, so I don't think that will happen. "I just want him to be close to my age and good to me."

She dismisses the archaic process of arranged marriages as if it's nothing. She has years of knowing the ways of the bratva world, whereas I'm still learning. I can't ask many questions or pry... if I value my life.

"I'd love to have a boyfriend who would bring me roses or those cute little squares of chocolate with caramel in the middle. Oh, and I love the raspberry-flavored ones. They're so addicting, aren't they?"

"You're a freaking twig, Izzy. I'd gain five pounds off of three of them."

She peers into a unique mirror with special lights. Her skin is alabaster, but by the time she finishes her handiwork, she'll look stage-ready to the point I'll only know her by her hazel eyes, mannerisms when she flirts, and her sassy voice when she makes a point.

"My boobs are nice. But my ass, well, it's not so little. If I weren't a seamstress, I'd be wearing ugly shit that hangs off me like oversized pajamas. Which, I don't mind, by the way." I love men's t-shirts, they're the best. I wish I had a boyfriend. I want to fall in love. I've thought I was in love a few times, but they just wanted to get laid. Other men seemed to like me, but they didn't have a backbone. I need a man I can respect, someone who will bring something to the table.

Alena snickers because it's a half-snort, half-laugh, and I go back to my room next to hers with a bathroom between us. It's the old Jack and Jill setup from the nineties, and someone spent a pretty penny on renovating this place.

"You look so adorable in your half-shirts and boy shorts. Pretty cheeky," she teases.

Yes, it is one of my favorite go-to's. I return to my room and spritz my hair with a mist to decrease the drying time.

"I'm blowing out my hair. Give me a minute," I reply. I flip the red switch on the beast of a dryer, which hurts my wrists if I use it for more than seven minutes. As I said, it's a beast, as in a dinosaur of dryers. The immediate hot air hits my hair like a cyclone, and I use my hairbrush to straighten it, hoping it doesn't come out frizzy. The dry time takes five to seven minutes. When I finished the dryer, I set it on the sink's counter and dipped a few fingers in a tiny jar. I gather a waxy substance on them, then spread it on my bangs which frame my face. I should get a trim and have it styled, but that costs money, and I need to save what I have. I make a note to treat myself to a salon when I get on my feet.

Alena's boy toys buy us drinks as they want to show off in front of her, and I'm okay with it if they don't expect something in return.

But I have fifty dollars on me just in case. It won't buy much, but I can suck down a ton of water in a few hours and act like I'm buzzed.

I've been out with her enough to know the Russians can hold more alcohol than I thought humanly possible. I don't know if it's the long, cold winters in Russia or if they drink to forget about the oppression in their country. Quite possibly, they like to drink. I can't figure out their culture.

With my hair finished, I pull the dress over my bra, which matches my bikini panties. Thankfully, the dress isn't tight, and it's shorter on me than it would be on Alena. She's more of a pencil skirt kind of girl, meaning her buttocks don't hold a candle to mine. She's heavy-chested, with a heart-shaped face, and whereas she has street smarts I'll never possess, she has a heart of gold when it comes to me. And I'd do anything for her.

I reappear in her doorway. Alena uses numerous brushes on my eyes and moves over them quickly. She has a knack for making them smoky, like in the videos I watch, yet I still manage to fuck up my eyes. I'm all thumbs, and my eyes are almond-shaped, making them appear smaller than they are. It's the gray-blue color of them I find unique. It's a recessive gene, and I didn't see it in any photo albums my mother had, and of that, there weren't many. She said her family disowned her, and she lost touch with them. One would think she was adopted, and no one had a camera. Thankfully, she had an older friend for us to live with, and I called her Aunt Emma even though she was not my real aunt.

"There," Alena exclaims as she straightens herself because I'm sitting on her padded seat at the vanity table. She had it custom-made before she moved in. I'm sure if you're going to remodel things, it's best to do them before you move in.

"It's time to leave. I called a car from Daddy's service. He wants us to be careful," she explains. Usually, we take the Metro. Now I'm confident we'll get into the club without waiting a minute. There are times like these when membership in the mafia has its privileges.

CHAPTER 4

DMITRY

I wheel my luggage to the bedroom and open it on the oversized bed. A bed this big is something one doesn't often see in Europe. We tend to be conservative, and space is at a premium. I pull out fresh clothes and lay them out methodically.

I step into the blue and white tiled shower and let the hot water run down my back. I could stand here all night, but I don't want to miss out on my mini-vacation and keep it reasonable.

I towel dry and run a solution through my long hair to slick it back on my head to keep it in place. I use cologne and head into the spacious bedroom. I step into my fitted jeans. I tug on a long-sleeve Henley over my defined shoulders, using a smaller-sized shirt so it will shrink my biceps.

I even sit on the bench at the end of the bed to put on my army-like boots that lace up. There are some habits I learned as a soldier that are hard to give up. The boots are functional and look good with everything but a suit. I give myself a once-over in the mirrored closet door. The shirt has wrinkles from being packed, and I smooth them down as much as possible. It will have to suffice for tonight.

I join Kirill in the spacious living room and judging from the butt in the ashtray, he's on his second cigarette. He offers me one, and I take it. I don't need it. It's a bad habit. I typically only do it when hanging out with other smokers. I inhale deeply and lean back on the sofa, blowing out a smoke ring.

"Man, I can't believe you have this place. It's sweet. Why are you stinking up the place?" I ask him.

He shrugs his shoulders, and I remember he was a bit of an entitled prick, but he taught me about American culture and how friend-ships are hard to maintain over the years. I stand and open the door to the balcony to air out the smoke-filled room. He joins me, and we're overlooking a green park with trees ready to bloom.

"We could be anywhere right now, but something about this reminds me of Europe."

"Do you miss living here?" He sounds concerned. His eyes search my face to see if I'm happy.

"Of course, I miss it. I'd be crazy not to, but family duty, y'know." I shrug and take another puff, lost in thought for a second.

"Tell me about it. Someone is skimming money, and they're very good. So good that our guy, Tito, hasn't figured out who it is."

"Who the hell is called Tito?"

"His mother is Latino. His dad is Russian. He'd get much more shit about it if he weren't such a big man." He chuckles at the irony of what he's implying.

"Big?"

"Oh, yeah, he's got a man bun and looks like a sumo wrestler. He'd make a great bouncer," he says with a chuckle. "His den of tech is complicated. He runs our computers and intel and helps with encrypted wire transfers."

I'm not surprised there are mixed marriages here, especially with the cosmopolitan world we live in today. Travel is easier and cheaper. Websites make it easier to form long-distance relationships that would never happen otherwise.

In Russia, we only marry other Russians. We want to know we can trust our spouses and that they understand us, all while keeping the bloodlines pure. It's the way it is. Family is everything. Outsiders are subject to suspicion, and I'd hate to be the one to bear the burden of all that scrutiny.

Even with a bratva don in the family, my loyalty might be questioned if I married outside the bratva. My family would accept the marriage, but the others in the bratva wouldn't be so forgiving. It's a nightmare I prefer to avoid. I wear my single status like a bulletproof vest. No one is getting through it.

We hang out, grab a late dinner, and Kirill drives us to their new club, where Kirill gives his car to a Russian to park. We can enter the club with our weapons if they aren't showing. This is one perk of the brotherhood and being part of the family who owns the club. Kirill opens doors. I'm proud of him for moving up the ranks so quickly.

Club 69 is all it implies, with metal poles for dancing on different platforms in what used to be an old warehouse. We enter through a side door reserved for Bratva members only. As long as we keep our weapons hidden, there's no issue. We don't like to advertise what we do. I don't know the players here, so I quickly take in my surroundings, the bouncers, and the exits.

"The number of people crammed into this place is insane," I yell close to Kirill's ear. It's impossible to be heard over the loud bass coming from the speakers. My eardrums are going to be useless for the rest of the night.

As much as I enjoy my visit, I don't enjoy being around this many people. Too many weak points can be exploited, and we're out in the open. I'm recognizable at home, but in NYC, no one knows my brother is the don in two European countries, per se. If I were to say his name here in mafia circles, they would know him because they keep in touch with their homeland as they all have family there. But most other Americans would have no idea I'm connected to a very prosperous and international Russian mafia family.

We continue to move about the club. There are private rooms for God knows what. I've seen places in Europe for the kinky dominant sex, and there are places where women are auctioned. I'm sure that would be harder to pull off here. I know they move tons of drugs through these city clubs.

I like moving, and I never put my back to a door, nor would any cop worth their salt. I'd rather face any threat than to be surprised by it. Call me paranoid, but I'm not trusting anyone other than Kirill. We've been through too much shit together not to let him into my small inner circle. I have no idea who his don has working here tonight, but they're sloppy. I see too many bouncers flirting with college-age girls to do their job correctly.

During a routine perimeter sweep, my gaze zeros in on two girls at the bar. One girl wears too much makeup for my taste, she's polished, and by the looks of it, she's a kept woman. If not by a husband, then it's daddy. The other girl is perfect, with dark hair with a slight figure. I love how she fills out her dress with her hips as she sits. Maybe New York has some hidden gems, after all.

CHAPTER 5

DMITRY

We take our seats in a private room overlooking the lower level of the most famous club in New York City. My jacket covers the fact that I'm packing an unregistered gun. We order a bottle of Vodka.

"Bring me your best champagne," Kirill adds before the waitress leaves.

I eye him, a question on my tongue.

"It's for my boss's daughter. They'll be here tonight. What woman watching her weight won't appreciate the low calories?" he scoffs with a mischievous grin.

"Do I sense a crush on this girl?" My eyebrows raise in surprise, and he shifts in his chair.

"Mm, dangerous. My boss's daughter. She'll undoubtedly be married off to someone now that she's graduated from one of those overpriced fashion schools. The girl is a smoke show, and she'll never have to work," he replies and shrugs. As if to say she wasted her time going to college.

"It's the new world. Even a caged bird wants freedom. I suppose it's an achievement, and it makes her fit in with her peers who aren't in the underworld. What do you expect her to talk about if she has nothing in common with the other women in her social circle? They are married to billionaires, attend charity events, and even start their own businesses. Clothing and makeup lines make the most money."

"Point taken," he says with a nod, conceding my point.

The waitress is scantily clad in fishnet stockings and lingerie, becoming a high-class hooker and befitting the club's name. I don't pay for sex, but I've seen men with their mistresses, and there's a close resemblance between the waitresses and prostitutes. I assume that's the point of the attire.

Knowing this is a mob-owned club, there must be rooms in the back for sexual pleasure, and God knows what else. We tend to use our London clubs to move drugs and launder money. It's the perfect environment to sell drugs under the guise of entertainment, and there are large crowds filled with millionaires and billionaires who don't care what they spend to escape their boring lives. I like working for my family and don't care to impress those who have had everything handed to them.

Scanning the bar, my eyes return to the two stunning girls. One has blond hair and is flirting with the bartender. The other waits patiently while observing the dance floor. Something beyond her obvious beauty gets my attention. She's dressed the part of a socialite, but I don't believe she's a part of that crowd.

A man approaches from her left. He's clearly out of his league but continues just the same. He makes contact, and I see his lips moving. He is undeterred by her politely avoiding eye contact with him. The blonde is unaware some unscrupulous dude is hitting on her girlfriend and continues to nibble cherries off a toothpick suggestively.

Meanwhile, the dude looking at her friend has the posture of intimidation. His feet are planted on the floor next to her, and he inhales deeply as that is the only way he can puff out his chest. It's like the mating season, with him showing off his dominance to impress her. Instinct tells me he's not there to impress. He's here to take. He wears gaudy gold rings on his right hand, and I imagine he reeks of too much cologne. She's avoided him thus far, but she can't any longer. As predicted, he grabs her wrist. I leap out of my chair, nearly dumping our table, and jog through the club to reach her.

"What the fuck?" Kirill says as he follows blindly one step behind me.

I reach the bar and clamp my right hand on the Russian's arm. "Remove it or die."

"Fuck off, kid," he says.

Now that I'm closer, I can see his salt-and-pepper hair and unkempt beard. I cannot know who he could be without a play-book of who's who. I doubt he's a brigadier or a capo. My gut tells me he's a creep with too much money. If this is a bratva club, it's for the elite. He doesn't fit in with the scenery.

He sticks his chin out and meets my gaze, his eyes like cue balls. "You got a problem?" he asks.

"I do," I say without blinking. The first to look away admits defeat. The same rule applies to dogs. This stray dog needs to be leashed, and I'm the man to do it.

"Please," the woman implores the man to let her go.

When he doesn't do what the lady asks, I pull a knife out of my back pocket.

"She asked nicely. Now we do it my way," I state in a deep, calm voice before stabbing the knife into the back of the hand he's carelessly placed on the bar.

The man now has a knife sticking out of the back of his hand. He yells again with excruciating pain as I clean my knife with a tiny napkin sitting on the bar. He relinquishes his grip on her arm, and I pull her to me as she slides off the barstool and into my arms.

Immediately, we're surrounded by men in suits and club members.

Kirill takes his place beside me, putting distance between me and the goon. I observe other men moving our way. I'm not sure if they are with us or against us.

"What's the meaning of this?" The head of security demands as three more security guards draw up behind him. We're outnumbered.

"She's mine," I proclaim without hesitation. I feel the girl's body stiffen against mine at the declaration. "She's not on the market. He didn't take the hint."

Something about this beautiful stranger makes me want to protect and possess her.

"Stand down." Kirill gives the order, and the man in control of the club's security nods his head once in our direction before he turns and gives commands in Russian to his henchmen to escort the man out. He's escorted to the closest exit, and the tense situation passes.

"Thank you, you didn't have to do that," comes the sweetest voice I've ever heard, and it's directed at me. "I would have made him leave," she states in a tone more suited for soothing crying babies than scaring off predators.

I am impressed with her courage, and she doesn't fear me is a plus.

Goons like the guy I just schooled prowl the streets at night, roughing up men who owe money to the bratva. By roughing up, I mean they break ribs and noses. It's only the first step of the process, putting someone in the hospital for months or worse.

"Right, like you're a match for a two hundred and fifty-pound Russian." This is my dumbass retort.

I'm captivated by her pale bluish-gray eyes and the level of vulnerability in them. I'm so tall she has to crane her neck to meet my gaze.

"Oh, my God, Dad won't be happy if I'm involved," her blonde friend murmurs, standing beside Kirill. "What the fuck did he want?" she asks her friend.

"I don't know. He grabbed my arm," she replies.

"No bullets were fired. It's no big deal," Kirill informs her. "I'm sure he was drunk."

"Probably," the woman, I assume her name is Alena, states. The blonde takes her friend's hand in hers. "Are you okay, Izzy?" She peers into her friend's face to make sure she's not in shock. I reluctantly relinquish my tight hold on her body, which is still pressed against mine.

Izzy's tight curvy ass is brushing my cock, making me hard. I allow my grasp on her to relax as I don't want to turn her off due to my boner poking into her back. There are rules to be followed in society, and introducing oneself with a hard cock isn't how I envisioned this. This is the only reason I allow Izzy to move.

"Yes, thank you. But what the fuck?" I'm so close I feel the tremor running through her body. "No one ever did anything like that before, and we've been to plenty of clubs over the years," she replies.

This is when I realize she's not in the mafia world. Otherwise, she'd be immune to a simple stabbing. "He's a stranger and thought he… he owned me."

I send a questioning look to Kirill.

"This is Izzy." He acknowledges Izzy. "And this is Alena, Mikhail Pasnov's daughter," he explains with a wry grin.

I assume correctly that these are the girls we were to mingle with tonight.

So, Alena is his boss's daughter, and her father carries weight. No doubt the men tonight backed down over her presence. She has a direct ear to the top of the bratva, and her father would have their heads on a platter like a goat at an orthodox Easter dinner.

"I'm Izzy," the shapely woman dressed in a beautiful off-white dress turns to me and politely extends her hand.

I take her petite hand and ignore the tingles in my groin. "Dmitry."

"Thank you again. I don't want any trouble," she murmurs. I lean in to hear her words as the music kicks up a notch, and it's hard to hear.

Izzy is refreshing. Russian women have a harshness about them. They do what is in their best interest to survive, making them angry, miserable, and anything but loyal.

Women who know me always want more, which might be why I've never invested in anyone since my girlfriend died. If I'm with a woman, it's only for a fuck. I've noticed lately that I'm beginning to feel empty after these encounters, and I'm often seen leaving clubs early to head home instead of hooking up with random strangers.

Plus, I won't be pitied for the scars I've covered with tattoos. Knife fights always leave a mark. I'm good with them, and they are easier to carry than guns, but every pro has a bad day now and then.

"Let's go to our table." Kirill extends a hand, suggesting the ladies go first, and we follow close behind to guide them.

Everyone around the bar area returns to their drinks, and all is forgotten.

We settle around the table, and naturally, Izzy sits beside me. I'm beginning to suspect Kirill of playing matchmaker and tip my head back to observe him. Someone in my family probably told him I hadn't been myself lately. I admit there hasn't been much time to hang out with my brothers like I usually do, and now that Nikolay is married, I see less of him.

Kirill is acting as if nothing is going on. However, my interest is piqued. Why Izzy? Why her, of all the people here tonight? She blends in as a local, meaning she isn't a targeted tourist, nor does she fit in as one of ours.

And the man who grabbed her arm? Was he sent here to create a distraction so someone could grab Alena? I study Kirill and wonder if he is guarding Alena under the ruse of a double date. I've heard she's opinionated, and her daddy always has people watching her. I also know how daughters hate to have security details on them.

Kirill is pouring the girls champagne and refilling our shot glasses with vodka. Alena is no longer concerned with the incident, and she's chatting with Kirill as if nothing ever happened.

The club is filling up, but I only have eyes for Izzy. I noticed her the minute she came into view. Izzy and Alena lift their glasses.

"A toast to the new graduates, cheers," Kirill says as we tap glasses.

"Thank you for what you did," Izzy says as she sips her drink.

"No problem. I'm sure he was looking for trouble," I say, knowing it's a lie. Men don't work to piss off the Russian mafia.

I'm convinced the goon wanted something. There would have been more questions if he were in the inner bratva. He's a rogue, and he tried to intimidate Izzy. What was he after? That leads to more questions. Something's not adding up, bothering me because I like details.

It would not surprise me to see a disgruntled employee make a move on Alena due to who her father is. However, I'm not sure anyone recognizes her as this is a new club, and mafia men keep their families out of the bratva limelight. They do social engagements and charity functions. The man tonight made a bold move. Or a desperate one. I'm not sure which. If anyone grabbed Alena like that, her father would see him dead before morning.

We listen to music and finish our drinks. Kirill pours more champagne into the girls' glass flutes, and we both toss back another shot of vodka. I never drink much when I'm in a new environment. I'm always on duty. It's ingrained in me.

I check the exits, and the group who caused the commotion is gone, but the bouncers are speaking into their mics which are clipped under their dress shirts. The wire between the ear and chest is the telltale sign of security. I'm sure the incident was noted.

"So, what's up now that you're out of school?" Kirill pushes the envelope, and I feel there might be some chemistry between him and Alena.

His flirting gives it away. He won't risk fucking Alena without her father's blessing. No, for him, he would have to court her formally. If Alena picks someone, it's on her. But a man in his position should follow the proper channels unless he wants to end up face-down in a canal, and there are plenty of them here.

Smart, Kirill, keep the girls busy while I check the temperature of the room. I thought this would be a simple job, a mini-vacation.

Now, I'm involved in whatever happens in his bratva, and it's more than the missing money. What am I missing?

Kirill carries the conversation. Izzy seems preoccupied with the earlier event as she drains half her drink in one gulp, places her hands in her lap, and fidgets with the lace of her dress.

I'm feeling relatively warm but can't take my jacket off as I have a gun clipped under it. After sipping her drink once more, Izzy is restless in her chair and decides to down it.

"You nervous or something?" My voice is low, my lips dangerously close to the ear I want to nibble.

She's vanilla and spice, a lethal combination of subtle sexuality, and my cock is straining against the zipper of my jeans again. Twice in five minutes, what the hell is wrong with me?

"Are you with Kirill?" Smart girl, she wants to know my connection.

"We're friends. I'm from Europe. Only here for a week or so. You?"

"I'm Alena's roommate. We just graduated."

"What did that Russian want?"

"He asked me my name, and I told him to fuck off. I think he saw my tattoo and grabbed my arm."

"What tattoo?"

She pulls the sleeve on her right arm up a few inches to expose an intricate tattoo of a bluebird. I want to touch her and decide to take advantage of the opportunity. I use my right hand, with scars over my knuckles and a broken pinkie finger, to hold her slight wrist. I observe the artwork, running my fingers lightly over the blue ink. Touching her makes my balls hard, and my cocks is pushing against the zipper of my pants. I'm sure I've got a zipper imprint by now.

A bird is a symbol that isn't meaningful to an ordinary civilian. She's the property of someone or someone's woman.

"Who are you?" I demand, fascinated with her. Who has kept someone under Alena's nose?

"I told you, Izzy, Izzy Lucci."

Her last name is Italian. She should be safe in this area of the city. Last I heard the Russians negotiated to form an alliance with the Italians. I slide my fingers under her chin and tilt her head back, and our eyes lock. "Why that tattoo?"

"It's for my mother. She had one with a cage, and she told me always to be free. I got it in memory of her. I miss her."

"She died?" I don't mean to be blunt, but it's necessary.

"Yes." A dark cloud passes over her angelic face. "It was a car accident many years ago."

"Was she involved with the bratva, the Italians?"

"No, she would never do that. She was sweet and down to earth. We lived in Connecticut."

Mm. I don't want to press and make her leery of me. Tonight is supposed to be fun.

I lean forward, refill the flutes, and pour another shot for myself and Kirill. I sip my vodka to keep my wits about me. When I return my attention to Izzy, the perplexed look on her face leads me to believe she's telling me the truth. I'm jaded. Maybe her tattoo is a coincidence.

"Let's dance." It's a command, not an invitation. I need to get away from the table and clear my head. I hate dancing, so this indicates how fuzzy my head is right now.

Izzy scoots off her chair and stands beside the table, waiting for me. She's not getting any further without me, either. Kirill glances in my direction, pleased we're hitting it off, before returning his attention to Alena. They seem to be enjoying a deep conversation, considering they have her father in common. I'm not surprised. Men who move up the ranks are a force to be reckoned with, and Kirill looks like he's on his way. Maybe he'll end up married to Alena, which would make them an influential couple in the inner circle.

I take Izzy's hand, and she doesn't pull away. Instead, she holds mine as my grip tightens. We snake through the crowd to reach the dance floor on the level below. I glance up. Kirill is still sitting with Alena. Techno music is new, but the beat is solid and easy to follow. I look down and take in her face. She gives me a smile, and I move my feet. This makes her happy as she returns the smile, sways her hips, and raises her arms in the air at the same time as the others on the dance floor. She knows all the current dance steps in New York City. I have a feeling this morsel will keep me on my toes. I didn't come here for a romance. An international relationship is the last thing on my mind. It's a complication I don't need or want. Besides, as my wife, she'd never be safe without me. This means we would have to be together everywhere, which would require picking a home country.

Given that she graduated with Alena, her education is too pricey for an average person not to make a living with it. This is another complication because my woman won't work. It's a reflection on me and my power. If I can't support my wife, I can't support the soldiers, and it would make me look weak.

Why the fuck am I even thinking about this? I find myself intrigued by this woman with the bird tattoo. I need to seduce her and get her out of my system. It's that easy. Bars are notorious for hookups, and yet, I'm getting lost in the music and the way her body moves.

She knows how to work her hips, and she swivels her hips and moves them in a suggestive circle. The next move puts her directly in front of me. Her firm buttocks rub my cock. And he rises to the occasion.

Fuck me.

I place my hands on her hips, and she wiggles them to the song's beat. *Holy mother of God.* I spin her around and lower my head into her neck, burying my face in her hair as my warm lips take that nibble of her ear.

"We need to leave," I say. "Now."

It's not a suggestion. I'm so excited I will explode the next time her tight ass brushes my cock. I've never been so turned on before. It's like I'm experiencing a contact high without the drugs. I need to fuck the hell out of here right now.

I grab her hand and lead her to the side door Kirill and I used earlier. I text an Uber. And Kirill. "Alena will take your purse home," I announce to Izzy as we stand on the curb.

My lips are on hers. Her lips are soft and yielding under mine. I press harder, wanting to devour every inch of her. Her arms slide around my neck, and my hands tighten around her waist.

The car pulls up. I open the door. She slides in first. I take a second to survey the landscape. Nothing looks out of place, so I doubt we're being tailed. I'm always working and decide that tonight I need to relax for a change.

I look forward to fucking Izzy. For some reason, I never want her to forget me.

I tell the Uber driver to take us to an intersection a few blocks from the condo to be safe. We get out, and I put my arm around her as we walk. I notice her soft skin is covered in goosebumps. The night air is warm by my standards. She's either cold or nervous. I pull her closer as we walk, leading us into the secure building with no visible doorman. I hope Kirill has control of the surveillance cameras out front and in the lobby. I don't want to be on video if I can prevent it.

We take the private elevator, and I press the button. As soon as the doors close, I turn, taking her by surprise. I pin her against the metal wall with one hand on her throat. She's under my control. Her slightly swollen lips are parted as if she's asking for more. One hand slides down her face, and the other holds her still. I bend my head. My lips cover hers. I kiss her gently at first. I nip and nibble, teasing her. My cock is engorged, and her hands slide around my neck. She wraps one leg around my hips and pulls me into her. She wants this as much as I do. She has no way of knowing I'm about to erase the memory of any man she's ever been with. I plan to tease her to frustration and leave her begging for more. By the time I'm done with her, she'll be screaming my name as she comes all over my cock.

CHAPTER 6

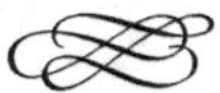

IZZY

*I*f Dmitry is hanging out with Kirill, he must be someone important. I've never been with a mafia man before. I was always afraid to get too close and get sucked into a world where I disagree with their criminal ways. I'm worried I'll lose myself if I become like them.

Tonight, their world spilled into mine. I'm not immune to danger, but this week has been intense. Between the stalker and the knife, I feel like my life is careening in the wrong direction. Does my friendship with Alena come with strings that will forever bind me to the mafia world?

I have no clue. All I know is that Dmitry's dark eyes see me. How did he know that man was going to grab me? Was he watching me? How could he do that with a knife and not be arrested? I know tonight is the first time I've felt safe since the stalker.

His English is good, but I picked up on what sounds like a Russian accent. I melt in his arms, and he can kiss me forever without breathing. The fact that he can stab a knife into a man's hand without blinking gives me a reason to pause. I've seen how brutal

Russians can be based on their reputation. Tonight, I have seen firsthand how brutal they can be. The violence was immediate and caused my heart to skip a beat. This man knows how to take control of a room, and he did it to protect me.

"You're beautiful," he murmurs. His hands are anything but cruel as he glides them over my arms and caresses my breasts, rubbing the nipples through my thin bra. I want to remind him we're in public, but the words die on my tongue because he's sucking it into his mouth. I can't resist him as he works my body into a fever I've never known. Oh my God, I'm in if this is what a bad boy is about. The elevator dings, and it's perfect timing. I need air. He gives my bottom lip a final nip before stepping out of the elevator and grabbing my hand as I follow him.

The woodsy smell of his cologne and expensive vodka drifts over me. I breathe him in, and his touch makes my panties wet. How long has it been? Too long. That's about to change. I'm done sitting on the sidelines, watching others have all the fun. I will be a bad girl tonight and walk on the wild side. What's the harm in one hookup? I want to savor tonight for all it's worth with this man who has shown he has a short fuse and can be ruthless when his demands aren't followed. I've never had a man defend me. It was exhilarating, empowering, and … a turn-on. Maybe women with dangerous men *do* have more fun.

He leads me into a large condo, and the kitchen lights flick on by sensor. The door locks automatically behind us like a hotel room. I don't have my phone or identification. I'm being reckless. I'm alone with a stranger, and my heart races like a Formula One engine. Dmitry empties his pockets onto the counter and pins me against the closest wall. He slips out of his shoes, removes my spiked heels, and caresses each foot after he tosses the shoe. Who knew this would send erotic shivers up my spine?

He finds the zipper in the back of my dress, and I hear it unzip. I moan against his strong jaw before he leaves a trail kisses down my neck, to my full breasts. He unclasps my lacy bra, exposing my breasts to the cool air. My nipples harden, begging to be stroked. I crave his touch. It's making my brain as fuzzy as a cotton ball.

He savagely grabs one breast. I gasp. I'm not used to rough sex, but heat fills my panties. I want more. I slip my arms around his neck, pulling him closer. Snaking a bare leg around his leg, I unzip his pants, slip my hand inside his boxers, and grab his rock-hard cock. When his lips latch onto my nipples, wetness gushes between my thighs, and I feel myself limp against the wall.

He catches me by scooping me up in his arms. I rest my head on his broad chest as he carries me like I'm light as a feather to a bedroom. He yanks the covers back with one hand and lays me in the bed with my legs dangling over the side.

He strips his boxers off and unbuttons his shirt, dropping it silently to the carpeted floor. In the soft glow of a night light in the room, my eyes drift from his brooding dark eyes to his broad chest covered with tattoos. His muscles flex. I hear my panties tearing after he slips a finger under them, leaving me exposed, physically and emotionally.

He drags me across the bed towards him. When my pussy is lined up with his cock, he kneels. Placing his hands under my buttocks, he angles me up towards him. I spread my legs, and he devours me. Arching my back, I grasp the sheets and ball them into my fists as the pleasure makes my head swim. His fingertips grip my thighs so hard it hurts. The bruises will be my reminder that this wasn't a dream.

He mumbles something in Russian and runs his tongue around my inner lips before focusing on my clit. He brings me close to climaxing, then pulls away. I want to slap him. How dare he deny me?

"Fuck me," I beg as I writhe with pleasure firing in every fiber of my being.

"Not yet, *dorogoy*," he says as he runs his tongue up my thigh and stands.

He rubs the tip of his engorged cock at my entrance, massaging my lips and clit. I take a deep breath and put a fist in my mouth to keep from screaming. My other hand grabs his chest hair, urging him to fuck me.

He bends over and softly kisses my cheek, then my lips. I thread my fingers into his thick head of hair. Our eyes meet.

"I'm going to fuck you hard," he whispers. He reaches for a condom on the nightstand, rips it with his teeth, and glides it on. He leans forward slightly and thrusts himself into my anxious pussy. I whimper. He's large, and I'm small. His eyes flicker with a mischievous gleam. "You are so tight. This might hurt."

I grab his shoulders to brace myself as he slams into me, and I experience his girth with a moan. It hurts, but it's the most incredible feeling in the world.

He doesn't strike me as a man with fuzzy feelings, but he asks, "Are you okay, Izzy?"

"Yes, yes," I assure him with the soft lilt of my voice.

"Fine," he says before he moves in and out of me, raising me higher and higher until my orgasm shatters me.

I cry out into the darkness as I clutch his shoulders. He pumps me a few more times before letting out a long groan, then shudders one last time before pulling me to his chest and gently holding me in his arms. I'm suspended in the air, holding onto his bulging biceps. The well-developed trapezoid muscles of his back support me.

"And now, how do you feel?"

"Amazing," I whisper. My mouth is parched from yelling and moaning while I clawed at his back during my final release.

"Good." He rolls beside me. "Do you need anything, my little bird?"

"Water, please."

He leaves the room without a sound. I hear water running in the kitchen faucet. He returns and hands me the filled glass. I guzzle it, then wipe the droplets off my lip.

I set the glass on the nightstand, and he pulls me back into the bed and places the covers over me.

"Go to sleep."

"You called me little bird. What does that mean?"

"Tomorrow, I'll explain more. We need to sleep now because I will wake you up for round two in a few hours."

"Oh," I reply. Now I'm not going to be able to sleep. *Fuck*, this man is a beast.

I have questions for him, too. I felt the scars on his chest, and I could tell one leg had suffered trauma, which left it slightly deformed. I wonder if he was tortured.

Sometime during the night, I'm awakened by a hand running down my arm, caressing my body. Immediately, I'm wet. I roll over, and Dmitry's face hovers over mine. He rolls on top of me, and his sheathed, hard cock enters me with one thrust, jolting my body backward. I gasp. My hands cling to his biceps, and my toes curl. I probably could have come without him, but when he thrusts in again, I'm happy I waited.

My eyes flutter open as sunlight peeks between the slats of the blinds. Dmitry is next to me with a cup of hot coffee. I sit up and take it from him. The smell alone is enough to give me a caffeine boost. He bought me coffee in bed. Will this man always surprise me? Or is this just to impress me?

"Good morning." He walks toward the open ensuite and starts the shower. "I didn't want to wake you up. You were very tired."

"I had no idea." I drink the coffee, trying not to choke on it as I take in his large frame. My eyes rest on a scar on his side that looks like a bullet hole and the incision from the knife used to remove it.

"Are those all from work?"

He must get asked this by every woman he's been with.

"Yes, some on my chest were accidental during training. Others are from knife fights where I didn't do good enough." He moves about the room methodically, pulling out clothing to wear. "Shower or more questions?" He sends me a look, but I can't read him. He acts like he's working again, and everything that transpired last night has vanished.

So, this is what it's like being with these guys. No wonder Alena hasn't formed any attachments to these men. They are unreachable. It's like a curtain comes down for sex, and then he shifts back to being curt and aloof. He doesn't impress me as a trusting man, especially when he's questioning me about my past. I'm glad he didn't do more to that man in the club. After I saw what he was capable of, I assumed he'd done this before. How many has he killed? I don't pretend to know what his life was like growing up in the bratva. I'm not sure I want to see that side of him. It scares me that his life is filled with so much darkness.

"Shower." I'll take the breadcrumbs he gives me. He's possessive and protective of me. I will figure him out as I go. If I'm to survive in his world, I can't let my feelings get hurt by his change in demeanor. Most men who have a hook-up would have skated out the door before daybreak. Dmitry cooked me breakfast.

We shower, both lost in our worlds, and he hands me a towel when he gets out. I dry off and have only the fashionable dress for the walk of shame home. I hope Alena is at the apartment when I arrive so she can let me in. What got into me last night?

Ah, the chemistry between us was thicker than Beijing's smog. I hope Dmitry isn't as deadly.

"Why the long face?" he asks as he tugs on his jeans.

"I only have last night's clothes. I can't believe I didn't even return for my purse."

"Nothing bad happened. Here," he says as he picks up his dress shirt and sends it flying at my head. "Wear this. I'll see what we have to eat and take you home afterward. You can put your dress on then."

I catch the shirt, and it's huge in comparison to my slight frame. He pulls a white t-shirt over his head and steps into jeans before he heads to the kitchen, and I'm left buttoning tons of expensive buttons. I sniff this shirt. It smells of him combined with the lingering scent of his cologne.

"You like the smell?" he asks as he watches me from the doorway.

Busted. Fuck.

"Mm. What's for breakfast?"

"That's what I was going to ask you. I can make eggs and toast."

"Perfect," I reply, acting like I'm not impressed he can use a stove.

CHAPTER 7

IZZY

*D*mitry makes me another coffee and adds Godiva chocolate liqueur to it. The coffee is made with the press of a button. I wouldn't be surprised to find an Italian barista living here, but then again, Dmitry is Russian. What do they drink when they're not drinking vodka?

"Do you drink more tea in Russia than coffee?" I ask.

"About the same. Why?"

"Just curious," I say. I'm perched on a stool, and even though it has back support, I prefer to put my elbows on the counter. My chin rests in my palms, and I study him with my eyes.

"Any other questions?" He turns and cracks eggs into a hot skillet while toast pops up from a toaster. He quickly butters the toast and returns to flip the eggs like a short-order cook.

"Nope."

"Well, eat up," he says, sliding the plate of food under my nose. I sit up and remove my elbows from the counter.

He remains standing, holding his plate in one hand, and passes me a fork with the other.

"Thanks." I begin to eat. I'm starving. I burned through those paninis before we left the club.

"I have questions," he says. His slight accent is seductive. I like the way the words surround me and make me feel like we're more than acquaintances. He has a confident demeanor about him that melts me.

"What?" I scoop eggs into my mouth. The seasoning is perfect, and I sneak a peek at the spice bottles he used. Garlic and steak seasoning? I've never thought of using that on eggs.

"I don't understand why you have that tattoo," he says.

"I told you, it's for my mom. It reminds me of her. She had a bird and a cage tattoo on her wrist. I mean, it is a pretty bird, it's blue. Besides, everyone has tattoos nowadays."

"I ask because the bird in a cage tattoo symbolizes women in the mafia. Our women are ours to protect, and we keep them in cages to keep them safe. Her tattoo implies she escaped her cage." His eyes are as cold and hard as black ice. Damn, it looks like he's ready to take my head off. *Men.*

I'm confused. My mother never told me the meaning of her tattoo.

"She was not the type to be involved with criminals. She was gentle, soft-spoken, and avoided attention. She bought her things at thrift stores because we didn't have much, so she sacrificed for me. It's pretty shitty that I didn't grow up with both parents. I'd love to have siblings, a family. I long to feel like I belong," I add in case he missed the point that my mother was different from the women he knows in the mafia.

Before Mom was killed in the car accident, she was involved with a long-term boyfriend and planned to marry. It's a shame because I liked him and would have loved calling him Dad. He was a successful investor on Wall Street. He liked all the modern Irish bands and used to sing me old Irish songs his grandfather taught him. Mom would laugh at his singing, but I know she liked it.

I shrug. "Well, I like my bird. Does there need to be more to it?"

He looks up from his food, swallows, and says, "Yes." His eyes seared into mine like hot pokers. He stands as he eats off a plate balanced on his hand.

"What's got your panties in a bunch?" I ask.

"I don't understand this phrase."

"Boxers," I explain. "Stuck up your butt crack."

He chokes on his food. After a cough, he speaks. "You Americans. Always so funny, eh?" He finishes his plate and puts it in a sink that looks like it's never been used.

"Well, you have tattoos, too."

"Yes, to cover scars and from a crazy trip to Miami with too much alcohol. But you're not one to do something like that. You like order. Everything you do is planned."

His eyes are on me again, and my jaw drops. *Shit*, he's profiled me. He's probably a hitman.

Fuck me.

I clear my throat. "Now you're a shrink?"

"I call it the way I see it, and I'm rarely wrong. You have some tough finger pads, which means your artwork is more manual labor than delicate work. You're not likely to get strong fingers from a paintbrush. Alena paints, and hers are still very…." He's toying with me now. "Feminine."

His eyes remind me of dark pools of death. They are so black, so deep, and I can't read anything in them. I wonder if he feels anything at all. He could be a psychopath, for all I know.

"Oh, so now I'm a cave dweller? Figures coming from a Russian. You're used to women doing all the heavy lifting." I finish the last bite of my food, which slides down my throat. He surprises me by grabbing my wrist with his cat-like reflexes.

Holy fuck. I jump from my chair so fast it flies backward, crashing as it hits the marble floor. I can't move. I pull my arm, but he moves quickly around the end of the island. My wrist is starting to hurt.

"What's the problem?" he mocks me with his sardonic tone.

"What do you want?"

"The truth."

"I told you the truth. Believe what you want, but I'm not one of your kind. I'm Alena's best friend. I have immunity."

"No one has immunity. You betray us, lie to us, we'll kill you just like we'd gut a fish for dinner."

Oh, fuck. Where is Alena? I'm with a madman.

"Let go!" I yell.

"That bastard in the bar left a bruise on your arm." He gently traces the mark with his finger. I notice his crooked pinkie for the first time. It looks like an old injury that healed wrong. He's full of battle scars and probably has a story to go with each one. "I should have killed him," he murmurs. "I'll have his head for that."

"Head?" I feel faint. "No, please. I'm sure he was drunk. I can't be responsible for someone dying. I've had enough of that."

"Explain." He releases me at last. I sigh in relief, rubbing my wrist.

Dmitry can be a scary dude. His mood swings and split personality have my head spinning. I'm struggling to determine which one is the real Dmitry.

"You have serious trust issues," I huff, determined not to give him the upper hand.

"You do, too. I don't think you've ever climaxed the way you did last night with anyone else."

"That's not for you to decide. I've had decent lovers." I stand with my chin up and chest out. *Dammit.* I'm still in his shirt, and it's hard to make a serious point when I'm not wearing panties.

His eyes catch mine, and we have a stare down. It's like a kid's game to see who blinks first. I never win these games. Besides, the winter air is too dry and makes my eyes water half the time.

I blink first.

"You have secrets." He moves to the kitchen, washes the plates and skillet by hand, and then sets them in the sink to dry. "What are they?"

"Well, if you must know. I think someone is following Alena."

"What?" He turns off the water and reads my face. "How can that be? Her father would be all over it. I'm sure she has guards she doesn't know about following her."

"I'm not so sure. She's very adamant about what she does. I suppose they could be good at blending in. Maybe she doesn't think about it as much."

"Mm, that's strange. I'd never leave anyone I love unguarded, and still, accidents happen." He grows distant. I'm sure there's more to that look than what he's sharing.

"No." I smack my hand on the counter. "You're not listening. Someone followed me, but I think they want Alena. I'm no one special. Why would anyone want me?"

He dries his hands and plants himself in front of me. His fingers are on my hips, and my pussy quivers with anticipation. We fucked our brains out three times last night, and I still want more.

"Why would someone be after Alena?" His warm breath brushes my face, but his eyes are fixated on mine.

"I don't know. I didn't ask questions, but someone followed me to our corner Italian grocery the other day. If I had my phone, I'd show you the picture. I acted like I was making a video for social media, but he hid his face in his hoodie. Big guy."

"The same one from last night?"

"I don't know. I never put the two events together."

"Maybe you should." His arrogant tone gives me a cold shower.

"You act like this is my fault!" I'm so frustrated that I pound his chest. He takes it and doesn't move a muscle. I may as well be pounding on an oak door. "I'm not connected. I'm not part of Alena's inner circle. I'm her friend, and I'd never repeat anything she says to anyone. I know if I did, I'd be dead, so *you tell me!*" I raise my voice to make my point.

He quickly catches my fists, gently holding them to his mouth, and I hate him for swiftly deescalating my anger. It's as if I were dusted with pixie dust.

The silence in the room is unnerving.

"You let me hit you," I whisper, lifting my head to meet his eyes.

"I did." His dark gaze is calm and soft. He's giving me a tiny opening into his gentler side, and I'm speechless. "I've been helpless before. I've lost many people, but two in particular. My world is dangerous. And I'm not fond of Italians, and you are Sicilian. Are you sure you're not connected to the Cosa Nostra?"

"Why do you think that?"

"You're someone, my little bird. The question is, who?

His eyes search mine. I can't hide my vulnerability. My heart yearns to know and understand his pain. "Who are you?"

"My last name is Volkov. We head the mafia in parts of Russia and London. My brother, Nikolay, recently took over as the don after my father was murdered in Volgrad. It was a car crash, made to look like an accident. That's usually how these things are done, so they don't look like hits." He kisses my knuckles and drops my hands before moving away.

"Do they do that here, too?"

"It can be anywhere. It's a way of eliminating enemies without starting a war between families. No proof, no guilt. Why?"

He lets go of me and walks to a large window, deep in thought. He impresses me as a man who knows what he wants before he goes after it. He's lived a lifetime, and he's not even thirty years old if one were to judge his age on his physique. I assume he's seen bad things like violence and death. But I know death, too.

"Why did you pick me up last night?"

"You wanted to fuck me as much as I wanted to fuck you."

I hope he didn't hear my sharp inhale. His words stung. I have to remind myself that he's higher than a soldier, and he's a made man for sure. No one stabs a person so swiftly and is prepared to go further without practice and balls.

He's honest, brutally honest. I don't know if it's better that he hurts my feelings now or lets me suffer an enormous heartache later. I need to stay away from this man. He's dangerous, and it's not just the physicality issue.

He turns. His face is stoic. I take in his dark eyes, and so help God, I want to run my hands through his thick hair.

"I need to get you home. I'm sure you have things to do," he says coldly. "Get dressed. I'll give you my jacket to wear over the shirt. I'm driving you home."

With that, my walk of shame begins.

"Did you text Alena to tell her I'm okay? Is she home?"

"She knows you're okay. I'll tell Kirill we're leaving now. He'll let her know."

"Fine," I reply, telling myself not to care. He's just another man who fucked me and left me. I'm a glutton for punishment, always picking the wrong guy.

It's for the best, and I prepare myself for the slew of questions Alena will bombard me with as soon as I see her.

True to his word, we leave a few minutes later. I'm wearing his dress shirt that looks oversized on me, panties, and heels. I'm a poster child for a backup singer in an eighties music video. He holds a suit jacket for me as I slip my arms into it. I'm making quite the fashion statement today, and I can't help but chuckle at the irony of it.

"Something amuses you?" he asks as he opens the door and looks both ways down the hallway.

"I love this fashion statement," I reply with a grimace.

"Ah, the fashion designer. Yes. I'm sorry I don't have a clothes closet for you to choose something nicer."

He's so fucking serious. Like, really? He flew here. I live here.

"No problem. I don't need much," I reply and stomp past him.

He takes the lead and uses a private elevator to access the parking garage.

"Wow, someone has perks."

The smirk he gives me makes me want to wipe the floor with him. "It's not my apartment, but membership has its privileges."

I hear a beep, and headlights flash in front of us. I've seen this car before, but I can't figure out why anyone would want to drive around in a Lamborghini. I'm surprised when he opens the door for me, and it opens like a regular car door.

"Must be a new model," I remark. I tuck my folded dress under my arm and use my other hand to balance myself while getting in.

Dmitry has his hand out to help. I ignore his offer of assistance and get in unassisted. He shuts the door, gets in the driver's side, starts the engine, gives it a rev, and backs out like a professional driver. We're not far from Alena's flat and buzzed in as we approached the door. I open it and walk in. We're on my turf. I know he'll understand if I'm not two feet behind him like a good little girl who does as she's told.

CHAPTER 8

DMITRY

I've never understood why American girls are so opposed to walking a step behind their men. It's like everything has to be equal for them. I'm unsure how Izzy's mother raised her to be independent and spirited. Unless it was a *fuck you* to her old man, who knows who that was. For that matter, who was Izzy's mother? What was her story? She's not here to tell us, so I have my work cut out for me. I thought Kirill would help fill in the blanks. However, Alena has a history with the family and gave me puzzle pieces.

I'm compelled to seduce Izzy again and tell myself it's only the intrigue of her tattoo. Tattoos are personal, some more meaningful than others. Her mother's tattoo was important to her, or she would never have put it on her flesh. I can't shake my gut instinct telling me she obtained the tattoo as a reminder of what she left behind. I can't determine the connection, but her mother knew our world. I'm sure of it. She could be a blood relative of any family, but my money is on the Sicilians. Was she born from an illicit union, or is she someone's crown jewel?

The part about the stalker was a surprise and gave me a reason to be concerned. We're all targeted at some point, and Alena is no exception. I texted Kirill that she could be in danger and needs to lie low with more guards. She's always been in an ivory tower. Even if she thought she was free, it was an illusion.

The door to the flat opens, and Alena greets us as she and Izzy share a warm embrace.

"Oh, my God," Alena squeals. She's not one to hide her emotions. "You two ditched us last night." She gives me a look that says *I hope you fucked her hard, you stud.*

"So, I take it you two had a good time?" Kirill asks as he gets up from the sofa in the living room.

"Yeah, yeah." I brush it off. Why is everyone making a big deal about last night? It was a one-and-done.

"Well, I, for one." Alena puts a hand on her chest. "Nearly had a heart attack when you stuck your knife in the hand of that burly Albanian, or was he from Russia? I couldn't tell in the dim lighting. But damn, that was something you don't see every day." Alena carries on about the night of the stabbing while offering us a mimosa.

"I'm good. Too much champagne last night." Izzy waves her off and heads down a hall, presumably to her bedroom.

I love her in my shirt and the heels. It's sexy as fuck, and my cock stirs as I watch her shapely legs move further away. A wave of regret floods my chest. I don't want her to be that far away. We're within a 1,500-foot radius of each other, and it's not close enough for me. She's mine. I marked her last night when I stabbed the stranger. She was mine when I sank my cock into her. I desire to be in her fully, without a condom between us. I want to feel her slick walls clenching around my cock.

As if I wished her to appear, she returns, dressed in a light sweater and fitted jeans that hug her curves in all the right places, making her ass look edible. I'd love to peel those pants off and sink my cock into her. He begins to thicken at the thought of it. *Fuck me.* I have to focus less on Izzy and more on my work. I have a job to do, and now, it appears, there are other issues in the bratva. I need to speak to Kirill and get some answers.

Izzy returns my jacket, and I place it on the back of the sofa.

"My shirt?" I lift one eyebrow as I question her.

She only shrugs. "Can I get you a bottle of fizzy water?"

"Sure."

She disappears, and Alena is right on her heels, no doubt to pump her for details about our night spent banging the headboard against the wall. Women do this in Russia and London, too. It's like a goddamn universal language, women wagging their tongues. Today, I welcome it because it allows me to ask my friend what's happening in the city and, more importantly, the bratva.

I don't want the girls to hear me, so I join Kirill on the couch and keep my voice low.

"Where did you sleep last night, here or home?" I ask out of curiosity.

"I crashed with a friend nearby. What's up?"

He punches my shoulder, and it doesn't even faze me—Americans and how friendly they are. I'm not one for hand-holding or affectionate taps like this. It occurs to me that I've had my hands on Izzy more in twelve hours than I've had them on anyone else in twelve months. What does that mean?

"Did Alena say anything about being followed this week?"

"No, but I noticed her father has more men looking after her. Why?"

"I'm not sure they are after her." I'm too big for Alena's modern taste in furniture and sit with my elbows on my knees. I feel like I'm in a kid's playhouse.

"Why?"

"Later," I murmur as I hear Alena's heels clicking across the tile floor in the kitchen. When they join us, I can't help but notice the slight flush in Izzy's cheeks.

Mm. She must have been sharing details. I sit back with one leg crossed over the other. I stretch an arm along the back of the couch to observe her. I didn't consider her a gossip, but nothing about her makes sense. It's as if her story has been contrived, but for what purpose?

"So, we had a great time," Alena speaks, giving us an authentic smile. From the dark circles under her eyes, I'm guessing they stayed out until the club closed. "Kirill knows tons of popular dances, and I have to say we made an impression." She curls up in a clear, lucite chair that looks as comfortable as a bed of nails. But what do I know?

Men like me only know fashion regarding custom suits, leather shoes, and Swiss watches that flaunt who's at the top of the food chain. Alena is wearing leggings and a red blouse. The top three buttons of her blouse are unfastened and reveal more cleavage than her father would allow.

"It's easy with you," Kirill replies. His voice is light and hints at a happy note. "Everyone had their eyes on you." He flirts. "Besides, you make me look good." He's laying it on thick, so he's still trying to get in her pants.

She blushes. "That's shit, and you know it."

That's part of Alena's charm. She knows she looks fantastic, but she's still humble about it. I decided here and now that I like her. How Izzy fits in, I'm not quite sure.

Izzy hands me a bottle of lemon-flavored fizzy water. Our fingers collide, and she flinches at the static electricity firing between us. I twist off the metal cap without getting another shock and then guzzle half the water. It's getting hot in here. Usually, I'd seek solitude in this situation and leave. The only reason to move is to obtain more answers from Kirill and ensure our coke deal is progressing as planned.

I stand, indicative of leaving.

Everyone stops talking and looks at me like I'm a buzz kill.

"I need to go. I have work to do," I explain as I look at Kirill.

"Yes, we do," he says, reluctantly standing up.

"But it's Sunday," Alena protests.

Is she upset that we're leaving so soon? I consider the fact that four is a crowd if she wants Kirill.

Izzy chimes in, "I have work to do, too. I need to look for a job. Plus, it's my day to grab a cappuccino and study fashion magazines."

Alena pouts, making her injected-filled lips look even more prominent. What is it with women nowadays? I love that Izzy is natural and doesn't need to compete with artificial enhancers.

We make our goodbyes, and I nod to Izzy. No sense in leading her on. She's a fool if she thinks it was anything other than a fling. It won't happen again. I can't handle another woman's death on my hands. On the flip side, what if someone *is* stalking her? Don't I have an obligation to keep her safe?

My first thought is that it's not my bratva or my problem. But I'm lying to myself. I might have a black soul that will go to hell, but women shouldn't pay for our sins. Love is the beginning of the end, as it sucks us in and destroys our souls when it's over.

We make our way to the elevator, and out of habit, I glance to the courtyard below for safety concerns. To my surprise, I see two men who don't belong. They are standing on the curb smoking, but they look out of place. This is not the type of neighborhood where men who look like they work nights would live or visit.

While we ride in the elevator, I ask Kirill to explain what's happening with his bratva.

"The Italians have been pissing us off lately, and we're all nervous about the latest cocaine deal. We need them to smuggle it out of the port and make sure it gets to London, where your brother's men will unload and distribute it. But, of course, they want a bigger cut than the original deal. It's a power play, a dangerous one. My mother's connections have broken down over the years. The Irish have been flexing their muscles to fuck with us. I get select intel, but I wouldn't be surprised if they know of the rumored alliance." He shrugs. "You know how it is. Everyone wants to fuck with us. The Albanians are a pain in the ass. They think they are contenders, but there is no way in hell we're giving them squat. I only hear bits and pieces from Mikhail. He's a good boss, but working with someone who advises the don is stressful. You know how that is."

"Yeah, only I'm family and part of the inner circle." I chuckle as the elevator doors open. "You know, should we pull the camera footage of the bar last night and find out who that man was? What if someone is after Izzy or Alena? We have a duty to make sure they're safe." We leave the building, and the men on the street light another cigarette. "Are the men on the curb with you?" I ask as I cast my head down so Kirill's glance to the street isn't obvious.

He looks to where I nod. "Those aren't mine. My guys know how to hide from Alena. She gets pissed when she knows her dad is having her watched."

The alarm on my Lambo goes off. We take our time walking to where it's parked on the street to make sure it's not a trap. The car belongs to Alena's dad, a perk that goes with Kirill's condo. Her dad keeps it parked there to avoid paying for storage.

I walk around the car, looking for anything suspicious. I bet someone touched it to fuck with me. City life feels more like an urban jungle between the car alarms, the sirens of the police, and the wails of ambulances. It's a constant noise that makes me miss my home in Russia.

Kirill looks around for his men.

"Fuck." He gets on his phone and calls Tito to see where everyone is. They reply that they were diverted from Alena's detail. "What the hell is going on, Tito? I want you to get men here now. I'm not leaving until someone shows up. Better yet, find out who decided this because her father will be pissed, and there will be hell to pay." Kirill is livid. "I need a smoke. This has never happened."

He pulls a pack of cigarettes from his leather jacket and puts one in his mouth. He offers me one, and I decline. It's a habit I gave up long ago, and I'm only tempted when I'm around others smoking. Besides, I'd rather be tasting the sweetness of Izzy's pussy than an ashtray.

"What now?"

He lights his cigarette, blows out smoke, and we square off, eye to eye. "We've been compromised somehow. That's my take. You?"

"Same. What would be the motive?"

"No clue. It's the first I'm learning of the situation. We know Izzy was followed this week. Alena mentioned it to me, so we increased security. She's Mikhail's daughter, but the don has children who live at his compound on Long Island. It's off the beaten path, but they are more likely to be kidnapped to obtain information on the elusive don. What would anyone want with Alena or Izzy?" He nods his head in the direction of the apartment building.

"No clue, but we need to get to work, and we can't leave until someone is here with them. Do you trust the men who will show up?"

Finished with his smoke, Kirill drops the butt on the ground and grinds it out with his shoe. "Probably not. I'm sorry, I had no idea shit was brewing before you arrived. But I'm glad you're here. You've been up the food chain and are more adept at the political game."

"Well—"

"Oh, yeah. What the fuck happened last night?" Kirill perks up in anticipation of details.

"That's off limits."

His face falls in disappointment, and I can't help but feel bad for him. "Fine. She's fucking amazing, but I can't be distracted."

"Oh, I know you. All work and no fun makes you a fucking drag most of the time."

I kick at the weeds growing through the cracked sidewalk. I pretend to look at my military boots and sneak a peek at the men on the curb.

Kirill gives a slight shake of his head. "They're playing it cool. I don't think we can leave the girls. Alena has to go to her father's until we resolve this. I doubt Izzy has anywhere to go."

"She's pretty much alone," I agree. "Did you know about the tattoo on her wrist?"

"I've seen it when I visited the flat, once when it wasn't covered. I've only been there a few times." He adds the last part to let me know he's not banging Alena.

"Is she honest?"

"Sure, never caught her in a lie. Why?"

"Something's off. I don't buy her innocent act. We need to get on top of the situation—the missing money and the men following the girls. It's difficult for me to trust strangers, you know how I am."

"I do. I think Izzy is honest." He paces the sidewalk. "Maybe we can park the girls at Mikhail's brownstone. They won't be happy about it."

"Safety comes before happiness," I snap.

"Huh, I thought you said it was just a fling. You're acting more like a lion protecting his mate." His face breaks out in a smirk.

"I don't fall for women. You know that."

"Yeah, sorry about that, by the way."

I nod.

"Let's get the girls. We can't leave them as sitting ducks. You need information from Izzy, so you drive her. I'll take Alena to her dad's and meet you both at the flat. Just make sure you guys are dressed." I don't miss the smirk on his face.

"It will be noon soon, so make it one o'clock?" I reply and ignore his slight. He doesn't think I can keep my hands off Izzy.

I like precision. I like order. I attribute it to making me a good soldier. We learned how to take orders in college. Over the years, our life experiences bonded us, and we remained friends.

"Great." He says as we casually double back to the girls. We use a back entrance this time so we're not as noticeable. Izzy buzzes us in.

"What's up?" she asks at the door.

I shove past her with Kirill close behind. Who knew we'd be back so soon?

"You were right. Someone is following you guys," I say, getting right to the point. I'm in my zone, running the risks and calculating what I need to protect them from the goons downstairs.

Alena acts eerily calm. She must be used to the drill. All she asks is, "How long am I going to be at Dad's?"

"A few days, maybe."

"Is Izzy coming too?"

"I need her with me for now," I interject. "But after that, yes, if that's okay."

"For sure. I'll grab my stuff. I'll be back in a minute."

Kirill follows her, and I follow Izzy.

She glares over her shoulder. "What? I have a hound dog on me now?"

"You'll follow orders, and don't be a pain in my ass," I inform her with a tone that indicates she better not fight me on this. Looking around her room, I see a sewing mannequin wearing an incredibly stylish man's suit. What Michelangelo can do with a brush, she can do with fabric and a needle. I wonder where this talent and creativity will take her. There is a rolling rack full of clothes for dancers and costumes for actors in the corner of her tiny room.

"You need to pack a small bag for a day or so, and I'm going to need more information from you."

"Like what?" She rummages around in dresser drawers, and I notice the shirt I gave her to wear home is on her bed.

She snatches my shirt and shoves it into her gym bag along with jeans, shirts, intimate underclothes, and a Ziplock bag already packed with toiletries. Maybe my shirt will make it back to me eventually.

"Did you anticipate this?" I ask, trying to remain objective and professional.

"I like to keep a bag ready in case we make a quick trip to Alena's house for the holidays, or I go to my aunt's." She shrugs and zips the bag shut. "It's efficient."

"The bag is a great cover."

"What do you mean?"

"There are men downstairs who aren't in the bratva."

She turns toward me, her face drained of color, and her eyes are as cold as a winter night. I know fear when I see it.

"So, we are being followed?"

Her eyes remind me of a clear and still natural lake at the base of mountains. I've only admired the views of this in pictures advertising the state of Wyoming.

"Probably," I deadpan.

Her blue eyes have a touch of gray. They are as mysterious, and so is she. Instinctively, I know I won't be forgetting her anytime soon.

I remember staring at her sleeping face as the sun warmed the morning sky. I wanted to hold her to me, but it was too personal. I'm going home after this, and as far as I'm concerned, it can't be soon enough.

CHAPTER 9

DMITRY

We are about to leave Greenwich when Izzy's stomach grumbles.

"You're hungry?"

"Yes, starving."

I'm amused she's hungry after I made her breakfast, but keeping up with me in bed burns many calories. We were both sweating and breathing heavily last night. Sex is sex. It's taking care of our needs, nothing more.

I don't know what love is, having only my parent's relationship as a model. They treated each other well. They had their ups and downs, to be sure, but they didn't cheat on each other, which is more than I can say for other married couples. A woman in the mafia can't cheat, but it's more commonplace outside the mafia.

Izzy gives me an address, and I talk into my phone to obtain directions. Modern technology is scary.

I've heard Americans get a dumbed-down copy of military-grade technology when the government has something better to replace it. It makes sense.

The funny thing about America is that their political shit is taking over, and yet their hunt for organized criminals is not their top priority. So, we're taking advantage of the situation and moving a fuck ton of drugs and guns right under their noses.

"The Lotus is your Thai place?" I ask with a voice bordering on disbelief.

"What? It's great food," she says.

"It's an unimpressive name."

"Well, it's the best Thai food to be had, you'll see."

"Is that a challenge?"

"Yes, in fact, I'll guarantee it."

"With what?" My smirk is taking over as my confidence never wavers.

"Um, maybe we just eat?" She gives me the side eye, curious if I'll accept her request.

"I'll say you owe me a favor if it's not the best food ever."

"Does your favor involve me naked?"

"Perhaps," I reply with a wicked grin. I'm not usually so chatty. Even though she's wearing jeans and knee-high boots, I remember every contour of her body like it's a road map to heaven.

"I stand by my claim. In the unlikely event you win, what do you want?"

"A blow job because I want those full lips of yours to feel how fucking big my cock is."

Thankfully, I'm driving. Otherwise, she would have driven the vehicle off the road as her jaw dropped to her knees.

A blank but defiant look emerges at last. "You're kidding."

"I don't kid about things that involve my cock. Besides, you are under our protection, but if you cross me, you'll be dealt with."

"Fine," she huffs. "If I win, I will tie your wrists to the headboard and torture you for hours." She crosses her arms in satisfaction, and I hide my joy that her punishment is one of my secret pleasures. Only I usually do the tying.

Fuck me if she doesn't keep my cock hard all the time. It's unnerving. We exit the car, and I pause to readjust my horny cock and pull my suit jacket out of the back seat after I slide my gun into the clip on my belt and the knife into my boot. I hope to God this distracts her from the bulge in my pants. I twist to make my way to the eatery and hold the door for her to enter. The aroma of freshly cooked food hits my nose, and I know she won this bet.

Fuck. My plan was to leave her without any strings attached. I should be working on Dmitry's issues, not losing my mind over the gorgeous woman at my side with her tight, tasty pussy.

Izzy orders for us, I pay, and we grab a table.

"How well do you know Kirill?" I ask, curious to see how close Izzy is to members of the bratva.

"Not well at all. I've seen him several times, but we don't hang out. Yesterday was maybe the second time I've seen him at the apartment. Why?"

"No reason."

"If you asked, there's a reason."

I sit back in the chair and observe her in silence. She's too intelligent to bluff.

"True. Do you know what's going on in his business?"

"Very little. Although Alena says she'll probably be married off soon. I mean, it's so barbaric, don't you think?"

"It's how our world operates. The women of powerful men make powerful alliances as bargaining chips. You wouldn't understand. We're from different worlds. Alena knows how it works and doesn't fight it."

"Maybe she should. I can't imagine going to the trouble of getting a college degree and not using it."

"Ha, most women attend universities to find husbands and drop out as soon as they find one. Every woman wants something from a man."

"That's not true. I don't." She acts like I insulted her.

"Says the woman who wants to tie me up."

"You started that."

"Do you always talk so much?"

"Probably. Why?"

I'm saved when our order number is called. I jump up to grab our food. She makes me nervous because she appears to understand more than I gave her credit for. I place the food on the table and return for our cold bottle of sake and two cups.

Izzy takes the food off the tray and sets the meals on the table. I sit again, busy myself with the sake, and glance out the front windows as I do so. It's a habit of mine to keep my eyes peeled for trouble. It's one reason I've lived this long—being diligent. Idiots are so predictable. The men from outside her apartment building are sitting in a car across the street.

We begin to eat. I have Pad Thai noodles with chicken, and it's delicious. Russian food is relatively bland by international standards. Things are quiet, and I realize food keeps Izzy from talking. We sip the sake and eat in silence.

I finish eating and put down my chopsticks.

"I need you to slide your purse under the table."

"What? I'm not doing that. Are you crazy?"

My eyes bore into hers. "I gave you an order, and you need to do it. *Now*. Without making a scene."

"What if—"

"Now, Izzy, no games. And if you don't, I'll be bending you over this table in two seconds, and you won't be happy with what I'm prepared to do in public."

Her eyes sprang open as wide as her legs when I satisfied her with my tongue. Without another word, she slides her purse under the table.

"Good girl. Now, wasn't that easy?" I say with a smirk.

She downs the last of the sake, crosses her arms over her chest, and pouts her lips. I resist the urge to pull her onto my lap and let her feel my hard cock under her ass.

Instead, I feel around inside her purse, trying not to be conspicuous.

"Ah. There it is, a tracking device." I pull a tiny tracker out and drop it into the empty sake bottle. "It was hidden in the lining at the bottom of your purse. Tell me why someone is tracking you. Are you working for the Sicilians?"

I eye her suspiciously. Could she be a plant? She and Alena have been in college for several years. It would be the perfect cover, acting like she needs Alena, getting into the inner circle.

"What? Are you crazy? Alena's father would kill me. I live with her for a pittance of rent. She has two rules, I can't have men over, and I can't tell anyone who I live with. It's for her protection, so I've never broken the rules."

As much as I'm an untrusting bastard, I believe her. So, what am I missing?

"Keep your eyes on me when I speak," I tell her. She goes to open her mouth.

"I don't have time to explain. Please do as I say until we're out of here. Do you understand me?"

"Okaaaay," she hisses. I figure she has a million questions running through that intelligent mind of hers.

"Keep your eyes on me and laugh like I told you a joke."

She chuckles and covers her mouth like she's laughing too much. It appears she can act too. I'm so fucked. She'll be running circles around me in no time.

"The men from the apartment complex are across the street. You'll get up and act like you are heading to the bathroom down the hall-way. Please go through the kitchen, out the back door, and wait for me in the alley. Can you do that?"

"Yes." It's obvious she's scared, and it's justified.

"Okay, I'm returning your purse under the table. Take it, then get up and leave."

She does as she's told, and I follow as soon as she's out of sight.

In the alley, I grab her hand and pull her past dumpsters smelling of rotting food. Two huge men block us as we turn the corner to double back to the car. The goons. *Fuck.* They are smarter than I thought. I'm sure the broken tracker tipped them off. *Shit.*

One has his hand in his jacket pocket, clearly concealing a gun pointed at me. "We'll take the girl."

"I think you made a mistake," I reply.

"Grab her," he says to the tall man beside him.

I'm surprised to hear a brogue accent. How did the Irish appear on Russian turf without being seen by the Bratva soldiers protecting Alena?

Izzy gives me a quick look, and I read the panic in her eyes.

"What am I to do?"

"Go with the man nicely, and we'll let your boyfriend live," the burly man with the gun stipulates.

He points with his gun to indicate that she needs to walk to his partner. As she takes a step, she trips on a crack in the pavement and tumbles forward. The man who was waiting for her takes his cue and reaches for her arms as she falls, giving me enough time to draw my gun. I shoot the first man in the chest, but not before he fires a shot. I hear the whiz, and a familiar burning sensation hits my left arm. The surviving man clutches Izzy to his chest as if his life depended on it.

And it does.

"You made a mistake." He pulls a knife from a side pocket in his coat and holds it to her throat. "Toss your gun. Now!"

His beady eyes dart. He had to make a getaway, but he lost his partner. The gunshots were bound to attract attention. We're going to be found out any second.

"Let her go, and I'll let you go. We can both live to see another day," I shout.

"I can't return without her." He begins to back up. But I know he has to get to his car, so I shoot his knee. He cries in pain, and his pocketknife slips from his hand as he falls to the ground, clutching his leg. Izzy tries to run, but his hand catches her ankle.

She screams and tries to kick, using her free leg as leverage, but her effort is useless. The man's large hands and tight grip are no match for her. I kick him in the face, and blood splatters everywhere. He lets go of her leg to protect his broken nose, and Izzy moves backward, step by step. I begin to kick the man in the gut and ribs. He groans. This isn't a clean hit, but I don't want to fire my weapon again. He pulls me to the ground, and I get him in a chokehold and snuff out his life. It all transpires quickly and quietly.

"Go to the sidewalk and cross the street, don't look back," I yell as I look for cameras and thankfully see none.

I use my shirt to wipe my fingerprints off the gun and approach the dead man, promptly putting my gun in his lifeless hand. I take his gun, wiping it down before I slip it into my hidden holster. "I'll be behind you," I yell to Izzy, hoping she will overcome her shock and do as I say.

I quickly look for witnesses. By some stroke of luck, no one is around, and more importantly, no one is filming this with their phone. I jog to a tree, yanking green leaves off it, and use them to wipe blood splatter off my boots. All the while, I'm keeping an eye on Izzy. She's crossing the road. I hold my breath. How deep is this conspiracy to grab her? How long has this been going on, and to what lengths will they go to get her? Strike that. I know what they're willing to do. These men have desperation in their eyes.

They might be indebted to the Irish and doing a job for them without the proper skill set.

I jog to catch up with Izzy. Even though my arm hurts like a son of a bitch and my damaged leg protests, we walk quickly away from the crime scene.

I text Kirill on my burner phone to get us. The cops will be here soon, and it's only noon. We have to be back at the condo to meet Kirill, and now, I assume Alena will be present.

"What was that? Who were those guys? You killed someone! What are we going to do? I can't go to prison," she cries, then sobs. Tears the size of pebbles flow down her high cheekbones. "I can't see," she murmurs and sobs even more as she brushes her hand down her face. Like swiping a bank card that isn't working, she continually repeats the movement.

I know from taking my first life that every emotion runs through your body when you witness a death that's violent and personal. You'd have to be a sociopath not to feel something. Then again, mafia organizations are known to have a few.

I wrap my arm around her shoulders to calm her, and we walk down a side road to wait for Kirill. He had to turn around to get us. I could call an Uber, but the driver would be a potential witness and a loose end. I don't want to take an innocent life.

Someone will need to get the Lambo from the parking lot, especially since it belongs to a member of the bratva's top men. I'll let Kirill worry about those details. I'm glad those decisions are not up to me because Alena's dad, Mikhail, will be pissed. I don't want any issues between their bratva and ours.

As we continue to a side street, Izzy rambles on in shock. She stops walking when she realizes I haven't said a word in three blocks.

It must be hard for her to look at me after I killed two men.

She turns to look at me, and for the first time, she sees the bloody sleeve of my jacket. "Oh my God, he shot you!"

She cries out and pushes my torn jacket away from the wound, observing the red, gaping hole in my arm.

I'm used to getting hurt. I'm not used to seeing the anguish in Izzy's eyes. Heaviness weighs on my chest like a cement block. I'm lost in her, her essence, the way she moves, the way she talks too much, the way sex is more than just fucking. I'd die if anyone hurt her.

Her body and spirit belong to me. She has no idea how deeply she's involved in my world. All I know is that she's never leaving it. She's the air I breathe. She's light to my darkness.

"You are mine, and anyone who touches you dies." Our eyes meet, and even with a gunshot wound, I want to kiss her lush lips and fuck her tight pussy until she begs for more.

CHAPTER 10

What the city lacks in trees, it more than makes up for in cars. They whiz by, going well over the speed limit and blowing through red lights. One takes their life in their own hands getting behind the wheel of a car here.

"We should have taken the subway. It's faster," I comment while looking at his bleeding arm, wishing I could make it better.

He's tough. I'm sure he's been through worse. He'll say I'm overreacting if I fuss or worry too much.

"And go where, exactly?" he asks, his dark eyes showing the strength and resolve of a battle-hardened soldier. "I can't walk around with a gaping hole, leaving a trail of blood like a bull in a bullfight," Dmitry says with growing frustration. He's cranky. One could argue he has reason to be considering the gaping hole in his arm.

I've heard it said it takes two years to figure out your partner, but with Dmitry, it's been less than two days. He never expresses himself and only speaks when he has something to say. He must be clever if he's been in the bratva his entire life because you don't last that long if you don't do your job well.

At least all this excitement has taken my mind off the pulsing at the apex of my thighs. I'm yearning for him to fuck me again. He's so large. I thought he would split my pussy in half.

When he took me from behind, he was balls deep inside me, literally. He pounded me so hard his balls were slapping my flesh. He was rough, and I liked it. The pleasure was mixed with pain due to his size and how deeply he was thrusting, but it took me to another world I didn't know existed. I screamed bloody murder when he told me to come. I'd never had a man order me to come, but I liked how it added an element of excitement.

"I'm too young for prison. I'll never make it." I worry out loud as if I pulled the trigger myself.

"They were going to hurt you, and the world is better without them. Remember that!"

Dmitry slayed them for me. Granted, they had a gun on him, but he risked his life for mine. I wonder if that's something I need to put on my list of requirements if a man wants to date me. Now I'm being dramatic. I blame my glib humor on the shock of witnessing such a violent act.

I'm not upset they're dead, and they got what they deserved. Maybe vigilante justice isn't such a terrible thing after all. How dare they grab an innocent woman off the street? And yet, I know it happens all the time with unfavorable results. What would have happened if Dmitry hadn't been with me?

"I think it's clear I'm the target, not Alena," I say, spitballing my thoughts and ignoring his dour mood.

If he wasn't with me today, I might not be here to complain about our predicament.

"Neither looked like the guy stalking me the other day or the man in the bar."

Dmitry is quiet, and I wait for him to say something. If I talk too much, he's guilty of not talking enough. Everyone has secrets, but this is carrying it a bit far, especially considering I'm part of what just happened.

"So, still no idea who wants you?" he asks.

I shake my head *no* and give him a blank stare.

Dmitry stands when he sees Kirill's car whip around a corner and immediately straightens his spine. I can see him wince in pain when he moves his arm.

"Where can you get that looked at?"

"We'll see."

"Right, Mr. Tough Guy," I mutter as Kirill pulls up.

We climb into his car like we just robbed a bank. Alena slides over to make room for me in the backseat.

"Right," he says as he gets in the front seat and nods once to Kirill in what I assume is a courtesy *thank you*.

"Are you okay?" Alena asks. "We were about to get on the freeway. I'm glad you caught us when you did."

"Yes, but Dmitry needs a hospital."

Kirill shakes his head. "No can do, princess. Gunshot wounds require too much paperwork, and the cops get involved. Don't you watch John Wick movies?"

"Oh, right. Well, we need to do something. You're a fixer or whatever."

"I'm on it. We have a doctor on call. And by the way, this was supposed to be a vacation for Dmitry. What the fuck happened?" Kirill barks.

I can barely hear Kirill's voice as it's noisy in the backseat. The muffler sounds like a jet engine at idle. When he puts his foot on the gas to accelerate, it sounds like a jet engine at takeoff. Men sure do like their muscle cars.

Kirill is checking his mirrors.

"Is anyone following us?"

"Not at the moment," Dmitry says, glancing toward me in the backseat, then out the back window. Looking for a tail, I assume. "What are you not telling us, Izzy? You're the target. What makes you so special?" His focus is back on me.

Shit.

"I have no clue," I murmur.

"Izzy, we need to know who's after you. These are dangerous men." Alena's eyes plead with me.

"Look, you know my story. I have a tattoo you think is a logo for the mafia. I got it in a tiny shop in Connecticut. I don't remember there being a warning sign about bird tattoos," I snap sarcastically.

The men speak to each other in Russian. Dmitry is getting Kirill up to speed. Meanwhile, Alena is asking me what just happened.

"It was scary. I mean, I had a knife to my throat, but I knew Dmitry wouldn't let them take me. I didn't know how it was going to play out. It happened so fast. I feel safe with him."

"There's no way you would have known what was happening. I'm sure it went down quickly," Alena adds, which makes me wonder if she's ever been in a similar situation.

"The man had an Irish accent. I think he's different than the man at the bar." I turn to Alena and see the genuine concern on her face. This is a first.

"Who would want to take me? I don't have any family, and I certainly don't have money. But I remember my Aunt Emma trying to talk me out of moving to New York City. She said my mom made her promise I'd never be in the city alone."

"Really? Shit. You never told me."

"I never thought much about it until now. I thought it was just bull-shit to make me stay with her."

"But you've been here for years. What changed?" Alena asks as she searches my eyes. I shrug before I glance out the window and try to identify any other clues, but I come up empty.

"What do you mean, Izzy?" Dmitry must have bionic hearing. I didn't realize he was listening to us.

"I don't know. I guess I wasn't supposed to move to New York City. I wasn't told why. I thought it was stupid."

"No, you wanted to attend school here," Alena says. "And there's nothing wrong with that. Could it have been a warning?"

"A warning for what?" I shrug. "I don't know any more than you. We've been roommates for years. We know everything about each other. The issue is that not much is known about my mother's or my father's family."

"We're here," Kirill announces as he smiles into the rearview mirror.

I glance out the window. "We're at an animal hospital," I mumble. Then I snicker for the first time since the shooting. Holy shit, it *is* like the movies.

"We need to stay here and wait. Are you okay?" Alena puts her hand on my leg, and I let her see my face so she won't worry about me. I shake my head to get rid of the cobwebs.

"Yes, my stomach feels like it needs to spew molten lava like a volcano, but other than that, I think I'll be okay."

We watch the men enter through the back door we're parked in front of.

"Why don't we go in?" I want to be there for Dmitry.

"The less we're seen, the better." She turns to me. "I have a feeling you are somehow connected to the mafia. Nobody will stalk you, put a tracker in your purse, and then try to grab you unless they want something. And they want it badly."

"Right. Well, I hate to break it to you, but I'm fresh out of explanations. I have no idea why they are after me. I thought they were after you. You're in the bratva. Your dad is high up there. And how did I become the bad guy in this?" My voice rises as I defend myself. Did everyone forget I'm the victim in this? Me and Dmitry? "I feel terrible he got shot."

"He's used to it. They all know what they signed up for. The only way out of the mafia is in a coffin. Everyone knows this," she says, sounding annoyed.

"Look, it's been a long day. I don't want this to affect our relationship. You're my best friend and my only family."

"I know. I'm stressed, that's all. The only thing going on with the bratva is a potential alliance with the Italians, and it's complicated because our mafia king, Alexsei Sidovo, doesn't have biological children to make a blood alliance with the Italians by way of marriage."

"He doesn't have kids?" How did that happen?

"He adopted two kids with his wife, who aren't his bloodline or Russian-born. The Russians and Italians are very Machiavellian when it comes to these things. Alexsei's son will never be able to take over as the don because of it, or so it's rumored. And he's not worth much in the way of an arranged marriage, either," she adds, which makes me wonder what else is wrong with him.

"And I thought I lived in a patriarchal world. I feel for kids born into yours."

She raises her eyebrows as if to say, Really?

"*Et Tu*, Brute?" she replies, but she smiles. I let out a sigh of relief. We're still besties. I relax with her flippant retort.

"So I guess you won't marry Alexsei's son, huh?"

"Who knows? I might be the sacrificial lamb. He's young. It might not be the worst arrangement."

The guys come out and get into the car.

I want to ask Dmitry how he is but decide to stay quiet.

"What is going on with the alliance Kirill? I know you must know something," Alena asks, relieving me of the duty to ask all the questions.

"Not much. Why?"

"I'm just spitballing, but something has changed somewhere on some level for Izzy to be in her situation—the tattoo on her wrists, the Irish mafia after her. And the guy at the bar grabbed that arm, so maybe he was looking for the tattoo. I mean, it's a brand. He must have known to look for it."

"Yeah, Dmitry mentioned it. I thought it was nothing. But the fact that she's been here for a few years with no incidents makes this more than just a coincidence. It's especially weird since all this shit is being stirred up between the mafia families." Kirill backs up the car and drives into traffic, following the speed limits and traffic signs. He doesn't even roll through an obnoxious stop sign.

"Right? I mean, how can it just be coincidental?" Alena slumps back in her seat, and I'm sure we're all wondering what we're missing.

"We're heading back to Dmitry's. We need to research shit." Kirill changes lanes and continues to check his mirrors as we zip through traffic.

"What are you thinking, Dmitry?" I ask, desperate to know if I will be alive at the end of the week.

"We'll figure it out. But you're staying at my place, and you're not to leave it." He swivels his head. Our eyes meet. "I'm not fucking around. You leave my side, and you might not be so lucky the next time."

My hardened stare softens like gelato on a summer day. I'm getting the impression that this isn't over for the foreseeable future. What has my mother gotten me into? It's the only plausible connection. I'm sure everyone in the car is thinking the same thing.

"Fine." My voice is a whisper, and with it, I promise to comply with his demands. I find my new world dangerous as fuck and oddly exciting. Or is it the broody man in the front seat who only smiles when he's with me?

CHAPTER 11

IZZY

When we reach the parking garage at the condo building, I unbuckle my seatbelt. Kirill walks to the trunk and retrieves a black duffle bag. Dmitry and Kirill visually sweep the cars parked in the oversized garage under the condos. Satisfied we have not been followed, they tell us to get out of the vehicle, and we follow them into the building.

Security here is tight as we pass through doors one by one, and I hear the click as it locks behind us. We pile into the elevator immediately in front of us, and Dmitry uses his card to make it work. None of us speaks. The tension inside the steel box is so thick that my body fills with a dull, painful ache.

When we get off the elevator, we are in a lighted hallway. I walk by Alena's side, thinking it would be cool if we were on a double date instead of running from people trying to kidnap or kill me.

"Make yourselves at home," Dmitry says as we enter a modern condo of black and white. I never paid much attention to it, as Dmitry had my full attention when I was here the last time. It's furnished and sterile looking. "There's a TV in the living room. Kirill and I will be working at the table."

He heads into the kitchen and takes a pill from a plastic vial. It must be an antibiotic or a pain pill the doctor at the vet clinic gave him.

Kirill pulls two laptops from his bag and places them on the dining room table. He enters the kitchen and retrieves a bottle of vodka I've never seen on a store shelf. He retrieves two chilled shot glasses from the freezer, puts them on the table, and fills them halfway with vodka.

"What are we supposed to do?" I whisper to Alena.

She shrugs. "I guess we're supposed to entertain ourselves."

I walk to the kitchen to grab a chilled water bottle from the refrigerator. Walking past the table, I overhear Dmitry saying, "She's only safe with me. My name is known by all the dons and top mafia families. I can protect her. Besides, your organization might have a leak."

Kirill seems to contemplate this as they both toss back the alcohol like it's nothing.

Leak? What? I share what I hear with Alena as I plop onto the leather couch beside her. She pensively takes my hands in hers.

"It might seem weird, but Dmitry is from a huge Russian family in Europe. If he says he can protect you, he can. They own the highest-rated hotel chain in Europe. Rumor has it they are expanding. His name is well-known in the right circles. The circles who govern laws and help officials get elected, if you know what I mean." She takes a breath. "I don't know anything about a leak, and I don't want to know. We're all safer not knowing the day-to-day operations of the mafia."

"Right, I get that."

"Let's get our minds off it. We don't have jobs to go to, and I'm sure my father has the building surrounded. You need a minute to process today. Trust me on this. I've heard plenty of men being baptized with waterboarding, and well, let's say we don't want to make waves."

I've seen what one gun can do, and the fact that it takes several men to safeguard Alena doesn't make me feel any better. The only one I can count on to keep me safe is Dmitry. He might not talk much, but he's a man who thinks quickly and acts with precision. Plus, he speaks the language of the criminal underworld, and I'm not referring to Russian.

I doubt this antiseptic condo is Dmitry's. He doesn't strike me as a man who cares where he lives. The lack of creature comforts here makes me believe this place is a secret hideout or short-term flop house.

I noticed none of that this morning because I was too fixated on Dmitry's six-pack abs and the scratches I left on his back. This makes me smile. It's as if I've marked him, too.

"I'm glad you're here," I say to Alena, not knowing what I would do without her.

"Me too." She reaches over and hugs me to her before she gets up to look for the remote. I lift the water bottle to my parched lips, and as I gulp water, my hand quivers. I hope it's a one-time occurrence. I'm still rattled by today's events and wonder when life will return to normal.

I snap out of my reverie when Dmitry calls me back to the table. He asks a million questions: Where I was born, my aunt's name, her address, and my parents' names. I don't know my dad's name, explaining that he died, too. When I tell him I have no other relatives, he drops his head into his hands like I'm the biggest inconvenience in his life.

"What?" I snap, thinking the worst, like, if he drops me, I have no one to go to for protection.

"You're killing me." He looks to Kirill. "Am I right?" Dmitry leans back in his chair and smiles like a dog sneaking a T-Bone steak off the counter.

"I get it, I do." He nods and cracks a toothy grin. "She's someone, all right," he says to Dmitry.

Then, Dmitry turns and gives me a look. And by look, I mean, he like really looks into my eyeballs as if they're a crystal ball and will tell him what he needs to know. "It's too convenient," he says before he sits straighter in his chair.

Kirill stands and begins to pace. "You're like a gift wrapped with the world's largest bow; someone is willing to do anything to get you. But why?" He spreads his arms to the side like he's parting the Red Sea.

"You're all so fucking dramatic!" I scoff.

"Maybe, but no one is chasing us with such enthusiasm. Well, maybe a few girls at the club, but…" He shrugs. "That's an everyday occurrence."

Is Kirill that famous? He wears expensive sneakers and drives a fancy car. Maybe this place is his, and he has serious cash. I can see why women would find that attractive. He's not my type, but he's easy on the eye. I saw him flash a wad of cash at the club, and the gold chain around his neck is a bit hinky, but it's not uncommon. I assume the *S* is for his last name, which is unoriginal if you ask me.

"So, if your analogy is correct, who am I a gift for?" I half laugh. "I've never had a huge Christmas or birthday party. My mom scraped by working at a diner."

"And you say she was killed in a car accident here in New York?" Dmitry questions me with his scrutinizing eyes. "That's rather convenient, don't you think?"

Does he still think I'm lying? *WTF?*

"It happens." But as soon as the words leave my mouth, the bits and pieces come together like the pattern of a dress. Each piece of fabric is cut, pinned, and then sewn together to make a dress. It's the same as solving a mystery. Details add up to pictures, and the facts tell a piece of the story until there is a complete story.

And more pieces are falling into place for me. There's the cryptic fear and promise never to move to New York City. Add to that my mother's untimely death in the city—when we never went into the city.

"Wait, was her accident a hit?" I turn to Dmitry.

"Now you're using that brain of yours." Dmitry rewards me with a smile of approval. I've noticed he rarely smiles. I pull up a chair next to him. Alena joins us and sits next to Kirill, filling the fourth seat at the table.

"We're checking her name in our database, and there's a Maria Lucci, who is supposedly fifty-three years old. That can't be," says Dmitry.

"She's not. I mean, she would be forty-three now. She had me at twenty. She was young. She said her family disowned her, and I assumed it was because she was pregnant and unmarried. She never wore a wedding ring or mentioned being married. There had to be someone in her life to wind up pregnant. When it rained, she'd get a wistful look in her eyes when we watched love stories on TV. She'd go through a box of tissues. She had a boyfriend, an Irish guy who worked on Wall Street before she died."

"You have no idea who your father is?" Dmitry's face gets even sexier when he frowns.

Is he doubting me? I'm insulted he thinks I'm lying. He must not get out much if he's questioning me because I have no reason to lie. I'm an outsider. Dmitry is a man who likes the safety of his family and is resistant to change. I know better than to think I can take a lone wolf like him and turn him into a domesticated lap dog.

"My dad passed away before I was born…." I answer, and at the same time, a chill runs up my spine. *No way!* Could his death have been planned? "Was it a hit as well?" A wave of nausea hits me, and I cover my mouth in case I'm sick.

"Don't know. We don't have a name for your father. There's none listed on your birth certificate." If Dmitry notices me turning green, he doesn't draw attention to it. Instead, he shifts his weight in the chair as if his leg or injured arm is hurting him.

"Mom said he was gone, and I would take her last name."

"Hidden in plain sight, your mother was smart." Dmitry pours more vodka into their shot glasses, and the two tap the table, say something in Russian, and drink.

"So, who am I?"

"We have no clue, but you must be part of a mafia family. I mean, we're going back twenty-three years, right?" Kirill states. I assume Alena's dad, Mikhail, must keep him around for his analytical skill set.

"Yes," I reply. He's wise to work backward to figure this out, especially considering we don't have much to go on.

"Wait, you mentioned an Irish guy. Do you remember his name? A Wall Street man? That sounds as fishy as a can of sardines." Dmitry leans toward me, and I smell the sweetness of the refined vodka as it mingles with the musky wood notes in his cologne.

"He was a regular Irish guy, James Murphy." I look around as if I'm stating the obvious. "Come on, aren't they all named Murphy?"

I look at Alena, and her face falls. "You've got to be kidding me."

"Yeah, I mean, it could be a coincidence. The Irish of New York are the Murphys," Kirill says. "It is common. But somehow, I don't think it is in this situation." He puts a finger to his chin and says, "Let me think a minute."

"Back in the day, the don was Alexsei's father," Alena says. "We were at war with the Italians, and each side sustained multiple casualties. Molotov cocktails were going off outside people's homes, and communities were in an uproar for more police protection. The incidents hurt businesses, and then the Feds came around to monopolize our our weakness.

"That's right," Kirill says. The light bulb over his head goes off. "They were looking to get someone low on the vine to turn. They probably wanted someone to spy on your organization, talk, or maybe both. RICO was big back then. It's still big, and it's how they break up the leadership, putting the don in prison. In the spirit of self-preservation, a temporary truce was made. And my mother, who is a Moretti, was a capo's daughter and married my Russian dad. The Moretti don is the same. He has kids. In fact, he has a son to take over for him."

"Right. Alexsei, his brigadiers, and advisors stay reclusive. It's that way for the top echelon of the bratva," Dmitry says.

Kirill nods. "I haven't even met the man."

Dmitry begins to type on his laptop. "I want to know who had kids back then. I'll search birth records." Watching his fingers fly, I'm impressed. He and Kirill are tech-savvy. I've never seen anyone fly between ten screens as quickly as this.

I sit, watching Dmitry with fascination. He's as good at this cyber shit as I am with a needle and thread. Glancing out the sliding doors to the small balcony, I notice it's getting late, and the sun is sinking behind the monolithic buildings, casting long shadows.

"Is the incident with the men in the alley over, or are cops going to bust through the door?" I ask, wondering how we got off scot-free.

The guys continue to tap away on their keyboards.

"It's been handled," Kirill murmurs without looking up. We're quiet, lost in our thoughts until Alena's stomach rumbles.

"Well, I haven't eaten all day, and mimosas aren't food." Alena stands and walks to the kitchen, opening the cupboards. "Gee, Kirill. Do you own stock in tin? Judging from the amount of canned food, I'm confident you will survive a pandemic."

"Oh, that shit is for emergencies. Why don't you two decide what we want to eat for dinner? It's getting late, and I think we should stay in. I'll have my man, Anton, pick it up, but I'll call in the order. Don't use your phones."

"Speaking of phones, I need to check them," Dmitry says.

I open my mouth to protest, but his *don't fuck with me* look makes me close it. Alena and I fetch our purses and bring them back to the table. I hand Dmitry my phone, and my fingers graze his. Like before, I feel a bolt of lightning, and goosebumps pepper my arms.

Dmitry pulls the cases off our phones, and Kirill runs a gadget over them. One more first to add to a surreal day.

"Clean."

Our phones are returned.

Alena uses her phone to look up local eateries. I sit down next to Dmitry and stare at his profile. He's the most intense person I've ever met and the only person I can count on to save me from the darkness that threatens to swallow me like quicksand. He's also the only person I'd follow into the abyss if he told me I'd be safe. I know he's not safe. He stabbed a man's hand, shot a man dead and choked the life out of another. Who else has he killed?

"I think you guys are going about this the wrong way," I speak confidently even though I'm not one to draw attention to myself. These guys can be intimidating, given the amount of testosterone between them. And they're big. If they were any bigger, I'd suspect them of juicing with steroids.

Dmitry looks my way and cocks an eyebrow. He crosses his arms and leans back against the wooden dining room chair. His stillness makes me nervous, and my knee bounces under the table. He's a statue as he waits for me to speak. His dark eyes lock on mine. Experience tells me mine are turning dark, like a storm on the ocean. My eyes always turn a dark blue when I'm excited, especially when it's sexual.

"What do you mean?" His warm voice soothes me like a hypnotist, and I find myself free-falling into his smoldering eyes.

Even with clothes on, Dmitry is the embodiment of a perfect male specimen. Naked, he's even more perfect, but that's because he makes me feel like a horny teenager. I should be running from him. I'm in over my head with zero street smarts and no criminal experience. And as far as sex is concerned, nothing before him is noteworthy.

Dmitry is a wet dream and a savvy business mogul whether he's in the bedroom or the boardroom. This man is on the chessboard of life, playing two moves ahead of his opponents. I hope he has an unbeatable track record because someone wants me. In fact, it might be more than one person. What did my mother do? Did she lie to me? And if she did, was it to keep me safe?

CHAPTER 12

DMITRY

"Why not consider who has the most to gain if the Russian and Italian alliance doesn't go through? If history repeats, the Russians and Italians will be at each other's throats. Who would benefit from that happening?" Izzy asks, putting an elbow on the table and glancing at Kirill.

She could have been killed today, and that scares the shit out of me.

"All the other mafia families would benefit if the Russians went to war with the Italians."

Damn, my arm is burning, and I'm tired of sitting.

"That's right. Because our fighting will take up too many resources," Kirill says. "The heat will be on us. The others would exploit it."

"Why don't you and the Italians get along?" Izzy asks, sending a quizzical look to Kirill.

Curiosity killed the cat. Maybe she's testing the theory on the belief that they have nine lives. It's a funny American saying, but nonetheless, everyone seems to love it.

In the past, women and children were off limits when retaliating between rivals, but it's no longer a code that's followed. If someone wants to get at my family, they can. That's why we keep the names of the head of the mafia confined to our top two men. There might be rumors, but soldiers will never hear our names from a Brigadier's mouth. It's a level of security we maintain to protect ourselves.

Kirill thinks it would be a good idea for Izzy's protection if I married her. My name is known by all the European rivals and the dons in the States, many of whom we do deals with to keep products moving. We've expanded over the years, and sometimes we include other mafias in our deals.

I've never been able to trust Italians after what happened with Polina. It all started at a bar with some Italian talking shit to her. Things got heated, and Polina wanted to leave. We went outside, and the idiot followed, pulling out a switchblade. It was game on, and he ended up on the wrong end of a knife—my knife. I didn't know that his *paisano* had snuck up behind Polina and slit her throat as retribution. When I saw her on the ground, there was nothing I could do to help her. The cops were on the way, and I had to leave her there, bleeding out. I never want to lose another woman like that.

I did what I thought was best for the Volkov family that night and killed the man responsible for taking her life. A message had to be delivered, and since that day, I have avoided places we don't own. We survive by trusting no one, which means everyone is an outsider, non-bratva members, especially Italians, as far as I'm concerned. I don't know why I had to have Izzy last night. She's so damn perfect that I couldn't help myself. It's been a long time since I made love to someone. I'd say *fucking*, but with Izzy, it's special.

I'm not sure why I have this fascination for her. Somehow, she ticks all the boxes. I love looking at her when she's sleeping and dancing, oblivious to anyone else in the room. Even now, I want to fuck her beautiful lips and have her swallow my cum.

We left the club thinking we were going home just to fuck. Only once we got into bed, I take my time with her, running my hands down her body and kissing her soft breasts, making her nipples stiffen under the slight brush of my hand. It thrilled me to no end to see her excitement build. She stirred emotions in me to a depth I've never known. I'm too possessive for her to ever be with anyone else. My cock marked her. It's no different than if I branded her arm.

"The Irish have always been a pain in the ass, but the Albanians, now there's a ruthless bunch." Kirill pushes his chair back and stands. "The Albanians are moving more drugs today than ever before. They used to stick to guns and human trafficking. The landscape is continually changing," he says as he begins pacing, probably to stretch his legs. We've all been sitting for over an hour.

My mind drifts back to Izzy, and I'm balls-deep in the mystery surrounding her when all I want to do is be balls-deep in her. I can't wait to sink my cock into her again. Even now, she's making me hard. I fight off the memory of her moaning under me last night to focus on what Kirill is saying about Santino Moretti.

I've heard of Santino. He was born in Sicily and moved to the States as a kid. The tradition of treating women as less than human continues in the land of opportunity. Sicilian women are expected to cook, clean, and breed, not give their opinion. They get knocked around by their man and get told to walk behind him, not beside him.

Kirill shrugs like it's unimportant, but pride and impatience can lead to an organization's downfall.

"What's the Italian don like now?" I ask curiously, expecting Kirill to answer, but Alena chimes in first.

"I haven't seen him in years. I hear he's mean and someone you wouldn't want your daughter married to. Good thing he's getting too old to knock women around like he did back in the day." Alena adds to the conversation, and I think she might know more than she's letting on.

"You know this?" I ask to see if it's a rumor.

"It was rumored—but credible. Women talk when we get together at charity events, weddings, and funerals. Mafia wives are kept on a short leash, so they look forward to anything that will get them out of the house. I hate all of it, but Dad makes me go." She glances at Kirill as if she needs his permission to talk. Is she checking his temperament?

"Why did you tell Izzy to hide her tattoo?" I ask Alena, suspecting she knew it was mafia related.

She shrugs. "I wasn't sure if it was a coincidence or not. I mean, I trust Izzy. She's my best friend. You know how difficult it is for me to have a friend and live a normal life, right?" Our eyes meet, and I understand. As a prized possession, her life is already planned. She will be married off to a brigadier, or what some call a capo.

I grew up much differently, with a loving mother and a father who had to toss us to the streets at a young age so we could live in the black world my grandfather and father built after the collapse of the Soviet system. We monopolized on the madness and made enough money to buy everything but our freedom.

A thought hits me like a lightning bolt. Maybe, Izzy's mother sacrificed a life of luxury, so she and Izzy could be free. Was her mother kept in a gilded cage? And if so, did she find a way out?

If I were trying to disappear, I'd change my name, move to an inconspicuous place, and work a regular job. She had to have known someone who could change her name and date of birth. That takes money.

I would be better at covering my tracks than Maria, but then again, I'm a professional. Someone was keeping her in a cage, and she escaped. This someone must've lived in New York, so Izzy was told not to move here. It would jeopardize her anonymity. This person must be connected and have power if her mother was that concerned. It's all assumption at this point, but I have a feeling for this because I'm entrenched in this world, not Izzy's.

Another question is, was Maria's car accident an accident? Maybe Maria was a neighborhood girl who got knocked up and bought off. The Santinos have been around forever. There's no end to what anyone with billions of dollars would do to make problems disappear. She might have been forced out of New York. Perhaps she embarrassed her strict father? It's evident to me that Izzy has Sicilian blood.

My thoughts are interrupted by Izzy's long sigh. She crosses her arms on the table and leans forward, burying her head in an elbow.

She's not used to this, and today has been overwhelming, to say the least. I cautiously place my hand on her back, something I never do. I can't resist the urge to touch her silky black hair, and I'm tempted to run my fingers through it like I did last night. I resist the urge to tug it like I did when I came so hard. I held onto the headboard while I pumped her full of cum. I want her under me again, with my hard cock pounding her tight pussy.

"You're exhausted, Izzy," I murmur.

Out of the corner of my eye, Kirill's face changes as he reads the situation. He shouldn't be surprised I've been interested in the gorgeous Italian he set me up with. I'm not looking forward to his comments the next time we talk. In our world, it's all about anger, hate, and violence. Everything in between is non-important. Trust and love are reserved for a few.

"I think you need to rest. It's been a long day."

"Yeah," Kirill says, closing his laptop. He looks to Alena. "I need to get you to your father's."

"Sure," she replies with a sympathetic look in Izzy's direction. "Stay in touch and let me know how you're doing. I'm sure Dmitry will do whatever it takes to keep you safe."

We all stand, and the girls meet halfway around the table and hug.

"Thanks for everything," Izzy says as Alena grabs her purse off the counter. Izzy busies herself, clearing the table of our shot glasses and vodka.

"Holy fuck, Dmitry, how are we going to handle this?" Kirill whispers as I let them out the door.

"I'll call Nikolay. There's only one way to protect her, and she won't like it."

"Sounds good. I'll leave Anton downstairs tonight. He can get you food, anything you need."

"Thank you both. Please don't mention this information to anyone. We don't know who we can trust." I look at Kirill. "We need to figure out how Izzy is involved in all this. Until we do, she's not safe. Alena, follow instructions. They might go after you to get to her," I say.

Alena nods. She's not the same party girl I met last night—the one who didn't flinch at me stabbing a thug's hand. Today she's quiet and reflective. Her friend is in danger, and there's not much she can do to help. I know how she feels. I'm not emotional, yet Izzy tugs at the part of my heart that holds a sliver of light.

"Later," Kirill says as he opens the door, checks the hallway, and tells Alena that it's safe to go.

I nod. At times, no words speak volumes.

When the door closes, I bolt the numerous locks. Then, I turn to Izzy and place my hand on her back. She's so petite. I'm surprised I didn't leave bruises on her neck last night.

"I'll help you," I softly mumble as I steer her into the condo and toward my bedroom.

Last night we were two strangers hooking up for sex. Was it only the raw chemistry between us pulling us together, or did neither of us want to be alone?

Izzy sits on the bed.

I remove my dirty boots quickly and leave them. I doubt she wants to see them again. I pull my gun out and lay it on my nightstand.

"We'll need to get clothes tomorrow. I don't want you returning to your apartment."

"Um, that's going to be an issue. Is there any way someone can get them?"

"It's too risky. You'll go shopping. Don't worry about the cost." I move around to her side of the bed and pull back the duvet. She bends over to take her boots off.

I'm compelled to take care of her.

"I'll do that."

"I can do it," she argues.

"I'm taking care of you tonight."

I take over and unlace her boots, tugging them off her dainty feet and setting them aside.

"You should change your shirt," she murmurs.

"Mm, probably," I reply.

"I'll help."

"No, I'm fine," I say, raising my arms to grab the top of my long-sleeved Henley and suppress a wince. It's stuck to the four-by-four bandage the doctor used to cover my stitches.

"Let me help, seriously." She huffs and stands. She's stubborn, and I know she won't rest until I let her help me. She gently pries my shirt off the bandage. "I never got an update on your bullet wound."

"It exited, no major damage."

"The bandage is full of blood. You don't want an infection." She inspects the bandage as if she's a nurse. "I'll take care of it."

Why am I agreeing? I grew up in Russia. We didn't even have bandages. When you don't have what you need, you make do. When you need help, and no one else is around, you learn how to do it yourself.

"I'm pulling it," she warns. Her sleepy eyes meet mine for a second, and we both look at the bandage.

"Don't yank at it," I say as I try to help.

She fiddles with the sticky side of the white gauze until my shirt breaks free. I swiftly pull the shirt over my head and throw it to the floor. I'll get it later.

"It's fine," I reassure her. "I'll get supplies in the bathroom. I'm sure something is lying around. I've been through worse." I turn to look at my shoulder, and we're so close I could kiss her lovely lips. I want to, but it's late. "You. Lay down."

She finally listens and gets into bed. As she lays her weary head on the pillow, I notice dark rings under her beautiful eyes.

"I'll have food brought in for later. Get some sleep. You're safe here." I tell myself that the kindness in her eyes isn't for me. There's no way she cares about me. I am unlovable, cruel, and brutal. She witnessed it first-hand.

What is hard to resist is my body. What I lack in charm, I more than make up for with a physique most men envy. Even though it hurts my bad leg, I work through the pain and deadlift weights. I have to stay strong, and I've built up my thighs so much that they rub together when I walk, altering my gait.

Izzy closes her eyes and drifts off to sleep within minutes.

I head to the bathroom, pick my torn and blood-soaked shirt off the floor and drop it in the motion-operated garbage can. I turn on the shower, and I step in and look for soap when the water is hot enough and look for soap. I find a cardboard box with a label that reads, *all-natural soap made with goat's milk and lightly scented*. I sniff it and find it refreshing. What will Americans think of next?

It lathers well and leaves no residue, only a clean, minty scent. I do my best to keep my stitches out of the water and pat the area dry before toweling off the rest of my body.

I dress in jeans and a crewneck shirt of stretchy material I find comfortable and realize I need to figure out dinner. Kirill said I could trust Anton to run errands and gave me his number. I take in the light rise and fall of her chest. Izzy is sleeping. I could stand here all night and watch her, but we need food.

I call Anton to come up. I don't trust a man until I see his eyes. When he arrives, the first thing I notice is his receding hairline. He strikes me as too young to lose his hair but otherwise nondescript. Blending in is essential in all areas of criminal mischief. He meets my steady stare with one of his own and doesn't back down under my intense scrutiny. He's passed my first test.

While I tell him what we need, he stands still, reminding me more of a soldier than a street criminal. I mean that as a compliment. Fidgeting means you're nervous, and if you're nervous, I'm nervous to have you on my team. I tell him to pick up steaks and tons of sides, enough for him too. It's going to be a long night. He leaves, and I return to the bedroom to check on Izzy.

She moans as she tosses in her sleep. It's not the pleasurable sounds I would prefer to hear. I walk to the bathroom to flip a light on, so she'll see where she is when she wakes up.

I trust no one outside of my family, and even at that, the further I branch out from my family, the more skeptical I become. Izzy doesn't fit into the fabric of my life, either. If I arrange a marriage of convenience, it will force her to be loyal to me, and she'll fall under my family's umbrella. If we're married, she can't testify against me, and no one can use her to get to me. I know how witnessing a murder can weigh on a person's conscience. Izzy hasn't felt the pain of torture, and I never want her to. Not only does marriage buy her protection, but it also buys us time to figure out who's after her.

Kirill's family has some pull, but he can't give her the level of protection like the Volkovs. I doubt he's suitable for her, his tastes lean toward flashier women, and only a full-blooded Russian will do because he's quite the company man. He has plans to move up in the organization.

This leads me to the other rule I hate to break: marrying outside the bratva. How will it play out within my family and my position of power? I will not tolerate anyone questioning my loyalty. Izzy would be the target of disdain from Italian and Russian families. Both will be wondering where her loyalty rests, and rightfully so. If she were Russian, she would know our culture because it can only be learned living in my homeland.

My gut tells me she's someone's daughter or granddaughter. I just haven't figured it out. I need to call Nikolay. It's late in London, but this can't wait until the morning.

He answers his phone and mentions he's getting ready for bed.

"I have a situation. There's a girl…"

"No, not you. You are the last one to ever let a piece of ass get under your skin." His rough voice has me thinking I interrupted him and Anya. The two fuck all the time.

"I know. And yes, she's a fantastic fuck, but I'm beginning to think there's a hit out on her. Either a hit or someone wants her for something big."

"Russian girl?" he asks, sounding intrigued.

"No."

His voice falls, "Oh."

We discuss the situation and spitball possible scenarios. I find them all unacceptable except one.

"You may proceed but know that you're making an emotional decision. The Dmitry I know never used to ask questions and would never get married. Just so you know, I am a man in love myself, so I understand."

"Don't worry. This isn't about love. I don't want the situation to turn on me. You know my rules."

"I do. It's a compromise, though, no?"

"I'm basing my decision on the circumstances," I reply. Am I pussy whipped? After one night? Not a chance.

"I see. Well, you'll be thirty soon enough. It's time you settle down. I hear the Italians are trying to get more money for the cocaine deal."

"I heard."

"Well, make sure the deal happens, or you and Kirill have another job."

"Tough to do here without starting a war. One is brewing as we speak."

"I feared as much. Too many hands are in this deal, and yet, it was one we had to take. It's like having too many women in the kitchen. They all think they are the best cook and know everything about cooking. It's the same with mafia families."

"What else is there for them to fight over? The mistresses are hidden, and they can't take the frustration of their empty beds out on anyone else. It's not like they don't know where their husbands are on Saturday night."

"That's true," Nikolay chuckles.

We chat, and I ask how Roman is doing in Russia, and he says surprisingly well. I say goodnight and hang up. When I hear Anton buzzing to come up, I look at the monitor and see he has his hands full.

He arrives moments after I buzz him in. I open the door, and the smell of good food immediately makes my mouth water. He tells me he ordered the juicy steaks from a place he knows and loaded me up with sides. There is enough here for Izzy to find something she likes. I pay him generously and thank him. He thanks me in our language and dutifully returns to his post until further notice.

I'm pulling food out of the bag when I hear a blood-curdling scream fill the condo. My heart drops faster than the food in my hands. Izzy! I go to draw my stolen 9mm Smith and Wesson and *fuck*. I don't have it on me. With care, I approach the room and see Izzy in bed, safe. I glance around the darkness for an intruder, which I know is impossible without a balcony. However, it doesn't keep me from grabbing my weapon as I place a finger on my lips for Izzy to remain silent.

After I've checked the closet and bathroom and deemed them safe, I return to her side to find her trembling. I sit on the edge of the bed and wrap my arms around her.

"I had a nightmare," she reassures me in a voice barely above a whisper.

"It's normal. They will eventually go away."

She nestles into my muscular chest. I pull her close and murmur into the top of her head, "It will all be fine, I promise." Why am I so protective of her? She's a stranger, and yet, I want to get to know everything about her. When in the past, I never cared so much for any woman.

CHAPTER 13

IZZY

"What do you mean I can't leave? I need to work. How can I do that under house arrest?"

"It's not house arrest the way you think. This is for your protection," Dmitry argues.

"I'm not Alena. I know she has more freedom than most girls in your bratva family, but I don't want any part of it."

"Mm, we'll see about that. You need to understand that you belong to me now."

"That sounds horrible. You can't just take me. I'm not a piece of property to be claimed or traded," I protest.

"That's how it is for now. Better you have a life to live than no one to mourn you at your funeral."

I screw up my face before exclaiming, "That's terrible!"

"Let's not forget that I risked my life for you."

"You'd do that for any innocent woman…" but my voice falters. It's no secret that Dmitry is connected to one of the more ruthless crime syndicates in New York City. By no means is he an angel. He may be demanding and exciting in bed, but he's dangerous and should probably be in prison. He's not your typical bad boy.

"You know what I think?" he says with a smirk. "You have daddy issues."

I'd love to slap that stupid grin off his wickedly handsome face. Something tells me he would be tempted to slap me back, so I clench my fists and control my impulses.

"What if you woke up one day and discovered your entire life was based on lies? I have no one to tell me the truth unless we find a living relative. Even if I were adopted, I'd have to have relatives somewhere."

But where are they? In New York City, more than likely, simply because of the directive to never come here. Mom had to be afraid of something.

"I could do a DNA test. It would turn up tons of people." I'm excited at the prospect of using technology to answer the questions burning inside of me.

"It's too late, our enemies know more than us, and they want you. If they find you first, I doubt you'd survive. These men aren't going to put you up in a fancy hotel or condo." He makes a sweeping gesture with his arm to indicate our comfortable surroundings. "They are killers who deal in human trafficking as a side business," Dmitry says with a sinister tone that sends a shiver up my spine. "Let's eat. You'll find something you like." Just like that, he changes the topic.

The atmosphere changes as our heated exchange ends, and he shows me to the dining room.

I may as well be a prisoner, trapped here with a man who can wreck me with one soft look, one touch, one word.

Resigned to my fate, I sit at a table crammed with enough food to feed us for a week. Dmitry hands me a plate, and I load it with a porterhouse steak, twice-baked potato, and creamed spinach. Hungry, I cut into the steak first. When I put the first bite in my mouth, some of the steak juice runs down my chin. To avoid embarrassing myself in front of Dmitry, I grab a napkin and quickly wipe it away. Who knew murder and mayhem stimulated one's appetite? Maybe this is why men like Dmitry do what they do; the excitement and stimulation can be addicting.

I chew and watch Dmitry eat slowly and deliberately. Maybe I was expecting him to eat with his hands. His gun is on the table next to his unused utensils. Instead, his manners are impeccable, and I wonder how he got into organized crime. Alena seems normal enough, but she's not running around at night playing butcher.

Nope, she's the opposite. Her drugs of choice: hot men and the hottest designer clothing and shoes. She told me about a secret place where she and her rich friends get their pick of the merchandise before it hits the public.

"Why are you so adamant about protecting me? I'm nothing to you," I ask to clear the fog of confusion between us. The entire day has upended my life.

"You don't know how to survive in my world. I know what it takes to survive. In time, you will, too." His voice is low, deliberately controlled, and I can't read his emotions. "To avoid being recognized, I keep a visible persona for the public. I use that persona to move about freely to carry on business. But our lower-ranking soldiers don't even know my name." He finishes chewing, puts his knife down, and gives me a soft look that brings warmth to my face and between my legs. *Damn him.*

"You are barely twenty-three years old. What do you know of life? Of love, of loss? Sure, you had it tough without your parents.

Losing a lover is just as painful. Have you ever been in love with a man?"

"That's personal." I shove a bite of mashed potatoes into my mouth to buy me time before he bombards me with more questions.

"Fine, I already know the answer." His glib retort tells me he never asks a question unless he knows the answer.

"I can tell you that leaders of the mafia families know my name, and when I show up, respect will be paid. We're the Volkovs from Russia. My brother Nikolay is the head of it." He gets up, returns with two small shot glasses, and pours from the same vodka bottle he shared with Kirill. He sips the sweet vodka, and I set my empty glass before him.

He raises an eyebrow in surprise but pours vodka into my glass without a word.

The smell is deep and rich, unlike commercial vodka. I take a sip, it's smooth like a liqueur, and my mind melts as it washes away my angst.

"You like?"

"Yes, it's smooth."

"Good, because I need to make you mine. That way, no one would dream of putting a hand on you."

Did I pass through some portal into medieval times?

"Whaaat?" I can barely control myself. "Mine? What the fuck does that mean?"

"We're getting married. It will be a marriage of convenience. I've discussed it with Nikolay. Kirill thinks it's a good move."

"What about me? Don't I have a say in this?"

He finishes his vodka. "No. You don't," he says without hesitation or care.

I toss back what's left of my vodka. "More vodka, please."

"You can have wine, the vodka you're not used to." He stands and walks to the kitchen. I hear cabinets open and close before he returns with two wine glasses and an open bottle of red.

"Enjoy a five-hundred-dollar red wine," he muses as he pours.

"Five what?" I almost choke on my spinach. I swallow and lift the glass to smell the bouquet. I might be young, but I picked up a few things from Alena.

"Stand." He has a way of demanding what he wants, and it's unnerving. And yet, I do what he says.

I stand and narrow my eyes at him. The soundtrack to *The Good, the Bad, and the Ugly* plays inside my head because he's on thin ice now.

"Relax, *Usha Uoya*. I will not hurt you. You're the only woman who makes me feel alive. I love to fuck you, and I will fuck you until the end of time." He lifts his glass. "I want your lush lips around my cock, and I want to taste your sweetness whenever I want."

I'm so close to him that I can feel the heat radiating off his broad chest. The liquor and his words warm me. What would he do to me if I displeased him?

My rational brain pools into a puddle between my legs. He runs his hand gently down the side of my face. His touch is as light as a cloud blowing across the sky on a summer day. I shiver.

"What do you want?" I ask with a whimper. His minty scent fills my nose.

"You," he growls. "We'll be married. You'll be safe. You can have a life, a new life."

"One in a gilded cage…" I murmur.

I want to push for more, but I doubt he can give more. He can't discuss a marriage arrangement like an average person. He's a beast. Everything is an ultimatum. Fake it with me, or you die is not what I call acceptable. I want to be loved, and I'm not sure he can love anyone. I'm his possession.

"You Americans are so dramatic. It's a trade-off, a fair trade." He raises his glass to mimic a toast and sips.

I sip the deep red wine, filled with body and flavor, the perfect ending to an exquisite meal. When I look up, I see the fire in his eyes. I sip again.

He takes the glass from me, setting it on the table next to his.

"It has to air out. We have time." His voice is husky. He kisses my neck. Is this why alcohol is called liquid courage? Because I will need a ton of it to get through the next few days. Maybe I can buy some time to figure things out.

He unbuttons my jeans and slips his fingers past my taut abs. I can't stop my moan when his fingers sink into my creamy wetness. My pussy betrays me as he gently massages my pink folds. His mouth takes a nipple between his lips and immediately hardens under pressure. I'd rather his hands were on them, grabbing and rubbing them raw.

"You want me, too. I want you dripping for me every day."

His lips are rough when they cover mine. It's as if I'm feeding a demon inside him that can't be filled. I want to remain cold and indifferent to thwart his control over me, but my resolve doesn't last. I submit to him, hating myself for my weakness.

He's the most virile man I've ever known, and I buckle under his warm lips as his tongue explores my mouth. I kiss him back; our tongues fight for control. It manifests the unspoken battle of wills that neither of us wants to lose.

He tugged my jeans off, and I remembered last night and how we fit together perfectly even though he has a porn star-sized cock. I rub my hand over the bulge in his tight jeans, slipping my hand under his balls, where I gently massage him through the denim fabric.

"You keep that up, and I'll fuck you right here, right now."

"Fuck me." I'm not sure what's stronger, my desire to challenge him or for his cock to be inside me.

He mutters something in Russian before lifting me to the counter, ripping my panties off. My ass smacks the cold granite, and he pushes his fingers inside me without warning. I gasp. *Goddamn, it feels good.* He moves his fingers, touching areas of pleasure. I tilt my pelvis to get more friction. I'm on the brink of climaxing when he pulls them out. When I open my eyes, he's tugging his shirt off, and then he takes mine off, tossing them on the floor.

"Spread your legs."

I move my legs as far as they will go and place my hands on the hard surface behind me, bracing myself. He wraps one arm around my waist and slides me to the counter's edge. His fingers thrust into me, going deeper than before, and when he pulls them out, our eyes meet as he places them inside his mouth.

"I could eat you for days," he murmurs as he licks his fingers with a salacious look.

Then, he drops to his knees and burrows his head in my pussy, and begins sucking. He's a thirsty man with a talented tongue. He licks around my outer folds slowly and deliberately, like he ate his steak. I ball up my fists, then put one in my mouth to avoid moaning. The pleasure keeps me in limbo, and I yearn for the release I crave.

He works his way up my body, kissing and nipping at me. I grip the counter's edge, not knowing what he will do to me next as he works up my body. He gently kisses me on the lips. His breath is warm, like a tropical breeze.

My bra falls away with one flick of his wrists, and my well-proportioned breasts tumble into his hands. He bends, squeezing my breasts with one hand, and his lips pull a nipple into his mouth. I hear his zipper and, by his movement, assume his jeans are off.

I arch backward. I need him. I want him to fill me with his huge cock.

His other hand is on my firm butt cheek, pulling me into his pelvis. My head tilts back, urging him to continue the pressure. He plays with my nipples, and they harden under his touch. I push my breasts into his capable hands. Hands that not only kill but hands that know how to deliver pleasure.

He nips at my nipple, and a flicker of pain shoots through my body. My nerve endings react as if they've received a jolt of electricity. He's driving me mad with desire.

"I don't have any more condoms," he murmurs.

"I'm on the pill."

The words leave my mouth no sooner than he firmly squeezes my breast, and I lean into it, pressing harder.

I wilt under him. The raging fire inside of me has been stoked. Now I need him to deliver the remedy to put it out before I incinerate.

His veined cock lays between my legs, the tip against my opening. I want to scream at him for delaying my gratification.

"I want to feel all of you," he concedes. "And I'm going to fuck you hard. You'll never look at another man."

And with that, he plunges into me, my insides part, making room for him. He fills me. My muscles tighten around him. He's so large that I gulp as he reaches places inside me no man has ever touched. I use my arms to support me as he pulls out, preparing for another long thrust he delays on purpose.

"Fuck me," I beg, breathless and dizzy with desire. All I want is for him to fuck me hard. I need to feel him in me and know he's committed to me and only me.

He plunges into me again, and my head jerks under the force of it.

My wetness squirts on his head. He moans. As I bathe him with my orgasm, my sexual appetite ramps to an all-time high.

His colossal cock strokes my clit. I grasp his biceps, digging my nails into his flesh as pleasure engulfs me. He buries himself deeper into me. I'm afraid he'll split me in half. And when I don't think I can take any more pleasure, he holds my ass steady with two hands, and with one last thrust, I shatter like a million stars.

He moans and shudders against me, his fingers digging into my ass. He groans again, and I wonder if he came twice. His hands relax when his body is satiated, but he still holds me.

I'm a goner. I'm addicted to him, to his cock, to him taking control.

"Time for a bath," he says in a gruff voice.

I know better than to argue. With his cock still inside me, he carries me to his bedroom. I grip his shoulders for support and allow him to carry me because my legs are weak. My arms are spent. I never knew I could become so exhausted after sex. We pass through the bedroom and enter a spacious bathroom with a jacuzzi bathtub. He sets me down, and I slide off his cock. Wow, it's still hard.

Fuck me and all that's holy.

While he runs the water, I sit on the chair at the vanity table. He turns on the jets, and the water swirls. Satisfied that the temperature is perfect, he finally lets me enter the warm pool of bubbles.

He joins me, bringing a washcloth and soap to gently wash my back. I pull my hair into a makeshift bun to keep it from getting wet.

He kisses my neck and whispers, "You're mine."

CHAPTER 14

IZZY

Dmitry lathers the soap and rubs it over my breasts as if we're making love and not taking a bath. My nipples respond, and I'm mystified by my body wanting him again already.

He takes his time washing my feet; oddly, it's sensual. His hand slips between my legs, presses his fingers flat against my triangle and slowly moves up my body. This time, he cups my breasts and gently massages them. I lean back against his chest as desire fires between nerve endings. I spread my legs without him asking, wanting more from him. His attention is intimate and thrilling. He submerges the washcloth into the water and rinses me by dripping warm water over my back. I've never experienced subtle arousal before. I want him so badly, but I refuse to beg.

I can't help but notice his scarred leg. I'm curious about it.

"What happened to your leg? Does it hurt?"

"Yes, when I overuse the muscles. Does it bother you to look at it?"

"No. What happened?"

"There was an attempt on my life during a dispute over territories. My car was hit intentionally and flipped before it burst into flames. I couldn't get out with the seatbelt stuck, and I had to find my knife to cut myself free. My leg got the worst of it when it caught fire before I could get out. The pain was bad, but the recovery was excruciating."

"Wow, and you have a brother?"

"Two. Nikolay and my younger brother, Roman."

"You sound close."

"We have to be. Our father was recently killed. Nikolay stepped up. We've all been groomed to run the business. We all have different skill sets."

"What's yours?" I ask, afraid I already know the answer...*killing people.*

"Kirill and I were part-time enforcers while in college at Princeton. That's where we met."

"Wow, Princeton is a school for kids in organized crime?"

"It's a good school, and it costs money. We don't have the same notoriety as the Italian American dons in New York who flaunt their extravagant lifestyles. We're the face of a legitimate business, importing and exporting, mostly liquor."

"And somewhere in all that, you manage to fit in drugs and guns?"

"Yes."

"I'm not going to Russia with you. You can force me into a marriage but can't force me to live there."

He's quiet.

"One thing at a time. First, we get married. Then, we have to find your family before someone else finds you."

His breath is warm on my neck, and he kisses my shoulder. His tongue moves over my damp skin, and goosebumps cover my arms.

I need to distract myself. If he knows I love what he does to me, I'll lose all my bargaining power with him for anything. There is too much at stake. I don't want to leave New York. I refuse to be dependent on a man. *Think, think, think.*

Family. What if I have siblings? I'm excited about having a family for birthdays and holidays. I wonder who they are and if I'll like them.

"You're quiet." His deep voice makes my nipples harden.

What is it about the timber of a man's voice that I find so attractive? Maybe I do have daddy issues. I picture him reclining in a leather wingback chair, smoking a cigar, and drinking amber-colored scotch from a rock glass.

"I'm wondering about my family. Will I fit in? Will I find aunts and uncles? What if they don't like me?"

"Then it's their loss. But you will always have a family with me."

"But your family won't accept me. Alena's family is tight-knit, and her marriage will be to a Russian no matter how she feels about it."

"It might take time, but family comes first. You'll see."

I allow myself to relax into his chest: the food, the vodka, the warm bath calming me.

"We still have wine to finish," I murmur.

"Let me get you out." He stands, water droplets streaming down the tattoos on his chiseled chest and six-pack abs, an incredible specimen of a man.

"What is the meaning of the tattoos? I can read the tat written in Spanish, but not the other one."

"It means beauty is brutal in my language." He towels off his chest and proceeds to his legs.

"Meaning?"

"Things in life that are beautiful can be lost. The brutality of life can take away all that we find beautiful and rob us of what we want most."

"What do you want most?" I step out of the water and stand naked before him.

"To call you mine." And with those words, my walls crumble.

With a soft towel, he pats my damp face, then my neck, and takes his time with my arms and legs. By the time he revisits my breasts, I'm breathing heavily. The towel brushes my nipples, causing them to pebble.

"See, you want me. You can't trick your body. Being near to you has the same effect on me."

No words are needed as his cock is hard and erect, and its head pushes into my navel. His cock is sublime. I've never had a man this big before.

I want him. I need him. I have no idea what I'm getting myself into, and the thought of being with him scares me. It's too late and too dangerous to go back to Connecticut. My only play is to stick by Dmitry. He will slay anyone who comes for me. With him by my side, I can come out of this alive.

"Kneel."

Fuck, he's hardcore. But I do as he says and drop to my knees on the bathmat before him. Is this the price I pay to live?

"Suck my cock."

My hand doesn't even fit around his thick nine-inch cock, and I worry how I will fit all this in my tiny mouth. Tracing the bulging veins with my tongue, I suck the pearly precum off the tip and swallow the wetness like its nectar from the gods. He doesn't taste bitter. I enjoy licking him. He has the most gorgeous cock with a slight curve. I wrap my mouth around the tip, go down two inches, and pull back. I rest my lips on his swollen tip, teasing him.

He pulls the comb from my messy bun, and my hair tumbles over my shoulders as I focus on giving his cock my full attention.

I inch further up his shaft and pull back, teasing him. He tugs at my hair, holding my head in place, making it impossible for me to play with him again.

He loves control.

"Fuck my cock, *Usha Uoya*." His words mean business. I can't say more than *please* and *thank you* in Russian. "I want you to suck me like your life depends upon it."

Fuck me. My pussy drips with anticipation.

I open my mouth to accommodate his girth and take him in as far as possible without gagging.

He groans with pleasure and pulls on my hair until it's taut. It hurts, and I can't tilt my head back without feeling more pain.

I flick the tip with my tongue and feel his body tighten. I move my lips up and down his shaft, swirling my tongue around him. With both hands tangled in my hair, his pelvis thrusts back and forth as he takes over and fucks my mouth.

I tighten my grip, trying to pinch my thumb and forefinger together, but he's too thick. I keep a tight hold on his cock until he abruptly pulls out.

"Bedroom. Now."

I feel the slickness between my legs as I walk to the bed, and he slaps my ass, which takes me by surprise. When I reach the foot of the massive bed, he commands, "Bend over."

His hand is on my back, between my shoulders, ensuring I comply. I press my face into the duvet and turn my head sideways, not knowing what is coming next.

"I'm fucking you hard, very hard," he says, his cock at my entrance.

He pushes the head through my soft opening and groans with pleasure before he ravages my pussy. His demanding cock should be registered as a lethal weapon because I'm sure it will be the death of me.

I cling to the duvet as waves of pleasure and pain ride over me, pushing all other thoughts out of my head. He thrusts deeper. I want to cry out from the pain, but the pleasure builds inside me, and I feel like I'll explode. I welcome his thick cock and enjoy hearing his balls slapping my ass as his grip tightens on my hips.

His cock slides over my clit, stoking it until it's about to burst. I'm climbing, yearning for more. I arch to give him more access, and he impales my love canal, finding parts of my anatomy I didn't know existed. I brace for each thrust and feel him quickening as my walls tighten around him. Pleasure courses through me.

Breathless, I gasp for air. My mouth is dry from all the panting. The velocity of him jars my body. He's a large man, and he packs a powerful thrust. Like a jackhammer, he pounds my pussy, making me tighten and quiver around him. *Fuck me and all that's holy.*

I moan, unable to prevent the strange guttural sounds from leaving my throat. I want to twist around to watch him drive me fucking crazy, but he holds me in place, so I can't move.

My clit swells and ripens as he takes long strokes, each more intense than the last. His hands move from my hips to the top of my shoulders to hold me in place as he pumps me harder, driving his hard cock against my walls and shredding my clit like a velvet rose petal.

I scream as I come. It's the most intense orgasm I've ever had. My body shudders and shakes until I fall into sweet oblivion. With one last push, his fingers grip my shoulders hard enough to leave bruises, and a low growl escapes his throat as he climaxes and spills his seed deep inside me.

His breathing is ragged as he kisses my neck, murmuring something in Russian. We both collapse and lay together for a minute before he slides out of me and lifts me onto the bed.

He lies beside me, with his hand between my legs, as his cum seeps out of me.

"Never forget who you belong to. You are mine and mine only."

Completely satisfied and spent, I drift into a deep sleep.

* * *

I WAKE up later and find myself alone. I get up, grab his shirt off the floor, put it on, fasten one button, and go looking for Dmitry. I find him sitting in an overstuffed chair in the living room, a glass of wine in his hand. He's pensive as I watch him take a sip.

His low-key energy matches the mood of the classical music playing softly in the background. I wouldn't know the difference between Beethoven and Brahms, but it sounds nice.

"I thought you might sleep the night." He stands, dressed in loungewear. "Would you like wine?"

"Yes, please."

"Sit," he says, pointing to the couch.

I sit on the end closest to his chair.

The sound the wine makes as it's poured matches the chill vibe in the room. He promptly returns and hands me a full glass. I stare out the window as he returns to his place. The moon casts an eerie shine over the city, making me shiver.

I take a sip of the red elixir and find he was correct about letting it breathe. It tastes different now, richer. The notes are more robust and dryer. It leaves a thick coating on my tongue. I rub my lips together, enjoying the notes of licorice and cherry mixed with Sangiovese grapes.

"Keep licking your lips like that, and I'll give you something else to lick," he threatens as he leans back in the chair and studies me.

"Mm, I'll lick anything you want as long as it tastes as good as this wine."

"I know a thing about quality wine, liquor, and women." When he lifts his glass to drink, his biceps bulge under the thin fabric of his fitted long-sleeve shirt. I have a feeling he bought the shirt for this very reason. He knows he looks good, and the shirt hides nothing.

I blush. His eyes flick over me, and I know he's ready to fuck me again. The man is insatiable.

"Why do you have a passport you've never used?"

Shit. When he eventually whisks me away to a different country, I can't use it as a justification to delay us.

"I'm serious about not going to Russia." I try to argue, but I'm too relaxed and realize I've never felt this Zen before. Endorphins, no doubt.

"That's not an answer."

"Well, you're smart. You figure it out." I sip more wine.

"Money."

I nod and curl my legs under me.

He nods and sits upright before leaning over his long legs.

"What did you want to do for your career?"

"I thought Broadway shows, fashion magazines, anything to pay off my student loans."

"Alright." He leans back, satisfied with my answer. "It will come in handy, your education."

"What do you mean?"

"We will have a huge wedding in London. You need to meet my family to make it official. Then we'll let the society pages work for us, places like Page Six."

"Look, we've been holed up here, and nothing bad has happened," I say as if there's nothing to worry about.

"Don't let the calm fool you. That's how everyone feels before the storm."

"Great, you're a poet now."

"No." He retreats into his thoughts, and just when I wonder if he's going to shut down, he breaks the silence. "Alena will help you pick out a new wardrobe."

"I can't look like her," I protest.

"I don't want you to. You're gorgeous and perfect as you are. I don't want a wife who's trying to be someone she's not. I can buy glitz and glamour. Only a woman who is beautiful both inside and out can be…you."

I scoff.

"What? Is that funny?"

"Yes, considering we're here because we don't know who I am. How do you know I'm a good person?"

A brief smile passes over his beautiful lips. "I see your point." He swirls the red liquid in his glass. "While I work with Kirill in the morning, you will go with Alena to shop for adequate clothing. She knows what you need. Two of Kirill's best guards will accompany you everywhere. No running away, no fucking around. Is that clear?"

"Yes." I agree because he's making it clear that there will be consequences if I disobey.

My heart soars at the idea of shopping, then drops at the thought of a wedding. Wedding ceremonies are about the bride and groom being surrounded by family and friends. It's a joyous occasion, but I'm not in a joyous mood. I'm not in love, nor is Dmitry. Plus, I'm being stalked, and two men are dead because of me.

"We'll need a marriage license. We'll have a quick wedding at city hall and fly to London for the big official wedding."

"Wait! So soon?"

"Do you have a death wish?" His dark eyes question my sanity.

"Well…" When he puts it like that, I don't have a choice.

"I don't think you do, my dear Isabella."

Damn, he's right. There's an inherent human condition known as survival, and for now, marrying this brooding beast, who professes to be my human shield, is the only way to survive.

CHAPTER 15

IZZY

I finish my wine, yawn, and politely cover my mouth. The events of the day are catching up with me again.

"Go to bed. I have work to do."

I raise my eyebrows and look at him, puzzled. "What work?"

"Don't ask questions you know I can't answer," he snaps and gives me a stone-cold stare.

"Fine. I'm tired." I would have said goodnight, but he was so rude I decided to give him the cold shoulder.

I head directly to his room and slide into bed. The soft sheets embrace me, and I drift off to sleep without worrying for the first time in a long time.

Sometime during the night, I wake and feel his arms around me and drift back to sleep.

In the morning, I find myself alone in the huge bed and look around the room, wondering if he has left. He's so secretive. I relax when I hear coffee beans grinding, knowing he's in the kitchen. I follow my nose to the aroma of coffee brewing, hoping for my caffeine fix sooner rather than later.

Dmitry pivots when he hears my feet shuffling on the tile floor.

"You're awake." He looks dressed to impress, wearing dark blue dress pants that fit his ass perfectly. He has on another white button-down shirt, leaving me to wonder if he has them in any other color. His suit jacket hangs on the back of a chair.

Maybe I was wrong, and he lives here. There are no framed personal photos, so it's difficult to tell who owns the place.

"Yep, alive and well," I coo.

He gives me a wry grin and turns back to the industrial-sized coffee machine. In less than a minute, he's walking toward me, carrying a cappuccino with a big dollop of whipped cream floating on top. My mouth waters as he sets the cup filled with creamy sweetness before me.

I gasp. This man is like a computer that's figured out my algorithm. How else would he know my fantasy? All I need now is a stack of fashion magazines to fulfill my dream.

He spins back to me, having grabbed something, and sets a stack next to my cup. I don't even know where to buy these magazines. How did he pull this off?

I dip my finger in the fluffy white cream and lick it. This is home-made whipped cream. The texture and taste are rich and creamy, not artificial like the commercial stuff from a can.

"I bet this cup contains enough calories to register as a dessert," I muse.

"Very funny," he replies and tries not to smile. "I was able to obtain some items from Alena's so you can change. Your dress is hanging in the closet. The other items are where you'd normally find them."

"Do you have elves?" I tease.

His face turns serious, his sweet demeanor—gone. "No, I have soldiers who do what I tell them. You should learn to do the same."

All right, then. I hunch over my drink, hugging it with my hands.

"No slouching. Volkovs don't slouch, and you will need to wear the appropriate clothing in public as you have a new position to fill."

He speaks like I'm an employee, and this is my first day on the job.

"Wait, did you get a job for me, too?" I mock him. This man can procure anything with the snap of his fingertips. Maybe the elves took care of that, too.

"Don't be so glib. Just because you're still alive doesn't mean you're safe. Everyone will be regrouping for another attempt at you."

Well, that killed my morning buzz. I hope I never become so consumed with work and whatever else he does that I lose my sense of humor.

He walks away, and without turning around, he calls out, "And wipe that pout off your pretty little lips before I fuck them."

I bolt upright in my chair. The familiar slickness between my legs is becoming increasingly difficult to ignore. What's more troublesome is how I associate it with him. No other man has come close to the way he makes me feel.

Fuck.

I practically inhale my cappuccino and return to the bedroom. I peek inside the closet to find my pink paisley dress. I designed and made it for my senior project. It's practical and can be dressed up or down, depending on the occasion. *Hmm...maybe Dmitry and I have more in common than I thought.* He has excellent taste in clothes, and he's meticulously groomed.

He's practical. I'm the poor version of him. I find heels on a shelf that match the magenta pink in my dress. They have red bottoms! Seriously? Is there anything that is off-limits to him? These shoes are divine! They easily cost a month's rent in the city!

I open the built-in cedar-lined drawers to find bras and undies. Everything is my size, so he's very observant. *No,* I tell myself, *he checked all your clothing.* Well, not him, but his soldiers. *Ugh.*

As I slip into my dress, I wonder what he was working on last night. From the undercurrents between Kirill and Dmitry, I can tell the two are as thick as thieves and go way back. I can't figure out why Dmitry is visiting and why he's helping me? It's not exactly tourist season when one would expect to have visitors flying into town.

Dmitry enters the room and tugs on his matching suit jacket. "Are you ready to go?" His eyes sweep over me like a landmine detector.

I finish applying a light-tinted cream to my face and dust on the bronzer. A sweep of pink lipstick is the color of an over-ripened watermelon, punctuating the fact that I'm done with my makeup, like always.

"Almost. Thank you for the shoes."

"As I said, you have a standard to uphold." His cold tone takes me by surprise.

It appears I'm his fuck toy, a whore by night and arm candy by day.

What role will I play once we're married?

"I think we need to talk about this marriage thing. We need rules."

"Rules? Interesting. I don't take orders from women."

"Not orders, it's a conversation, in case we get stuck together in this fake marriage. You never mentioned if I can return to my life when this fiasco ends."

As I slide a foot into a shoe, I hold the doorframe for balance. The inside of it is soft like butter.

"I'll think about it. But I never said anything about fake."

I bend to lift the second shoe, sliding it onto my other foot. I straighten and smooth my dress, knowing his eyes are on me.

"You're beautiful," he says with a softness to his voice. I can't bring myself to meet his eyes.

With three long strides, he's in front of me, close enough to smell his musk and the notes of sweet tobacco. He places two fingers under my chin when I refuse to look up and tilts my head back. I refuse to meet his gaze and close my eyes. I can't face him. I can't be vulnerable. I can't risk being left again. If I fall for him, it will destroy me.

"I don't say words I don't mean." His deep, deliberate tone conveys the seriousness of his words.

My breath catches in my throat. I'm nervous. My stomach churns. I feel exposed because he knows my body better than me and reads my mind like a football playbook. I've never had a long-term relationship. We're heading into a potential lifetime commitment, and I barely know him. He was thoughtful enough to make a cappuccino and serves me in bed. This freaks me out and impresses me at the same time. How does he know I love cappuccino? His attention to detail would make him an excellent detective.

"I know." I open my eyes and meet his. I find his are warm, soft, and even kind. I can't be vulnerable. "Can we go now?" I change the subject because dwelling on his words will only set myself up for disappointment.

He turns abruptly. I follow behind him, my heels clicking on the tile floor.

At the door, he makes sure the way is clear before we enter the hallway. In the elevator, the forced proximity is overwhelming. I feel trapped, and my heart races.

He turns to me. "I love the design of your dress. You're very talented."

"Thank you," I reply, unsure how he knows stuff he shouldn't. Does he know who my mother is? Would he keep that information from me if he did? Does he have an ulterior motive for rushing into marriage? Arranged marriages still happen, especially in the mafia world. Women are treated as possessions, used as needed and dispensed with like an old prescription bottle. Take two pills as needed and dispose of the bottle after expiration.

"What are you thinking about? You're too quiet." His deep voice commands an answer.

"How did you know I have a passport?"

"I'm a great hacker. It's one of the reasons I started working security for my brother after the accident with my leg. I oversee the books and launder funds. Besides, anyone can do what I did. Few can do what I do now."

"And what exactly is that?"

"For now, keeping loved ones safe and tracking down thieves."

The elevator dings, and the doors open. Dmitry exits first.

Loved ones. He must know what love is. I'm not sure I do. My mother loved me, and she's gone. Dad is gone. I can't lose Alena. Everything I've been told my whole life seems to be a colossal lie. I have to know the truth. If I find my mother's or my father's family, maybe it will fill the emptiness I live with daily.

I want to ask Aunt Emma questions, but Dmitry said it could be dangerous. Whom do I trust? The person who raised me or my spanking new fiancé?

We arrive downstairs, and a black Escalade pulls up. Dmitry opens the door for me. I climb in, and he sits beside me. He tells our driver, Anton, to take us to a location on Broome Street.

"Alena will be there to take you to her secret place." He hands me a black credit card. "Spend. I know you're not used to blowing money, but I want you to buy everything you like and get some fun stuff I'll enjoy. Stick together."

"I got it."

"Hand me your phone." I pull it out of my purse and hand it to him. Our fingers brush, and for some reason, I don't want him to leave. Is it because I feel safe with him, or is there more to it?

I'm being silly. It's as if I'm a teenager with her first crush.

"Should I text you my number?"

"Nope, already have it," he replies and returns my phone. "Call me if you need anything."

"Okay."

The car stops, and I see Alena standing with two huge men wearing dark sunglasses and dressed in black, clearly bodyguards.

Dmitry gets out and takes my hand to help me. These heels are treacherous. One wrong move, and it won't be pretty. When we reach the curb his lips cover mine in a deep kiss that makes my pussy tingle. Then he's gone, leaving me wanting more.

Damn him.

I decide I will buy sexy clothes he'll love and drive him crazy. He deserves to be teased, too.

"Izzy." Alena squeals and throws her arms around me like I've been missing for days. I wrap my arms around her.

"I'm sorry I didn't text you back last night. Dmitry has kept me busy, if you know what I mean."

She links her arm through my elbow. We walk with the two men flanking us. I notice they're wearing ear devices like government agents.

"Man, he's intense. So, now you get to see what my life is really like. We have two bodyguards, and we can shop for whatever you like. We're not here to worry about prices, and we're not finished until you are buried under the weight of the shopping bags. You need a ton of stuff, like elegant cocktail dresses, party dresses, and formal dresses. I could go on and on, so let's get started."

Alena is on a shopping high. She's dressed in a black pantsuit with gold buttons down the top jacket. It must be made of fine wool due to its thick, soft-looking texture. Her trench coat is open but matches her outfit. She could pass as a modern-day slayer of vampires with how she carries herself. I wish I was that confident.

"Dmitry requested I buy something for him."

"I'm sure he did." She scoffs. "So, tell me what he's like. He's so mysterious."

"Yes, he is. Do you know why he's here?" I ask as we take a corner and walk down an unfamiliar street.

"He's working with Kirill on something. It's best not to ask questions."

"I get that. Do you think I'm related to the Morettis?"

"Maybe. If you are, it's better your mother left that crazy father of hers."

"That bad?"

"Really bad. The worst. I heard one of his daughters died under mysterious circumstances, and there wasn't even a funeral. No one talked about it or asked questions. I was just a kid, and it was the first time I'd heard of anyone dying. I don't know any of the Morettis. In fact, until now, I kinda forgot about them. They've had bad blood with the Russians since the beginning of time. They only tolerate each other for lucrative deals."

A chill runs up my spine at the thought of domestic violence. Was the daughter murdered? Was it covered up? Am I being too nonchalant with Dmitry?

"I'm sure there are things that never make the papers. The Morettis sound like bad news."

"Yes. But today is our day, we're here to have fun, so we're going in here." She stops in front of a shop I've never seen.

The guard has us wait while he does a security sweep of the building. I glance at Alena, who seems completely unfazed. The man returns a minute later, and they escort us in.

The shop is in an old brownstone that's been renovated. Natural lighting from the windows brightens the original brickwork, and the eclectic copper and porcelain globes give it a nice touch.

"I never knew this was here," I say, looking around at the clothing racks.

"Yes, so this city doesn't function unless we get our cut. We give some of it back by sponsoring new fashion designers. That's why I wanted you to go to the bar with me and make contacts."

"Holy shit. I'm so stupid. You should have told me all this before."

"You want to do everything on your own, you're so independent, but friends and husbands help each other. It lightens the load, y'know?" She smiles as we descend upon the nearest rack.

I flip through the dresses and run my fingers over the silky fabrics, all well-known designers and pieces not in the boutiques yet. We're getting first dibs. When I check the price tag, I cringe at the cost.

"Don't worry about the money." Alena playfully slaps my hand off the tag.

"I can't help it."

"Here." She hands me a bunch of dresses on hangers. "These are for evening events and dinners.

I look at the beaded cocktail dresses and wonder if we'll be dining at the Ritz Carlton.

"Oh, you need some suits as well. Those are in the back. The lingerie is on the top floor." She winks at me, and I wonder if she and Kirill are banging yet.

"So, you and Kirill?" I ask as we head to a dressing room large enough to accommodate a couch.

"Just friends. He likes to see me."

CHAPTER 16

IZZY

"I think he has a crush on you. Do you think you will be married off to him?"

"No, my husband will probably be a capo. I don't know. Because of the stalker we believe is pursuing you, I can't sneeze without everyone hearing. I have bodyguards everywhere I go."

"I'm sorry."

She gives me a look that lets me know this is nothing new.

"No worries. I'm worried about you."

"You mean the testosterone, fists, knives, and guns?"

"Exactly. You need to be careful of making him jealous. These men are possessive. If you so much as look at another man for too long, it will be an issue."

"That's ridiculous."

"No, these men are territorial and—"

"I'm his property."

"Yes."

Alena plops on the couch while I slip on the first dress. It's crepe and beautifully cascades over my curvy hips, accentuating my waist and boobs. It's amazing how a well-cut dress fits perfectly.

"That's you. I love it." She claps her hands together in glee. "Next!"

I slip out of it and go through her picks to find she has excellent taste.

A friendly saleswoman helps fetch different sizes, and eventually, we have enough suits, shirts, and dresses. We leave the pile of clothes with her and head to lingerie.

This section has everything and anything. I want to surprise Dmitry and pick up a sheer slip made of mesh. My nipples will show through the material. I hold up a piece with leather straps and wonder how to wear it.

"Oh, that's awesome. You step into it. I'll show you."

Back to the fitting room we go. Dmitry will like that it's crotchless, and I like how the straps hold my breasts in place and make them look even bigger.

"Is this too much? I mean, am I sending the right message?"

"It says *fuck me*. Isn't that why you left the club with Dmitry? It will be a nice surprise for him on your honeymoon."

"At the club, I wanted to get laid. It had been so long, and our bodies have this incredible chemistry. It was too loud in there for words."

"Sure, sure, he's hot, let's face it. He has piercing eyes and a brooding temperament. There's something sexy about the strong, silent type. I'm surprised he hasn't had dinner with the don yet."

"They do that?"

"Sure, it's all hush-hush. His brother is in charge in Russia and London. They're bigger than us."

Now I know why I was paired with Dmitry and no one else.

"Once I'm married, how does everyone learn about my protection?" I ask.

"There will be announcements in the papers and on social media. The word on the street goes through the top men and trickles down. Trust me. No one wants to piss off the Volkovs." She shrugs, trying on an outfit of black leather with silver studs and a collar to match. Who knew bedazzling was still in?

"That's hot," I comment.

"Thanks. Oh, we need to get you shoes and coats too. It's the end of the season. I know of a place that has them at reduced prices."

I buy crotchless underwear and a matching bra. I pick out a leather bra and thong as thin as a slingshot. This should make him happy. The entire time I pick through lacy underwear, I wonder—am I buying this for me or to keep the fuckfest going?

CHAPTER 17

*A*lena's bodyguards walk us to a waiting black SUV with blacked-out tinted windows. High on retail therapy, we clamor in, giggling like schoolgirls while the men pile our shopping bags in the trunk and hang our dresses safely inside garment bags onto the hooks behind us.

"We might need another vehicle," I tease as we buckle ourselves in.

"Right?" She snickers.

"I don't even want to think about how much we spent."

"Don't. As they say, you have to dress to impress," she points out as the vehicle pulls into traffic and crawls through the crowded city streets. I don't even own a car, parking is a bitch, and the cost of going over a bridge is highway robbery.

My phone pings, alerting me to a text.

Dmitry: *How's your day going?*

Me: *Good. You?*

Dmitry: *Fine. We're going out to dinner tonight, just us. Eight p.m. Be ready.*

Me: *Fine.*

"Let me guess, that's the dashing Russian. I heard he's as cold-blooded as a Siberian winter with his personality, but I imagine he's hot as a brick oven in bed," Alena teases.

"Hm. Well, he's hot as Hades in the bedroom. And he has the longest dick I've ever seen. Not that I've been with that many men, but I did watch Sex/Life streaming on TV. He's like, that big."

Alena's jaw drops with a glint of envy in her eyes.

"I'm getting an education today. Holy fuck. Tell me more."

"He's very… demanding."

"You've got the hots for each other." She rubs her palms together, excited for me.

"Doubtful. We're practically strangers. Plus, it's a forced marriage, and I have no interest in going to Russia."

"It's kinda exciting, isn't it? The dashing stranger with the big dick who knows how to use it."

"Yes and no. I like that he's very perceptive about people. But he scares me because I think he knows me better than I know myself."

"I just hope the person I'm forced to marry is nice," she says.

"Given what I've heard about the Morettis, I imagine the men bring that mean shit home, huh?"

"I don't know what comes first. Do they start off violent or become violent? Lots of mafias started as street gangs. When the gangs form alliances with other families, they become a mafia. By sticking together and getting organized, they make more money. Along came RICO, and they diversified into money laundering and investing."

"Yeah, real estate, shell companies, and legit businesses."

I look out the window, and the plight of the homeless people on the street doesn't go unnoticed. I could be out there. Maybe my mother was homeless at some point. I may never know what she lived through as a single mom. She was probably alone and scared, raising me by herself.

We were very close and did simple things for fun. I wonder what happened to her in New York. Was her death an accident or intentional? I may never know. Years have passed, and technology and forensics back then were primitive compared to today.

The vehicle stops abruptly, and one guard opens the door and beckons that it's safe to exit. The other guard opens the door to a nearby store, and we make the dash inside. This one is dedicated to outerwear, so picking out a trench coat and purchasing shoes for every occasion is easy. My weakness is my love of boots. I throw a few pairs in for me, then feel guilty about the added expense.

"Don't be silly. He wants you to have nice things," Alena says as we check out.

"Oh, by the way, I'm trying to get Dmitry to agree to a verbal contract. Y'know, I think we need some boundaries and to discuss our expectations."

"If he does that, you're ahead of the game. Arranged marriages are for alliances or to buy peace. And even those are done with a handshake. The less paperwork that can incriminate everyone, the better. You won't find contracts. Everything rests on a person's word."

"I never thought about that."

We leave digital footprints everywhere. Hell, there's probably a tracking chip in my underwear. How would I know?

We pile back into the vehicle and head to a late lunch at a place Alena suggests. As soon as we walk in, I see it's upscale, so I'm glad to be dressed appropriately. There are white starched tablecloths on the tables and a quaint bar with dark wood that looks like it's been here for a hundred years.

We ask the waiter for water with cucumbers, and when he hands us the menus, I notice there are no prices. Well, the food can't be free, so this must be one of those places I couldn't afford to eat at until today. I order a chicken salad, knowing I will be eating later with Dmitry.

"How are things going with your parents?"

"Not too bad. I can do without their arguments, and I hate not being able to come and go as I used to."

"Even when you thought you were, were you really? I find it difficult to believe your father doesn't always have eyes on you."

"I'm sure he does. It's a lie I tell myself to try and forget I was born into the family," she says, leaning in, her voice just above a whisper in case anyone is listening.

"I don't want to leave the States. Dmitry says we have to go to London and have a wedding there to make it *official*." I make air quotes with my fingers, rolling my eyes when I say the word *official*. "I never dreamed my first trip overseas would be for my unwanted wedding."

"It is the way." She grins at her Star Wars reference. "I hope I get to go. Who's planning it?"

"I have no clue, but Dmitry has two brothers, and I gather the oldest is married."

"Hm, well, I'm sure they know what they are doing. I'm told they own numerous companies, including high-end hotels. Maybe you'll live in one of them like Eloise at the Plaza. No wait! I can't have you living overseas." She reaches across the table and clutches my hand, giving it an affectionate squeeze.

"See, this is why we need to hash things out now. Once that ring is on my finger, I don't have any bargaining power," I add.

"Good point."

Our salads arrive, and we dig in, chewing in silence as we're both hungry.

"This shopping works up my appetite," I comment as I spear the chicken on my plate. They could have given me more meat for what they charge.

"Tell me about it. Wait until you attend the boring events." She gives me a grin. "Misery loves company. Oh!" she exclaims. "The Met Gala is coming up. It's a huge charity event, and there is a red carpet. I wonder if Dmitry will take you."

My face pales. I lean across the table. "Okay, bad guys want me dead. Why would I show up on a red carpet?"

"It's very public. It makes the statement you need to send."

"The one that says I'm untouchable?"

"Exactly. See, you're catching on. I've never been on a red carpet. You should do it. It would be such a rush to walk the same carpet as the celebrities."

"They do wear incredible dresses," I muse.

Alena knows I watch all the award events on TV to see what they're wearing. I sketch designs in my notebook and scribble notes only I can read because of my atrocious handwriting. I'm always thinking about new designs and want desperately to be a fashion designer. I never tell anyone because I feel like a failure for graduating without a job. The stagnant economy is making my prospects worse as each day passes without a response to my myriad of job applications.

"Are you allowed to go back to your condo?" I ask.

"No, you?"

"Off limits. However, Dmitry managed to get this dress out." I glance down and realize it's one of the few items I own. I don't have much, but what I have is mine. "But I still need my sketchbook and birth control pills."

"That shouldn't be a problem. The pills should be a priority unless he wants to get you pregnant. Kirill said he's never had a serious live-in girlfriend, so the fact he has you holed up is newsworthy."

I give this some thought. The sex is great, but there's no way we're soulmates. I don't think Dmitry is capable of love. Lust, yes. Love, no.

Alena insists on paying for lunch. We pile back into the SUV. When Anton pulls in front of the condo, Alena gets out to hug me good-bye. A deep voice behind me says, "I'll take her from here."

Dmitry.

How did he know I was even here?

"Hello, Alena. How are you?"

"Great, thanks." She answers as if she expected to see him here.

I hug Alena. We promise to see each other soon. Over her shoulder, I see two suspicious men on the opposite street corner. Since the shooting, I've been trying to be more vigilant about my surroundings.

"And be better with answering a text," she yells as she climbs into the SUV.

"Dmitry, are those your men over there?"

"No," he replies, his tone sharp and annoyed as he slides his arm protectively around my waist.

I don't know where they came from and haven't seen any suspicious cars parked on the street. Anton gathers my loot, and we follow him to the private elevator.

Once we're inside the condo, I take off my shoes and head to the bedroom to change into loungewear. Dmitry stands outside the closet where I'm dressing.

"How was your day?"

"Good. Yours?"

"Interesting. This place is Kirill's safe house. No one knows about it, so why is someone standing across the street watching this building?"

I lean against the doorjamb of the closet and face him. Damn, he looks good in anything he wears, and I swear he has his suits and shirts made by hand.

"And?" I ask, not following the point he's trying to make.

"I'm using a laptop from the Sidovo Bratva. Kirill got it for me so I can access their records for an issue I'm helping him figure out."

"A big thing, right?" I sense the level of concern and urgency.

"Yes, and I found the issue last night. Now someone knows about us, you, and where we are."

"Fuck." It's as if the air has stifled my lungs instead of feeding them.

"Yes." His face is focused and calculating. "I'll find a way to divert them, but it's also why we should be at the MET. You'll need a dress. It's—"

I cut him off. "I know what it is." My heart leaps at wearing a one-of-a-kind dress. But where do celebrities get dresses for the event?

"Great. We don't have much time to prepare for it." He walks to his nightstand, where his gun rests, and picks up a dark gray ring box.

Nervously, I wait for him to return.

"This is your ring. Never take it off. If something should happen to you, I have a tracking chip in it."

The thought of being abducted makes me nauseous. He said there's a calm before the storm. I saw the men outside. This isn't a practice drill.

"I have my own laptop now, one that can't be hacked, and your chip will ping to my phone and watch. Never take this ring off."

I notice he is indeed wearing a new watch. Wow, he's not fucking around.

He opens a box with the initials HW and pulls out what looks like a three-carat diamond.

"Part of the package deal," he says as he slides it on my ring finger.

Tears well in my eyes. I blink them back. This isn't how I imagined my engagement. I deserve love, and this is not a love match. I want a man I love, a house with a white picket fence, and beautiful babies to love with all my heart. I want the entire package.

His hands are gentle as he brings my fingers to his lips and kisses the ring. "I promise to put your life before my own." He releases my hand, letting it fall to my side. And without another word, he turns and leaves.

Alone and in shock, I lift my hand to the late afternoon light. The ring feels heavy. The setting is made of platinum. It's exquisite, with sapphire baguettes on both sides of the square-cut diamond. Dmitry strikes again, knowing what I like. The ring couldn't be more to my taste if I drew it myself.

The HW initials must stand for Harry Winston. I cannot imagine what this ring cost. A tear drops from each eye, and I wipe them away with the back of my hand. I guess this means there will be no further negotiations. Alena did say men set the pace and lead the way, just like on the dance floor.

I pull myself together and go searching for Dmitry. I follow the TV sounds and find him watching the news with a pensive look and a rock glass of scotch in his hand.

I stop walking and freeze when I hear the broadcaster say a familiar name.

"James Murphy, that's the same James Murphy my mother dated." I stare at the picture on the flatscreen TV. "James is older, but that's him," I say, sending Dmitry a wary look.

Hearing this, Dmitry's face hardens. "He's wanted on fraud charges related to a pyramid scheme, and the FBI wants to question and possibly arrest him. The problem is, he's gone missing. What aren't you telling me?" He closes the distance between us and grabs my arm. Under furrowed eyebrows, his eyes are darker than a moonless night.

"Nothing," I insist. "I only know his name, I told you. He sang funny Irish songs to me as a kid. He didn't stick around after Mom died. He didn't even show up at the funeral." I pull my arm, and he lets go without seeming to notice.

"Fuck. The men in the alley were Irish, too." His dark mood lifts as he directs his rage back to the bad guys instead of me.

"What does it mean?"

"The Irish want you. That's a given." He tosses his scotch back and sets the empty glass on the coffee table.

He notices me shaking and pulls me into his strong arms. I lay my head on his chest.

"What have I done? I wasn't supposed to be in New York City. I don't understand why this is happening."

"I'll figure it out. Until then, I'm requesting more men. I'm going on the laptop Kirill gave me and booking tickets to Vegas. Now that we know this computer is compromised, I can use it to trick our adversaries into thinking we're going to Vegas.

"I haven't figured out how the Sidovo Bratva and the Murphy Clan are connected. It's possible they both know of your existence. I'm here to find the missing money for Kirill. The money is being embezzled, and it's worse than Kirill thought. Tito, the man who does his money laundering and IT, is covering the loss with bogus charges. He put the laptop together for me and made it powerful enough to hack into other systems. That's how I realized my moves were being tracked. It won't be long before Tito knows I'm on to him. I need to figure out who his accomplices are."

I plop onto the couch, suddenly exhausted. Dmitry has been busy, and he's learned so much in just a day.

"The MET Gala is tomorrow night. I have a dress being delivered here in the morning. Tonight, we're going out to a famous place for dinner so you can pretend to be the happy bride-to-be. We need to celebrate our engagement, and the word will get out. Tomorrow, on the red carpet, pictures will go internationally. Then, we're flying to London. It will be safer for us there."

He kisses the top of my head.

"Is James still alive?"

"If he is, he won't be for much longer. If he worked for the Murphys, he's a relative, and he stole from his family. The penalty for that is death."

"No! I exclaim in a muffled protest.

How could the nice man I knew as a child meet such a fate? Did Mom know he was connected? She had to have. She waited so long to have any man around us. I'm sure she checked him out. I sob for my mother, for James, and for myself. There is overwhelming evidence that I'm not safe around anyone other than my fiancé and Alena.

"Is Kirill safe to be around?"

"I think so, but I'm not taking any chances with you." His arms pull me tighter to his solid chest. "Don't cry. Your gorgeous face will be swollen. We'll be fine. Take a bath. I have calls to make. You need to rest before dinner."

I'm not good at taking orders, but I'm too tired and scared to complain, so I do as he says. The warm bath eases the tension in my body. My mind is another matter. I worry about James, or rather, Jimmy. Sure, he might have stolen from his own, but maybe there is a reason. I would love to find him and ask him if he knows who I really am.

The bath water grows cold, so I get out and dry off. With the large towel wrapped around me, I pad into the closet where I left my purse. Finding my phone, I text Alena to keep things about me to herself. I doubt Kirill is an issue, but I'm not taking any chances. I put on one of Dmitry's dress shirts and slide between the cool sheets. I close my eyes, but sleep eludes me. My mind spins, worrying over what will become of James and if he's put the Irish on to me.

CHAPTER 18

DMITRY

I shower and change while Izzy sleeps, her black hair creating a dark halo around her serene face. I'm an asshole for forcing her into my world, but there's no other way to keep her safe. I can't slay every soldier. Two mafia families are looking for her, and I don't have the home-field advantage. If not for me, she would have disappeared, and I don't want to take odds on her still being alive if that were the case.

I assume the Irish want her due to her connection to James Murphy. I can't figure out how Tito figures into the missing money. Is he watching me in order to follow the money trail that leads to him, or is he collecting information on my whereabouts, or Kirill's, and quite possibly, it's about Izzy?

Love is brutal. It can be kind, but not in our world. We live by our codes, codes that make it difficult to navigate the world outside of ours. Our society worships money, just like billionaires who thrive on their fortunes. In order to be successful, we bend some rules and enforce others. The general public has no idea how this gets done and what we do at night. We all have blood on our hands and too many secrets to tell.

Izzy is the light in my world, a beacon of hope for a brighter future instead of a certain death. My cock hardens at the sight of her. Her voice, filled with sweetness and innocence, forces the air from my lungs. She's intoxicating. She's independent. I fear she will always want to leave me. I've no doubt I'm the darkness that her mother wanted to protect her from. No matter how much her life is in danger, I'm a selfish man to take an innocent. But I get what I want. I wouldn't be where I am today if that weren't the case. We learn early in life to take what we want.

I look at her, and she stirs before her sleepy eyes open and meets my gaze.

"Dinner?"

"Yes. I'll wait for you in the living room." My cock twitches. I need distance between us or I'll fuck her again.

I rummage through the liquor cabinet, pull out top-shelf whiskey, and tip it into a waiting rock glass. Drink in hand, I walk to the large picture window and stare out at the skyline.

My brother texts and learns that the Irish are a source of contention.

Figures, he responds.

We had a run-in with the Irish in London a year ago. Things got quiet, but now they're causing problems in the States. *Fuck me.*

The date for the wedding is set, and Anya wants to know Izzy's preference for flowers and colors.

I text: *I'll send it when acquired.*

My brother makes a crack about fucking my new interest, then tells me to use the family jet to get home safely. I thank him and sign off.

I sip the liquor and settle onto a chair that swivels around to the window. What will my life be like in London with Izzy? There are plenty of women in our circle whom I've fucked. It might be awkward for Izzy to meet past conquests.

I swirl the liquid in my glass and zone out. Now I understand how men who fall in love become weak. We'll do anything for the woman we love. In one respect, it's a weakness, but protecting my own has never been a question, and I have to rise to the occasion for Izzy.

I sense her presence and turn around to see her standing before me, looking gorgeous in an elegant dress. Half her hair is piled into a knot. The other half cascades past her shoulders. Her lips are red, and the rest of her makeup looks very natural.

"So?" She twirls with a clutch in hand, showing off her dress, but it's the last thing on my mind.

"You wear it well, Isabella."

Her eyes shy away from mine, meaning she's not accustomed to hearing compliments. I have more where that came from, so she better get used to it.

"Time for dinner," I reply, setting my glass down. She turns toward the door, and I slip my arm through hers. We quietly ride the elevator and find Anton waiting in a Range Rover outside.

* * *

THE RIDE IS quiet as Izzy takes in the city lights. Anton pulls up in front of Maesto's to let us out. I possessively place my arm around her waist and guide her into the restaurant. We are seated immediately. I order a bottle of red wine I know she will love.

Seeing the ring on her slender finger, I take comfort in the fact she is mine. Mine to fuck and mine to keep.

"I've been meaning to ask you something."

"Anything."

She leans toward me and lowers her voice. "Will you find my black book of sketches at Alena's condo and grab my birth control pills?"

*Interesting...*my wife wants to continue to work and not have a family.

"I'll see what I can do," I reply, knowing one of those two items will never make it to the condo.

"Great." She smooths her dress down on the sides and rests a hand on the base of her water glass. She's relieved, and I wonder how long she has thought about this.

Our waiter arrives with a bottle, uncorks it, and pours a sample. I swirl it under my nose. The robust notes engulf me. I lift my eyes over the glass and am surprised to find Izzy observing me. I withhold a smile but admire her beauty. I think my sex kitten likes me.

I sip the wine, nod to the waiter, and he finishes the pour, then sets the bottle on the table. I order an appetizer of oysters Rockefeller, wondering if Izzy has ever tried them.

"My mother and sister-in-law are working on our wedding. You'll like them both. We'll be married in two weeks."

"So soon?" She was eyeing her wine until her eyes returned to me. Her dainty hand encircles the stem of the wine glass.

"You have an alternate idea that will keep you safe?" She's not out of the woods, and she bloody well better well understand she is mine and that I call the shots.

She picks up her glass and stares into the sea of liquified grapes, shaking her head. "No. I guess I don't."

"Let's toast to an agreeable future together."

Our glasses touch, and I long to have her fingers wrapped around my back as I fuck her again. I can't get enough of her. God help the man who tries to take her away from me.

"Cheers," she murmurs, and we both sip.

She sets her glass down and gazes at the reflections of candlelight dancing off her new ring.

"I take it you like the ring?"

"Oh, it's more than adequate."

Adequate? What does that mean? Men like me don't settle for adequate. We need to conquer and win at everything. My eyes narrow as I attempt to read her mood.

"I can get you whatever your heart desires." I offer to get her what she wants. I want her showered in gems and diamonds. She'll have everything needed to be happy in her gilded cage.

"Oh, no. The ring is gorgeous," she replies, her voice becoming dramatic, proving to me she loves it. She fidgets with the ring as she speaks.

"Will they really take me?"

"We've been over this. You saw them on the street corner. Do you want more proof?"

"No, I get it. It's just so… surreal."

I understand she's spent her life thinking she is less than everyone else. Little did she know, she was someone's princess and hidden under everyone's nose. Does she know more than she's telling me?

It's a question I ask myself every day. It's not in my nature to trust. However, if I'm to start trusting, logically, it should begin with my wife.

"I've noticed you're wearing a subtle fragrance." I change the subject.

She lowers her head demurely. "I love lilacs because they are blue and don't overpower my senses."

"What else?" I inquire.

"Roses, for sure." She chuckles. Her nervous laugh tells me she hasn't received many bouquets. I'll have to make sure I change that.

The oysters arrive, and Izzy gracefully places her napkin in her lap.

"Have you had these before?"

"No, I've seen them."

Right, money is her obstacle, and it makes me deliriously happy that I can shower her with anything her heart desires.

I pick up a shell and slide the oyster into my mouth. She watches, then picks one up and delicately lets it slide into her mouth.

"So?"

She swallows. "Very good."

"Well, there are more," I encourage her, and she lifts another one to her lush lips and opens her mouth. The very mouth I'd like to fuck again.

The waiter comes by, and Izzy studies the menu before ordering a porterhouse and sides. I grin. My little bird enjoys a good meal.

The conversation is nice as she asks me about England and my family. Our food arrives, and she waits for me to lift my utensils before she cuts into her steak. We make light conversation, and she seems to be at ease with me.

Dinner is over, and she can't finish the amount of food on her plate. I bet the chef loaded our plates, knowing I was there. Our family owns several businesses, and anything that can bring in cash to launder money is a winning proposition. Restaurants go under all the time, but we funnel money into ours. And we own this one, and many others.

I order champagne and propose a toast when it arrives.

"I'm going to be tipsy with all this alcohol," she warns. I think my little bluebird is having a good time.

"Doubtful. You don't impress me as a person who will ever be out of it in public." I can't help but grin, knowing how she comes undone for me in the bedroom. The mere thought of her yelling for me to fuck her makes my cock hard.

Men with wives are escorted to tables, but they can't pass ours without glancing at Izzy. I'm angry they are so brazen to ogle her with their unabashed eyes—men like me, who are used to getting what they want. I suppress a territorial growl. I turn my attention back to Izzy. I do believe my princess is enjoying herself. She wraps a strand of hair around her finger, and God, I want to fuck her right on the table. She has no idea how seductive she is without even trying.

New York-style cheesecake with fresh berries shows up without us asking. She can't finish it and adamantly refuses to take it home. I don't get a bill but leave hundreds of dollars on the table to tip our waiter.

I'm slightly buzzed as Anton drives us back to the condo. The guards are waiting for us outside to inform us that the building is secure. In our private elevator, Izzy stands with her back to the wall, and I stand close enough to nuzzle her neck, inhaling the soft scent of lilac and vanilla.

My cock is hard. I want her. I grab her wrists, and her clutch falls to the floor. She lets out a surprised gasp, and my lips cover hers. I hold her arms over her head, my pelvis pinning her against the wall. I slip my tongue into her mouth and taste the raspberry from the cheesecake.

I will devour her. My free hand slides down her body, over her hips, hips that will widen when she delivers my son. I cup her ass, holding her immobile. She has nowhere to go when my cock presses into her abdomen.

I'm drunk on desire. Feeling the heat between us, she clutches my neck and grinds her pelvis into mine.

A raspy groan escapes my throat. *Fuck.* If the elevator hadn't dinged, I would have her stripped naked and carried her to my bed. My breathing is ragged as I pick up her purse, and we make our way down the hall, kissing and groping each other like young lovers. I slip my card into the lock, pull her inside, and let the door close and lock behind us.

The kitchen's recessed lighting paves the way to the bedroom. She unbuckles my belt and unzips my pants. I step out of my shoes and slide my boxers off, shedding my jacket as I nuzzle her neck. My pants fall by the wayside as I pursue her. She turns. I unzip her dress and kiss her supple neck. The material slips off her delicate shoulders and drops to the floor. I'm shocked when I take in my soon-to-be wife, scantily clad in crotchless underwear and a matching lacy bra.

My cock twitches and swells even more as I run my hands over her breast, knowing the thin fabric is the only thing between me and her full perky breasts. I cup one tit, squeezing it hard to show my desire to have her. I flick one strap off her shoulder and push the fabric away to expose her breast. I lock my lips on her hard nipple, flicking it with my tongue. Her back arches slightly, and I run my other hand over her lacy bottom, grab her tight ass, and give it a firm squeeze. I let out a groan that sounds more like a growl.

I slip my fingers into the warm nest between her legs. She's dripping for me, and it makes my cock throb. We've worked our way to the bed. I put a foot on the mattress, grab my cock, and rub the tip around her velvety entrance. I push the tip past her folds, knowing my precum could get her pregnant. The thought of impregnating her is making me harder than I thought possible. What better way to keep her tied to me after the threat is gone?

I nip at her nipple, and she yelps. My lips move up her neck.

She pulls back. "What about a condom?" she suggests.

I let out a low chuckle. "Do you want me to stop, Izzy? I know you want me just as much as I want you. You can't deny it." I let go of my cock and cup her pussy, flicking a finger over her clit and feeling it harden in anticipation.

I palm her wetness and run my fingers around her lips, slick with her clear, sweet juice.

She moans and arches her back, offering up her pussy. My finger slips inside, and I finger fuck her, making her twist and moan before she collapses on the bed.

I lay over her, pulling her arms over her head. Her knees are together as she writhes under me, her body twisting. Her desire is evident.

"Ahh," she gasps, her head rolling side to side in slow motion.

"Tell me what you want. I will never take you against your will. But say it because I need to sink my cock in you."

"Mm." She moves her legs apart, her hips lifting off the mattress.

"Use words, Izzy."

I place my swollen tip inside her pussy. Her wetness bathes me. *Fuck*, I'm about to take her regardless of what I promised.

"Izzy." Unable to hold out much longer, I can barely speak.

"Fuck me," she begs at last.

My cock slams her so hard her head almost hits the headboard. "Oh," she gasps as I fill her with my girth. Her walls are warm and inviting. I groan as I lose myself in her.

I tease her, holding her arms at first as she twists under me, her urgency becoming evident as her walls grip my cock. I drop my mouth to her breasts and tug at her nipple, making her moan with pleasure. She's ripe for me, but I delay her gratification. I release her hands, and she immediately clamps them onto my back, digging her nails into me like a cat scratching a post. *Fuck, that's hot.*

I grab a fistful of hair with one hand and slide the other under her toned ass to cradle her for my next thrust.

She moans softly. Her eyes are closed, and her neck is exposed. I suck on it, leaving a mark. She lifts her hips for a better angle as we fuck each other, spellbound by our desire and lust. I feel her clit quicken and pull out, slipping down to her shaved pussy. She spreads her legs wide, and I have her for dessert. I nip at her swollen clit, and her body is on the cusp of convulsing. I run my warm tongue up the inside of her thigh and lick everything but her clit, teasing her.

She grabs a fistful of my hair and yanks me up.

"Fuck me. I can't take it anymore," she wails.

I resume my earlier position and slam my cock in her hard. Her screams of pleasure echo off the walls of the room. Her eyes shut, and her body spasms with euphoria. I continue to thrust over and over until she stiffens as a wave of more orgasms erupts on my cock. I can't hold back and bury my head in her neck, groaning like a primitive animal as I come, spilling my seed inside her. My heart is racing, and my head feels like it will explode.

I'm spent. I can't move. I can't catch my breath. My legs feel like overcooked spaghetti. I lie on top of her, still buried inside her love tunnel. With reluctance, I pull out and roll to her side.

She reaches down and gently squeezes my slippery cock, still hard and covered with her cum.

I've never lost control with a woman, and I'll be damned if I start now. That doesn't stop me from pulling her into my arms. I enjoy the feel of her breasts firmly pressed against my chest, and my cock stiffens again. If this continues, I'll have a difficult time getting any work done.

I leave her side long enough to check the door and turn off the kitchen lights. I return and pull her to me. She doesn't resist, so she's either too tired or she's becoming comfortable around me. I hope it's the latter of the two.

With a long-satisfied sigh, I drift off to sleep. My gun is on the nightstand, and I hope I won't have to use it again.

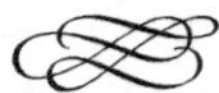

IZZY

Dmitry reminds me that the MET Gala is tonight and tells me to get undressed for a dress fitting. I do as he instructs and wait in the bedroom, wearing only a bra and panties. I hear voices, and a stylist brings in a beautiful red sleeveless gown with a beaded bodice. Dmitry watches from the doorway as she helps me into the dress and zips the back. I swear he's enjoying this.

The dress fits perfectly around my bust and has a long train of satiny material that stretches out behind me. A built-in corset pushes up my breasts, making them appear bigger and my waist smaller. I may look like Jessica Rabbit, but I feel like Cinderella going to the ball.

I raise my eyes, seeking Dmitry's approval. His arms are crossed over his chest as he leans against the door frame, his eyes feasting upon me. My nipples ripple under his intense gaze.

"You're so beautiful, Izzy."

He's said this twice now. Am I really beautiful? The fact he says it makes me smiles inside.

"The dress," I say, and he interrupts me.

"The dress is exquisite because you're wearing it."

Dmitry's phone rings, and he leaves the room. I can't help but wonder how he has so many people available to produce what he wants from thin air. Maybe it's better that I don't know.

The woman helping to fit me is older. I ask her for her name, and she informs me it's Vera. She's as direct as she is efficient. I'm envious as she rattles off the names of designers she's worked with in the past. I tell her I appreciate her working with me, especially last minute.

Vera singsongs and talks to herself as she works. I stand patiently, waiting for her verdict on my new look.

It suddenly occurs to me I will be rubbing elbows with TV and movie stars tonight. How did I get in the limelight? Dmitry is my connection, but who does he know well enough to get an invite to a star-studded affair that's been planned a year in advance?

In addition, I can't help but wonder how much the man is worth. I've never stumbled across the name Volkov, and I'm too afraid to look him up on my phone.

Vera tells me to stand up straight and that people need to have better posture. She's right. I stand taller, and she pulls shoes out of a bag filled with sewing supplies. I slip then on. They are oddly comfortable for being four-inch heels. She checks the length and nods with approval. You would think it's tailor-made, the way it fits like a glove.

Vera bustles around and tells me to raise my arms and bend as she checks to make sure everything is snug. Satisfied with her results, she informs Dmitry it's perfect. He hands her a roll of bills, and she scurries out of the door.

"This is insane," I exclaim.

Dmitry's hungry eyes rake over me. His face darkens as he moves across the room to unzip me. I'm excited by the fact that he's so close to me. His hand pushes aside my hair to find the zipper, and my body tingles.

"I thought you might like to get out this morning, so I'm taking you to the Channel Gardens."

"Really? I get a hall pass?" I chuckle.

"What's a hall pass?"

"Oh, right. Well, when you're in class, you need a pass to go to the bathroom or your locker. It's called a hall pass." He looks at me, confused. "Never mind. Getting out of this condo would be great. I like feeling safe, but it's feeling more and more like solitary confinement."

He looks hurt, or is it my imagination?

"I mean, you're great, really," I babble as I step out of the gown.

He hands me the dress to hang up and disappears. I place the dress in the closet and leave it swaying on a hanger before tossing a t-shirt on and shimming into my jeans. Should I wear flats or sneakers to walk in a garden? I decide on my new sneakers, in case we walk on the grass.

I look for Dmitry and find him in the kitchen on the phone. My black notebook on the counter catches my eye. That's weird. It wasn't there earlier this morning. I proclaim him a magician with a proclivity for sexual tricks. As long as he's only having sex with me, I'm fine with doing it multiple times a day. I feel a slickness between my legs whenever I'm around him or thinking about him. Everything about Dmitry fills me with desire.

Then it hits me. My birth control isn't here. I want to ask him about it, but he's still on his phone, speaking in Russian. He sounds annoyed, so maybe this is not the time to ask.

Shit. I slip into the bedroom and call Alena.

"Izzy, how are you?"

"Okay, I guess. Um, is there any reason why Dmitry would want a kid?"

She laughs. "What are you talking about?"

"He didn't bring me my birth control pills like I wanted. I'm curious why he would risk getting me pregnant."

"Shit. This is newsworthy. Normally, bratva men only want kids to continue the bloodline."

"So, I'm a bitch in heat?" I bemoan my worst nightmare.

"Well, that's a way to label it. I seriously doubt he views you as a dog, Izzy. I think he's into you, and it's romantic."

"I'm too young for kids."

I sit on the bed. Damn him for making me want him. Now I need to start keeping my legs crossed.

"That's what everyone says, and then they end up forty years old and hiring a surrogate to carry their baby."

"I don't have to wait that long. This is not a real marriage, and I'm not having kids with him."

"Bratva men get what they want. Why do you think they give us everything we desire? It's the buy-in to be with them. We're bought and paid for, Izzy. We have very little free will. If he wants a kid, he'll have one. But wow. I did not see this coming."

"Right?" I sulk.

The sex is exceptionally hot. Maybe the added risk of pregnancy gives it an element of danger. Or the fact Dmitry screams danger, I'm not sure. I decide I'll make him pay for this. Ideas run through my head. I could tell the pharmacy I lost my pills and have them deliver a new pack, but our location is a secret. Can I risk it? He'd be so pissed if I disobey him.

"What's happening with you? I'm sorry I've been out of touch lately. Dmitry keeps me busy."

"I can only imagine. Is it really hot? I mean, hot enough to steam the wallpaper off the bedroom walls? I imagine with his wild hair and the brooding eyes, he's got a hint at some level of kink."

"Maybe." What is she talking about? Kink? Oh, lordy, there are no butt plugs in my future. Pinning my wrists and arms was intense. Making me wait before he satisfied my lust was very hot. "I'm so screwed. I can't deny him anything, Alena," I whisper into the phone as something occurs to me.

Do I love him? The thought of having his baby is romantic, and there is a tingle between my legs at the thought of a mini-me running around. If he wants to be bound to me by blood, he must care for me.

"What's up with you and Kirill?" I decide to change the conversation back to her. I'm in over my head with this man.

"He's working. I'm sitting here buying things online and charging it to my daddy's credit card."

"Any idea who he's going to have you marry?"

"Jury is out on that. I'm getting bored. I can't go to many places. I mean, Daddy has to understand these thugs are after you, not me. However, he's being very adamant about where I go. I can't wait for this to be over."

"I imagine when we leave for London, these nameless, faceless men will realize I'm gone and give up. Then things will return to normal," I add optimistically.

Dmitry has altered my life forever. I doubt anything will ever be normal again. Whether it's necessary or not, I'm stuck with him.

"I'm going to miss you when you're off having a European adventure."

"It won't be much of a vacation. I'm getting married and meeting his family. What if they don't like me?"

"They will. Keep your chin up, girlfriend. You need to remain positive. I'm sure his family will love you."

The idea of faking the marriage and lying to his family gives me a sinking feeling in my gut. It's deceitful, and I value honesty above all else, which brings me back to my mother. Was she honest with me and Aunt Emma? I brush this off as Dmitry hangs up the phone and announces that we are leaving in a few minutes.

I've never taken the time to visit the gardens. It's more of a tourist attraction, in my opinion, and because of that, it will get busier now that the weather is warming up.

As if on cue, Alena yawns and says her mother is calling her. "Gotta go," she adds. I say bye, and we hang up.

Dmitry waits for me in the doorway.

"Coming," I say as I grab a purse and transfer items from last night's clutch before following Dmitry to the car.

Anton drives us to the Channel Garden and pulls up in front of a door that reads Staff Only. None of us work here, and yet someone on the other side opens the door and lets us in.

Dmitry looks comfortable in his jeans and a button-down dress shirt. Taking my hand, we slowly stroll along the walkway, enjoying the blooming spring flowers. The kaleidoscope of colors is breathtaking, and I comment on the waterfall, and we pause under arches covered with tea roses. I wonder how long it takes for everything to grow. To be this perfect, there must be greenhouses and minions of gardeners behind the scenes.

"It's time for lunch, let's grab a bite from a street vendor, and we'll head home."

"Okay." I follow him and notice Anton. He and another man are following us, keeping a watchful eye on the people around us.

"Are we safe here?"

"As much as we can be. He reaches for my hand and surprises me when he pulls it to his lips and kisses the engagement ring.

"Tonight will be fun. Relax."

"How do you know so many people to arrange all this?"

"Years in the making. My father was a powerful man and traveled internationally. In fact, we have a house on Long Island, but we're not using it because it's too far away. I wanted to be in the city this week."

It's only a train ride, but I see his point.

* * *

BACK AT THE CONDO, Dmitry has a glam squad drop by. One girl does my updo, and the other does my makeup. When I take one last look in the mirror, I don't recognize myself. My skin is flawless. My eyes pop, the gown is stunning, and I look fabulous. I inhale deeply to fill my lungs with air and calm myself. I'm going to the MET. I'm filled with excitement as I never dreamed this would happen to me, and to have the handsome Russian escorting me is icing on the cake.

Dmitry catches me fussing with my hair, making sure it's not falling out of the bun.

"Stop fidgeting, Izzy, you're beautiful. I don't care if a hair falls out of place. Nothing diminishes how gorgeous you are."

"I'm nervous." I fidget with the fabric of the dress, then decide to grab my new matching clutch from the counter.

"I'd be shocked if you weren't. Nothing to it. If anyone asks, we met through friends, fell in love, and decided to get married."

"Got it."

"Let's go." He opens the door, and we take the elevator to the parking garage, where Anton is waiting for us in a limo.

There's chilled champagne, and Dmitry pours us each a glass of bubbly. This is my first time riding in a limo, and I take the glass from Dmitry. It will suffice to calm my nerves. I never knew what I missed out on with my senior prom until now. It was the talk of the town when the star quarterback and his girlfriend arrived in one for prom. I went with a girlfriend, and there was no limo for us.

"You're so beautiful. Happy engagement," he says as I hold the stem between my thumb and two fingers.

I have no idea what to say and nod.

We touch flutes. I quickly sip the golden alcohol. When we finish our cocktails, I put the flute down. I can't drink much without it going to my head and decide to err on the side of caution.

The closer we get to the MET, the worse the traffic becomes. At some point, we join a long line of limousines and continue to inch forward. I crane my neck to see who's getting out of the cars ahead of us. Some people look familiar, but most don't because I've been busy with school, and I'm no longer up with the who's who in Hollywood.

It's our turn to get out, and I'm terrified I'll fall on my face. My mouth is bone dry, and I want to vomit. Dmitry senses my panic and squeezes my hand. I look down and notice he wore cuff links with rubies to match my red dress. Men with earpieces open the car doors. They're probably security or event coordinators.

I step out, afraid the ground will move. This is surreal as flashes on cameras pop. I manage to get out of the limo, and Dmitry has his arm gently around my waist, guiding me into the sea of paparazzi.

"Smile. I thought you'd enjoy this," he says.

"The gowns, the tuxes. Oh, my."

I scan the horizon. Single women, men, and couples are standing and talking to reporters. I smile. I need to enjoy my five seconds of fame. Someone obtains Dmitry's attention. We pose, pointing our toes toward each other and smiling at the photographer who snaps numerous pictures. I glance up at my fiancé and catch him smiling.

Dmitry slides his hand into mine. We wait our turn on the red carpet. My palm is sweaty, but he doesn't seem to care. He squeezes it and gives me a reassuring smile. I smile back. I can do this. Remembering Vera's words, I pull my shoulders back and stand taller.

Someone behind me says something, but I can't hear it due to the commotion. How do stars do this? I'm overwhelmed by the perfume and cologne floating in the air. I glance over my shoulder and discover an event coordinator spreading the train of my gown behind me. An ephemeral breeze blows my way, and I catch a whiff of Dmitry, him, mixed with sandalwood and musk. Our eyes lock.

I'm smitten with his dark, brooding eyes and sexual vibe. He looks dashing in his black tuxedo.

He leads the way, and I walk beside him. We're next. I pray I don't trip in my heels. When we reach the steps—and it's a repeat of the lights from cameras and overhead ones staged to light the vicinity. I'm blinded. I blink and try not to squint.

"Smile," Dmitry murmurs as his head dips into my neck.

The tantalizing manliness of his aura sweeps over me. He's so intimate and comfortable with me. It's as if we've been together forever. We pose once more for the camera crew.

My sleeveless dress doesn't cover the tattoo on my arm, and I wonder if this is on purpose. The message is loud and clear: *Here I am.* If you come for me, my future husband will come for you tenfold.

I discreetly turn my arm to make sure the cameras capture the image of my bird tattoo. And just when I think our time on the red carpet is finished, a woman in the crowd calls Dmitry's name.

Dmitry stops and greets the woman. I wonder if this is a liaison from his past. She asks him about the recent sale of a hotel property to another well-known international hotel chain. He plays the billionaire smoothly and explains that the deal will allow him to downsize and focus more on his family. With that, he brings my hand to his lips and kisses it.

When the reporter asks if he's engaged, he replies, "Yes, I am. This is Isabella Lucci, my future wife." His radiant smile makes the woman happy.

"Congratulations. How does it feel to be marrying into the Volkov family?"

"Fantastic." I smile nervously, sticking to a one-word answer.

She moves the microphone back to Dmitry and asks another question. I can't hear their words. The noise from people behind us leads me to believe someone famous is getting out of a limo. I'm about to turn my head, but Dmitry pulls me closer to him. As we break away from the reporters, we continue to walk the red carpet.

"Don't look behind you. Keep moving forward," he murmurs. I walk beside him, following his lead. We walk the red carpet, and at the end, I slip my phone out.

"Time for our picture." He dutifully takes my phone and holds the camera high, snapping a few pictures of us.

Satisfied, we continue off the carpet and circle back to the waiting limo as I inquire about the dinner reception.

"Too dangerous. We'll pick up food on the way home and leave in the morning. I'm afraid it's an early night for you. Besides, the rubber chicken and a drop of pea soup aren't what I'd call food."

I take it he's done this before, and I wonder who he was dating.

CHAPTER 20

DMITRY

I'm relieved when we're heading back to the condo. I send Anton into the restaurant from last night, and he returns with my pre-ordered dinners to go. Izzy is famished and dives into the burgers made of the best beef money can buy.

"Thank you for the MET. Is it strange that I enjoyed visiting the garden more?"

I knew my little bird would appreciate the beauty of the roses and spring flowers in the Channel Garden.

"No, in fact, I prefer it too." Something about the quiet atmosphere of the garden inside a city buzzing with life creates a calm oasis, like the eye of a hurricane. I never felt uncomfortable when we walked together in silence. There was no pressure to carry on a conversation. With Izzy, I can be myself. She seems to tolerate my brooding and moody nature.

Her phone dings with a text message alert.

"That's probably Alena."

She pulls her phone out of her purse to text a reply.

"I'm sending her pictures," she warns me.

I nod. She's vivacious and so full of life. I'd feel bad about dragging her into my world and would avoid it at any cost had I not been totally consumed with her at the club.

I grab a burger, and we talk as we eat. She's still high on the stars she thought she observed. I have no idea. I'm from Europe, and I usually don't watch pop culture shows. I have no idea who's a rapper or actress. Crazy Americans with their reality TV shows. Today, they are dubbed into foreign languages and on international airwaves in days, not months.

We finish eating the fries, and I discover we both like them without ketchup. Izzy tidies our food containers into the large bag. It's nice that she's conscientious of the men who pick up after us.

We make our way into the condo without incident. Izzy asks for my help getting undressed. My cock hardens at the thought of seeing her naked. You'd think she'd be out of my system by now, but that's not the case. There is no way I can forget about my little bird. I'm drawn to her like the moon pulls the ocean tides. I can't explain it, but Izzy is mine. I am a possessed man. She's my addiction. All I can think about is sinking my cock into her again.

I unzip her dress, and my cock swells at the sound of the zipper. I drop a kiss on one shoulder and let the dress drop to the floor. It's a one-of-a-kind Versace and cost thousands of dollars, but I have more important things on my mind than hanging it up.

Her phone pings.

"Everything okay?" I ask.

"Oh, yeah, Alena wanted to make sure we got home. She's so jealous we went. She saw us in the event videos and texted some to me."

"We're fighting world hunger. What's not to like?"

"So, now that we're out and the engagement has gone viral, am I safe?" Izzy asks, tossing her phone on the bed. She turns, and it takes all my willpower not to drool at the sight of her firm breasts filling her bra to capacity.

I chuckle. My princess thinks social media will fix her problems.

"I'm the solution for your problems, Izzy," I growl. "No one will touch what is mine, and you have been claimed as mine."

Goosebumps suddenly sprout on her arms as I hold her hand and gaze into her eyes. She focuses her attention on my chest. She begins to unfasten the buttons of my white shirt. My cock yearns to be free. She wants me as much as I want her. I don't know what is more thrilling, the thought that she's making the moves or the fact that I know her pussy is wet for me.

I slip a hand behind her head and pull pins out of her updo, allowing her long tresses to tumble around her shoulders. My cock twitches.

I rip off my tux, tossing it on the floor next to her dress. Izzy reaches for my cock, grabs my swollen shaft, and glides her hand over the head and back again. I moan. I'm so hard I could pound nails into concrete. *Fuck me.* I have to have her. I don't think I'll ever get my fill of her.

I grab her wrists and twist an arm behind her back, then manhandle her to the bed so that she's bent over with her face on the mattress. I love her like this, under my control, wearing only panties and heels. My balls tighten at the view of her perky ass in the air. I want to bite it.

Her breathing is choppy, like a sea of lust. Happy with her compliance, I release her wrist to unsnap her bra. I greedily grab her breasts from behind and massage them in my large palms. They are exquisite, warm, and silky to the touch. Her nipples harden beneath my fingers.

"What do you want, Izzy?"

"You, only you," she murmurs into the duvet cover.

My heart skips a beat and drives my desire to an all-time high. I'm not a man without a past. I've done enough drugs to know she's the only one who can make me this high.

I roll her nipples between my fingers, making them hard as I grab her firm ass cheeks and line my cock up to her entrance. She arches her back, yearning for my cock to fill her.

I plant a hand on the middle of her back. My breathing is labored as I use my other hand to glide my thick cock inside her wetness.

"You're wet for me, good girl."

"Fuck me, Dmitry."

I rub the head of my cock, covered in precum, inside her swollen lips.

Without warning, I thrust my cock into her inviting opening, causing her to scream with pleasure. I'm large. Even with her wetness, I'm sure it's a mixture of pleasure and pain when she screams again, and it's loud enough to alert our guard stationed outside.

I grab her breasts with both hands and massage her nipples into hard peaks. She makes guttural sounds under me, and I sink my cock into her again. My balls are hard and smack into her glorious ass.

Fueled by her body's response, I pump her like a man driven by the devil. She moans into the mattress, her hands clutching the covers as I pound harder with each thrust. She writhes under me. I feel her clit tighten on my cock, sending chills over my body.

I'm on the verge of coming, but hold off. With one hand on her shoulder and another on her hip, I continue with my powerful thrusts until I feel her clit quicken. She screams and squirts her love juice, covering my head. Her muscles tighten around me like a boa constrictor. Her body quivers with another round of orgasms. I thrust one last time, holding her in place. With one long, loud groan, I shoot my load past her swollen lips and hope my seed impregnates her.

I shudder one last time before pulling out. I walk to the bathroom and grab a washcloth and wet it with warm water. I return to find her lying under the sheets, but I pull them back to wipe cum off her thighs.

"Good night." I drop a kiss on her lips.

"You're not staying?" Her sleepy voice sucks me in, but I have work to do.

"I'll be back in a few minutes," I lie. I'm going to stay up and work. Besides, she'll be asleep in no time.

I text my brother and learn the jet will be here first thing in the morning. I pour myself a vodka and use my laptop to cross-reference Moretti's daughter, Martina, with Izzy.

I'd swear Izzy belongs to the Morettis. However, Martina passed away before Izzy's birth. She was nineteen years old and died in a car accident in NYC. It must have been a bad accident because it was a closed casket. The funeral was held at a catholic church in the city. A brief obituary appeared in the *NYC Times* newspaper. After that, there was always tension between the Italians and the Russians.

It's odd how the names don't match, but speaking from experience, fake news reports can be bought. What is Santino up to? By all accounts, he has a son to take over after his demise. What happened between the two families that could not be fixed with a simple sit-down? When the Italians used Kirill's mother to patch things up with the Russians, it only managed to stop the bleeding. It didn't mend the wound.

I wonder why Alexsei isn't more visible. There aren't any pictures of him online, and information on where he went to school isn't public. It's safer living away from the spotlight, so is he trying to fly under the radar, or is he a recluse?

This is not unusual. The bratva men do not like to be in the media. They are a stark comparison to the Sicilians who run their side of New York City and are known to be flashy and vocal. You don't have to be part of the mob to know about the Gambino crime family and the Teflon Don.

Looking at online images of Alexsei's wife, Llea, it's evident from her frozen face and puffy lips that she overdid it on the Botox and fillers. She's had so much work done on her face that she could go into witness protection. Born in Russia fifty-five years ago, she dresses impeccably. She throws fundraisers to raise money to help inner-city youth. Ironic considering she's part of the reason inner-city neighborhoods are riddled with drugs.

Sure, if we don't supply the drugs, someone else will. The drug of choice is constantly changing. Twenty-five years ago, cocaine was big, and today it's heroin. Europe is making coke popular again, but cheaper drugs like meth and fentanyl can be made rather than imported, keeping down our costs.

I down my vodka and close the laptop, disappointed I could not make a concrete connection between Izzy and the Moretti family. I'm not giving up. Merely shelving it for another day.

Tomorrow will be a long flight. The fact that Nikolay sent the jet is a generous gesture. Maybe he is excited about gaining a sister-in-law.

I turn out the lights, check the door, and ask Anton if the building is secure. Confident we're fine for the night, I call Kirill.

He answers on the first ring. "What's up? I saw you on TV. That's amazing."

"I hope it works, for now. I need to buy time to figure this out."

"I have men watching the airport tomorrow. They're new to the organization, and no one will recognize them. I have a contact who can get me a list of the passengers."

"Sounds good, but considering how easy it is to get a fake ID, it's better to have boots on the ground. A fake driver's license is expensive, but anyone with the money will gladly pay whatever it takes to avoid leaving a trail."

"Okay, keep me in the loop and text me when you are home."

"Will do."

I'll leave my gun here, and Anton will dispose of it for me. The jet will have weapons for me in the baggage hold.

I crawl into bed next to Izzy and lie there, unable to shut down my overactive brain. I sigh, eyes wide open. I end up staring at the ceiling. I roll over, drape my arm around Izzy, and cup her breast. *Fuck*, I want to take her again. My cock twitches behind her silky soft buttocks. I resist the urge to fuck her and will my boner to go down. Izzy needs to sleep without interruption once in a while. I'm so screwed. How can I be expected to sleep beside her every night and not fuck her? My blue balls ache, and I wonder if she would be mad if I woke her.

A good fuck always relaxes the body. I'm sure it would help me sleep. However, I don't want her to think I'm a Neanderthal and stick to my original decision to leave her alone. Closing my eyes, I imagine my new home in London with Izzy. I smile, knowing she'll love it.

CHAPTER 21

IZZY

*D*mitry is dressed in tight jeans and a pullover that hugs his broad chest. He hands me a cup of cappuccino. I pull myself into a sitting position before I take the cup from him.

"Thank you. What time did you come to bed?"

"A few hours after you, why?"

"No reason, just curious."

"Did you miss me?" He strokes his freshly shaved jaw with the back of his fingers. There's a hint of mischief in his salacious grin.

Is he teasing me? My eyes haven't left his physique, yet I sip the warm drink.

"It's chilly in here," I say to change the subject and stop feeding his ego.

"I just turned the heat up. The temperatures dipped last night."

"Wait, it's dark out. What time is it?" I always had a routine, coffee, workout, and attend classes. I never sleep in late.

"It's five in the morning. Anton is making sure the electronic gates are manned, and no one can get in and take what is mine."

I flinch. He's referring to me as if I'm a possession.

"My hope is to have two weeks in London before they discover we've left the country. That's overly optimistic, but still, I want time with you to get settled before the wedding."

"Oh, you want the bad guys thinking we went to Vegas," I say to let him know I've been paying attention.

"Exactly." He grins, and I take that as a win.

I can't take my eyes off him as he leans against the bedroom door. I am keenly aware of the package stuffed in his tight jeans. How does he manage to get something the size of a toddler's arm shoved inside his pants? Dmitry's not only hung like a porn star, he knows how to use it, and I'm putty in his hands. No other man has ever given me multiple orgasms, but I'll never tell him. A man with his self-confidence doesn't need to know how much I crave him.

I have to remember he's a killer of men, but in his defense, his latest kills were to save me. Thankfully, my nightmares haven't returned. I'm sure having Dmitry lying next to me every night helps.

The way he makes me feel safe makes our forced marriage more palpable. It's not in my best interest to go it alone. I doubt I will ever return to my normal life. Honestly, it wasn't all that special. I had a college degree but no income, nor did I have a way of paying off my student loans.

Dmitry walks to the bedroom window and peers through the blinds, separating them ever so slightly. His movements are slow and deliberate.

He turns back to me. "The flight to Vegas is at nine. We need to leave soon so we can fly to London close to that time. There's a convoy of cars waiting downstairs who will distract any tails when we leave." He gestures with his hands as he strides across the room, explaining the plan to me.

"Some vehicles will go to LaGuardia. Others will go to JFK and Newark while we head to Teterboro, the private airport. They won't be able to follow all the cars."

My jaw drops.

"Private jet?" I squeal. "A private airport?" This is how movie stars and rock stars travel and why they are rarely seen on commercial flights.

He smiles at my silliness, but I don't care. He's gorgeous when the corners of his mouth turn up and a seldom-seen dimple appears on his right cheek. His teeth are perfect, and so is his wavy, dirty blond hair. No one should look this good at five o'clock in the morning. The faint smell of him mixed with mint and musk swirls lightly in the air.

"Do you feel warmer?" he asks, his arms folded over his chest.

I wonder if he was ever in the army because when he stands, he never slouches. His feet are always firmly planted just so, and he crosses his arms defensively. Maybe he was in the Russian army, maybe not.

"Yes, thank you." I try not to stare, but it can't be helped. He fills the room.

His no-nonsense approach to our predicament is very comforting. Unexpected events do not easily rattle him. His past is unclear, and he never volunteers personal information.

"No problem," he replies. "I suggest you get dressed. We need to pack and get out of here within an hour."

I throw back the covers and leap from the bed. If I linger, Dmitry will find a way to seduce me before breakfast. He has a way of making it impossible for me to refuse him. It's not that I don't want him. The issue is that I do. And if he ever finds out, he'll always have the upper hand.

I scamper into the bathroom. I take a quick shower, washing my hair. I remember seeing a blow dryer under the sink. I can't look like shit when we arrive in London. I towel dry my hair and pick up another thick towel to dry myself.

I run conditioner through my hair and blow it out with the hair dryer. I use my fingers to fluff it and wonder what my mom looked like in her twenties. Maybe someone in New York City recognized me because I look like her. I know we shared the same thick, black hair.

I walk into the closet and pull new panties out, and they match the bra I always wanted but could never afford. I tug on jeans and a long-sleeved shirt, throwing an oversized sweater over it. Alena helped me pick out these clothes. She does have good taste, expensive, but good. I don't know what it is about me. I'm great at dressing others, but not myself.

I check my look in the bathroom mirror. Layering clothes is always the way to go when the weather is fickle. I apply moisturizer to my face along with foundation. I even use a bronzer. Why not splurge on the best products Dmitry's money can buy?

Satisfied with my look, I duck back into the closet to pull on socks and grab a pair of low-heeled suede boots. I hear Dmitry moving about and peek in to catch him packing his silver laptop into one of two matching roller bags. One must be for me.

"How am I to fit everything into this tiny thing?"

"You don't."

I freeze, my eyebrows raise in disbelief. "You just bought all this stuff," I argue because it seems silly to leave it behind.

"I know. Take your necessities and a few outfits. You won't need anything else," he replies flatly, showing no emotion.

"Am I walking around London naked?"

He sets his luggage on the floor. "Of course not. It's too cold. Everything is taken care of." He rolls his luggage across the tile and parks it at the door. "Your clothes will be shipped."

"What will I be wearing, exactly?"

"The best of everything." He smirks, flashing me a naughty smile.

My face grows warm under his suggestive gaze.

"Is this entertaining for you?" I put my hands on my hips as I face off with him.

"Kinda." He shrugs on his way to the kitchen. I watch him put glasses and soap in the dishwasher and push the start button. He looks up at me standing in the doorway. "Go. Pack. We're leaving in twenty minutes."

Shit.

I return to my closet and take one last look at the red dress I wore to the MET. It breaks my heart to leave it even for a week. I want to make works of art like it one day. Sure, it's a pipe dream. But I need to have goals. Inwardly, I wonder if it's another dream that will never come true. I run my hand over the fabric, remembering the night and the incredible sex we had as soon as I stepped out of it.

Dmitry's phone rings, and he answers in Russian. I need to learn some of the language to understand what he's saying.

I busy myself with packing my toiletries from the bathroom. I grab my phone that was charging by the bed all night and pack the charger. I realize I haven't had time to check in with Alena.

She won't be up, but I text her anyway. *Heading to London with the billionaire.*

Come to think of it, he probably *is* a billionaire, or his family is.

I open my luggage on the bed, tuck my intimates in a side pocket, and choose a few outfits in the closet that will fit. I still have his dress shirt and tuck it under my clothes. He doesn't have to know I've kept it. I'll be happy to have it on nights he'll be out. It will remind me of him and prevent any more terrible nightmares. I'm assuming he has work to do and won't be babysitting me. I'm equally sure he'll always have a man to guard me.

I slip my black sketchbook into my purse with the intention of working on designs during the long flight. Lately, I've been too distracted to be creative. I finish looking around the room for items I might have overlooked, and Dmitry is suddenly next to me, closing my suitcase.

I glance at my phone screen, noting the time. We have ten minutes before I fly off into the unknown with the mafia enforcer.

I follow Dmitry to the door. He opens it, and Anton enters.

"Hello, Izzy," Anton says.

He's dressed in a black suit and has a mic in his ear. Our plans this morning require a coordinated effort, so the drivers need to be able to communicate with each other to avoid a tail.

"Hi, Anton." I smile at the man who's kept us safe this week. He's in great shape for his age, mid-forties, if I had to guess. Grabbing our luggage, he heads to the elevator.

I'm sad to be leaving New York but understandably excited for my first real adventure since leaving home.

"I trust you have my passport," I ask Dmitry.

"Of course," he replies matter-of-factly.

"Did you get to enjoy yourself? I mean, your trip was about visiting your friend, Kirill."

"I met you, didn't I?" He answers with a riddle. I watch him fiddle with his phone and imagine he's closing a huge deal or arranging a drug shipment. Who knows? I follow Dmitry's lead and grab my purse from the bedroom, double-checking to ensure my cell phone, charger, and wallet are in it.

I'm cautiously optimistic we'll have fun in London.

"Are we going to eat before we leave?" I ask as he types on his phone.

"There's food on the plane. Is that okay?" He looks up from his phone, sends his text, then slides it into the pocket of his jeans. Grabbing his long coat off the dining room chair, he turns to me. "Did you bring a coat? It's still freezing in London this time of year."

"I don't have one here," I reply defensively, but it's not my fault. How was I to know? Things are moving faster than the speed of light.

Our eyes meet, and his softens. His face is long, even angular. I wonder if he looks like his brothers.

"It's fine. You can use mine. A car will pick us up at Heathrow. Everything is set for our arrival."

"What do you mean? What's everything?" I search his dark brown eyes for answers, but he's guarded. When will he trust me enough to confide in me?

"If I tell you everything, it will ruin the surprise. Don't you like surprises?"

"Normal surprises, sure. But, in case you haven't noticed, my life has turned into an action-adventure movie." I scoff.

He holds his coat open for me, and I slip inside the cashmere warmth. He's close, so close I feel his body heat. *Damn him.* Sex appeal drips from him like an elixir that cures loneliness.

Am I lonely? Yeah. I've gone almost a year without sex. That's not normal. The only men I am friendly with are Alena's friends, and that lasted until school finished. Most of them were busy working. Everyone seems to be moving on with their life, but I'm stuck in the past and have no idea what my future will bring.

I'm jobless. My life is a colossal disappointment. I can't even contact my aunt due to safety concerns, and to top it off, my fiancé isn't hiding the fact that he wants to get me pregnant. I wrap the coat around me and tie the belt. It's comfy and smells of him.

Dmitry moves stiffly to the door.

"Does your leg hurt?" It's then that I realize the cold might affect him physically.

"Nothing to worry about," he replies. But from his pained expression, I can tell something is hurting.

Dmitry opens the door, and I walk to our private elevator.

In the forced proximity of the elevator, I remember the last time we were here and how we almost had sex. I close my eyes, and euphoria wash over me. Suddenly, his lips are on mine. My eyes remain shut. I know where he is and snake my hands around his neck and through his hair. His fingers trace a line between my cheek and neck. Our tongues dance playfully. He opens the front of my coat and leans his pelvis into me.

He's hard with need. I reach down and grab him. The soft moan in his throat tells me he's enjoying this. Our mouths ravish each other, smearing my lipstick for sure. The elevator dings, and he pulls back, exiting as if nothing happened, but his lip color tells a different story.

Anton is waiting in the garage, and for once, I wish the elevator had gotten stuck.

I lag behind him. The mixed signals are confusing, one minute wanting me, the next minute walking away. He's a tease.

He waits for me at the open car door.

"What's wrong?" He asks. "You were happy a minute ago."

I pull my shoulders back and hold my head high. "A second ago, I thought I would get fucked."

"Patience is a virtue, or so I'm told." His eyes twinkle with a devilish glint. He's playing me, and we both know it.

"I'm nervous this won't work," I say, getting into the SUV. He slips in beside me and closes the door.

Anton speaks into a mic attached to his collar and puts the vehicle in gear, and we join a line of identical black SUVs. This reminds me of a funeral possession, and I desperately hope it's not a bad omen. I clutch my purse.

"It will work," Dmitry murmurs taking my hand in his, then giving it a tiny squeeze.

It's as if he can read my mind. His presence calms me. I relax against the seat. The drive to Teterboro is as smooth as can be expected with city traffic.

"Is someone following us?"

"Not if everyone did their job," he replies, and I notice a slight nod from Anton, so I'll assume we've cleared the riskiest part of the plan.

"So, what's there to do in London?"

He releases my hand. I didn't realize I was gripping his so hard.

"I'll show you around when I'm not working. You'll have a guard with you when I'm working."

"And what do you do all day?"

"All in good time." His voice is patronizing as if I'm an inquisitive child.

"It's all on your timeline, not mine," I voice my displeasure.

"Is that so? Well, maybe there are a few people in New York who want to meet you sooner rather than later," he threatens.

"Speaking of them, any word on James?" I wonder if he carries secrets with him. I wonder how he and my mother met and if she knew he was connected to the Irish mafia. She never went into the city, so it's possible she never knew the truth.

"Kirill is looking into it. His men know a few Irish. I'm sure we'll learn something soon."

"And, just so we're clear, I wasn't looking for deep pockets when we met. It was supposed to be just a hookup."

His eyes narrow on me. "Oh, really, that's all it was?" His disbelief confirms that I can't fake anything around him.

"Well, it seems we're stuck together for the foreseeable future. But the reality is that I need a job. I can't live off of you. I want to design clothing, and I think I'd be good at it. I could work from home, even." Maybe I overstepped. Does he even have a home?

He remains pensive.

"I have debt, Dmitry, lots of school loans. You don't want the government looking for me."

He gazes out the window, and his voice is cold when he says, "Your debts have been paid."

I'm stunned. Of course, he knew I owed money. He probably knew how much, down to the penny.

"I didn't ask for you to do that," I say while staring out the window, unsure how to feel about it. Should I be annoyed that he is so presumptuous? Or should I be happy he fixed my problems?

"You didn't ask. But it's been handled. It's all about the optics," he says. "I can't have the government poking into my affairs."

Damn, I could have unintentionally exposed him and his family if I had defaulted on my loans. He handled the loans to keep his family's ill-gotten gains off the fed's radar. Why am I disappointed it wasn't out of chivalry?

"Where do I figure into this?" I turn to him at last, no longer worried about what he sees in my expression.

"I'm older. It's time to get married." He turns to me, slipping his hand under my stubborn chin. "You're more beautiful than you know. What man wouldn't want to give you the world?" His words strike a chord in me.

My heart races, and my pulse quickens. The familiar slickness between my legs returns.

I'm speechless.

"Just as I thought, you like me, Izzy. If I were to slide my fingers between your legs, I'd find you wet for me."

I'm about to turn my head away, but he drops a light kiss on my lips. My bottom lip quivers with anticipation.

Is the bed in the jet big enough for two?

CHAPTER 22

DMITRY

nton announces the coast is clear when we arrive at Teterboro Airport. There is still one SUV in front of us and one behind us to ensure we weren't followed. So far, our plan to send identical cars to different airports seems to have worked.

Izzy can't resist staring at the waiting jet as it glistens in the morning sun on the tarmac. Anton carries our suitcases onto the plane while I wait with Izzy at the bottom of the steps. When Anton shakes my hand to say goodbye, I thank him for keeping us safe and hand him a wad of bills. I won't be needing this currency when we touch down in London.

"Close your mouth," I whisper to Izzy as she places a foot on the step.

"I can't believe we're doing this."

"Well, get used to it. You're going to be a Volkov."

We reach the door to the plane, and Izzy stops so abruptly that I almost run into her. Being this close makes my body zing with energy. I can't wait to share my life experiences and show her new things. This desire to include a woman in my world and bring her into the family fold is all new to me.

"Wow! This is amazing. I never dreamed I'd fly in something like this."

I peer over her shoulder and see lots of glossy wood and four cream-colored leather seats, two on each side of the aisle. Behind them is an eating area with a polished wood table and overstuffed booths. Beyond this is the entertainment area with a couch and a flat-screen TV mounted on the wall. Without looking, I know there is a bedroom complete with a full-size bathroom. The best part about flying private is not sharing a toilet with hundreds of other passengers on a commercial flight.

"Let me take your coat. You won't be needing it," I suggest.

"I feel underdressed," she murmurs but allows me to slide it off her delicate shoulders.

Doesn't she know she's beautiful no matter what she's wearing?

"You're fine. You always look gorgeous. Make yourself at home. I'm going to check on the food my brother preordered."

Opening the coolers in the galley, I find them fully stocked with seafood and beverages. It's a long flight, so we need plenty to eat and drink.

For billionaires, a private plane is a home away from home. This home comes with wings. My brother likes what our money can buy, and to his credit, he didn't skimp on transportation.

Izzy makes her way to the leather club chairs.

"I assume we need to sit here for takeoff," she says, making herself comfortable.

"Yes, but you have a minute to check out the plane if you like. There's even a bedroom in the back."

"I'm fine," she says, dropping her purse on the plush carpeted floor and buckling her seat belt. "I believe you." She glances at me and winks. "There will be plenty of time for that later."

Is she for real? I don't know anyone who wouldn't explore first.

I walk past her and make my way to the bedroom. I hang the coat in the closet and check the outfits already hanging there. I open a dresser drawer to make sure her sleepwear and a change of intimates are here, and they are.

I send a text to my brother.

Dmitry: *Everything went according to plan.*

Nikolay: *Great, see you in the morning, he replies.*

I return to Izzy and sit in the club chair next to her. I'm like a kid who's waited his entire life to celebrate his birthday. I feel guilty like I did all this for myself to enjoy her shocked expression. The reality is that I made sure this flight was perfect for her.

"How long before we take off?" Izzy cranes her neck to look out the window. There's really nothing to see yet, just a sea of concrete.

"Soon. Once we're in the air, we can eat. Are you hungry?"

"Yes, and a cup of coffee would be great."

"I picked food I wanted to share with you."

"You did, did you?"

"Yes, it's a cosmopolitan theme. I think you'll be happy." I'm nonchalant. If I were in London or Russia, I would order from my favorite restaurants. I told Anton I wanted the best place to deliver the food this morning.

She has yet to learn that I spoke to Anya and Nikolay about her career ambitions. They wanted to know all about her and what she wants to do with her degree. They contacted a designer to set up my house in preparation for our arrival.

"Oh, just so you know, my mother and Anya have booked a venue for the wedding. Most places are booked a year in advance, so we were lucky to get a cancellation."

"That's nice of them. Is everything already arranged, or do I get a say in anything?"

"There isn't enough time. Anya hired a professional wedding planner, but I'm sure you will be involved."

"Oh." Her mouth makes a cute oblong "O" shape, and I want to kiss her full and luscious lips.

I haven't shared with Izzy the ulterior plan behind the large wedding. I'm waiting for the right time to tell her it's a setup. I can't overload her too soon with details and risk her being upset and refusing to marry me. If she bolts, I can't keep her safe. I can't let anything happen to an innocent woman who never asked for the events that have transpired. I'm protective because I know what men like me can do to someone like her. She's an easy target; without my intervention, she would have already been snatched. By whom and for what purpose? I still need to figure it out.

"How long is the flight?" she asks, checking the time on the phone.

"Depends on how fast we fly and the winds. I expect we'll arrive in London around eight or nine at night. I have a car picking us up at the airport. My guard, Milan, will meet us there. You'll like him. Give me your phone."

She hands it to me.

I type on her keypad. "You have Milan's number now. If you can't reach me, you can call him. I'll also give you the number of your guard, Erik. I don't want you going anywhere without him."

I hand her the phone. She accepts it and manages to avoid my hand. It's a pity, as I'd love nothing more than to touch her. Does she know I'm obsessing over her? She fiddles with the buttons on her armrest as she tries to figure out which controls the recline, the footrest, and the electric window shades.

She's like a kid with a new toy. I would never take her as someone who'd do something she doesn't want to unless her life was in danger. She's fortunate she fell into my lap, or rather, my bed. Too many men out there wouldn't treat her like the princess she is.

I imagine she's nervous about leaving her best friend and her only home. I'm still perplexed why she chose to go to college in the city after her mother told her not to. She could go anywhere for her degree. Why there? Everyone knows New York, Milan, and Paris are fashion meccas, so maybe that had something to do with her decision. It was close enough to home to be safe; if it didn't work out, she could return to Connecticut.

The captain announces we'll be taxing to the runway. I reach for my seatbelt and secure it over my lap. The plane lurches forward like a race car and bounces over a tarmac that has seen one too many winters.

We're picking up speed, and Izzy clutches my hand with a death grip. I glance over and see her face is noticeably pale. She's looking straight ahead and murmurs, "I've never flown before."

"It will be fine. We'll be in the air soon." I gently squeeze her hand.

"Promise?"

"Yes, and in a minute, we'll be able to move about the cabin as if we're on land."

The plane lifts off, the g-forces pushing us back in our seats. Every-thing smooths out, and the only thing we hear is the roar of the engine and the sound of the landing gear being stowed.

"Great, because I have to pee."

I'm glad she feels comfortable enough around me to overshare.

Turning my head to hide my smile, I gaze out the window and watch the New York City skyline get smaller and smaller as we climb higher and higher through the clouds. When the turbulence is over, the pilot announces that we can move about the cabin freely.

"Okay, you can…pee, now." I let go of her hand and unclip my belt to get up too.

"Thank you," she says with an urgency that borders an emergency. I swallow a chuckle and step aside to let her pass me.

While she's gone, I move to the dining area and set the table with linens, china, and silver utensils. I find fresh daisies in one of the refrigerators and place them in the center of the table. I know she'll love them.

I also find fresh crepes and a glass container filled with red caviar. Always a stickler for detail, I plate the crepes, spreading them out symmetrically on a small serving dish. Glancing toward the bedroom, I know I only have a few seconds. I quickly put the food on the table along with a plate of freshly cut fruit, then grab a bottle of champagne, a bucket of ice, and two flutes.

Just as I finish placing everything on the table, I catch Izzy out of the corner of my eye and intercept her before she reaches the area.

"I have food." I step back and turn sideways so she can see the table is set for two. "Sit."

"You did this?" She gives me a questioning glance.

"Of course. I hope you don't mind that we don't have a stewardess. I thought we'd use the time to get to know each other."

She tilts her head back and appraises me with her eyes. Her stare lingers, and I forget the pain in my leg. She's like a drug that eases my pain and makes me see a future I never envisioned.

I need to get a handle on my emotions before we land. It's not like me to be so... malleable. Suddenly, I remember every etiquette tip my mother drilled into us and later reinforced in boarding school.

"Mm," she murmurs as she picks up the bottle to read the label.

"I opted for champagne instead of cappuccino, but I can make some if that's what you prefer." Why am I droning on about coffee?

Because I know she loves it.

The table is perfect. I've been to enough fancy parties and fancy restaurants to know how to plate food so it looks pretty. As they say, we eat with our eyes first.

"Oh, I forgot the mother-of-pearl spoon." I return to the galley and retrieve it from a serving utensil tray.

Izzy is watching me with an amused expression.

"What?" I ask, holding my breath. I'm not sure if her wrinkled brow means I did something good or if I fucked up. I'm on a tightrope, waiting for the verdict.

She chuckles. "My goodness, you put a ton of thought into this," she exclaims as she slides into the leather booth.

"I did," I concede and release my breath slowly. I join her in the booth and sink the tiny spoon into the caviar.

I can't let anyone know how important she is to me. Although, I'm sure Kirill has an idea.

"This looks incredible. I know that's caviar, but I've never tried it." She gives the bowl of caviar a skeptical look.

"I hope you'll like it. We eat it on crepes in Russia," I explain, using the spoon to spread a dollop of caviar on top of the folded crepe. "Try it." I set the delicacy on her white ceramic plate.

I stand to grab the champagne bottle and un-twist the bail around the cork.

"Is that safe to do on a plane?" She picks up the crepe and eyes me.

"No, I have to make sure I don't hit a window." I swipe my napkin from the table and drape it over the cork.

"What?" Her panic amuses me.

"Relax, I know what I'm doing, and you need to learn not to question me."

"So I fit in," she states as the crepe passes her lush lips.

"Yes. You might get the cold shoulder from the women in your circle because you're not from Russia, and in all likelihood, you're the product of an intercultural relationship. If you are Sicilian, that will cause suspicion and skepticism." I pop the champagne, and it fizzes into the napkin.

"You think I'm part of the Moretti family?" She takes a bite of the crepe and chews it with satisfaction written on her face. Good. Enjoying our food is the first step to adapting to our culture.

"It makes sense, don't you think?" I fill her champagne flute until the golden beverage is a few inches from the top. I pour one for myself and set the bottle in the ice bucket.

"What are we toasting?" She's finished her crepe and is holding a strawberry.

"Well, we've been in forced proximity for days and haven't harmed each other. That's worth celebrating, isn't it?"

She nibbles the strawberry, making her lips red and juicy. I want to fuck her mouth so bad that I lean over the table and take the strawberry out of her mouth with my teeth. I chew, swallow, and go back for more. This time, I cover her kissable lips with mine.

The taste of her mixed with the sweetness of the fruit and my raging hormones led to us ravaging each other. Is she just private jet horny, or is she truly into me?

I don't care. She's mine, and she doesn't have a choice. No one will ever know what it's like to sink their cock in her. I'll erase the thought of any man who's ever been with her.

Her fingers are in my hair, and she pulls me closer.

"Let's grab the champagne and caviar and move this to the bedroom," I suggest.

CHAPTER 23

IZZY

Dmitry snags our champagne and swigs some out of the bottle as he leads the way to the bedroom.

All I hear is my heart pounding in my ears and the low hum of the plane as it makes its way across the sky. He reaches the bed before me and hands me my drink.

"Here's to us," he says in a wicked, low growl.

I'm at a loss for words. Am I toasting to us? Our glasses clink, and I take a few sips. Dmitry finishes his drink, takes mine from me, and deposits the glasses on the nightstand. Scooping me into his arms, he dumps me on the bed.

"I'm going to take you inch by inch."

His threat sends shivers up my spine. I've never had a man command the bedroom like him. Hell, I've never had multiple orgasms, either. Dmitry is bringing me to life. When I walk into a room, he eye-fucks me even when I'm fully clothed.

"I want you to scream my name." His voice turns raspy against my ear as he nibbles and tugs on my ear lobe.

He strips off his shoes, socks, and jeans. I pull off my top and unfasten my bra. My breasts tumble out, warm and full. He shucks his briefs, and I can't help but drool at his huge, throbbing cock. I grab him, stroking his enormous length when he leans over me.

The sound of his breath makes when it catches in his throat gives me satisfaction. He may drive me crazy with his lust, but I'm beginning to think I have the same effect on him.

His mouth finds my nipple, and he sucks it while his hand massages my pussy with his palm and fingers. I feel my excitement gush between my legs. My ovaries are exploding as his skilled tongue flicks over my hard nipples.

My fingers are tangled in his hair. I yearn for more, but he stops and stands.

What?

He pulls my buttocks close to the edge of the bed. "Spread your legs, princess."

I love the sound of his deep voice. My labia swells as his commands float over me like thunderclouds. He has the unique ability to give an order that makes me eager to comply. What can I say? He's a leader of men and the boss of my vagina.

I spread my legs. He kneels on the plush, carpeted floor and pushes my thighs further apart. The thrill of his touch makes me arch my back off the bed. I grab his hair and fist my hands in its thickness.

His tongue is warm and gentle. He circles it inside my lips and edges closer to my core. His tongue becomes more demanding as he reaches my clit and inserts two fingers inside me, thrusting in and out as he flicks my clit until it hardens. He sucks on it, and I moan. *Fuck me.* I've never known pleasure like this.

I raise my greedy vagina to feel more. He thrusts his fingers deeper, finding my G-spot and rubbing my clit with his thumb. I am so close to reaching a crescendo when he stops. *Dammit!*

I open my eyes, and he's above me, licking his fingers.

"You taste sweet," he murmurs. "Roll over."

I roll to my stomach. I need him to pleasure me and release me from this ache.

He stands behind me, his hard cock rubbing between my ass cheeks.

"I'm going to take you hard and fast," he rasps as he plunges into my pussy. I buckle under the force of him and how big he is as he pushes against my walls. My love muscles grip his pulsating cock as ripples of euphoria build.

His hand is in between my shoulder blades, pushing me down, and my nipples find the friction from the duvet pleasurable as he thrusts in and out of me. I cling to the cover like it's a lifeline. My brain explodes into fireworks, and I scream loud enough for the pilot to hear as I come on his cock.

"That's good, princess. Now, I'm going to fill you with my cum." He slams into me, shoots his load, then roars like a lion mating on the Serengeti.

He pulls out and leaves for a second before he returns with a warm cloth, wiping me and pulling me onto the bed. My legs are shot, and I welcome his strong arms lifting me. He places me in the center of the bed and lies beside me, pulling me to his chest. My head rests on his shoulder, my cheek in the crook of his arm. I glance down and run a finger over a scar, tracing its path as I'm lost in thoughts of nothingness, satiated and content.

"Are you okay?" he asks.

"Mm," I murmur. Maybe being with him isn't so bad after all. He's my beast, and I'm falling for him.

"What are you thinking?"

Hearing his accent, I'm reminded that he's returning home to his family, and they will be speaking Russian. I won't be able to follow their conversations and will be in the dark, always the outsider.

"Have you heard from Kirill yet?"

"I probably have an update on my phone. However, it's in the other room. I'll let you know."

"Okay." I'm overwhelmed by my growing feelings for him and need a distraction. I pull myself into a sitting position. "I'm hungry. Can we finish breakfast?"

He looks like his feelings are hurt, which frankly confuses me.

The crease on his forehead disappears, and he rolls out of bed. "Let's shower and dress. There are PJs and lounging clothes in the drawers for you."

"Really?" How thoughtful. I get up and walk to the dresser. I assumed the drawers were empty. What will he think of next?

I open a drawer and find several lounging outfits with matching tops and bottoms. I select an outfit the color of heather and lay it on the bed.

I hear what sounds like light summer rain and realize Dmitry is warming up the shower.

Is it me, or is it the two of us together that makes everything in life sublime?

I go to the bathroom and slip into the shower next to him. He rubs soap over my body. If he keeps this up, there will be a round two.

After we've dried each other, I slip into new panties and the outfit. I could get used to this. I hear people complaining about flying commercial nowadays because of the overcrowded planes and weather delays that turn into cancellations with no way of getting home.

Dmitry pulls on a t-shirt and black joggers. We're both barefoot, and he grabs our champagne glasses while I follow him to the breakfast he prepared. I slide onto my seat and dive into bagels with cream cheese and smoked salmon.

He refills our drinks, and I take a few gulps of the bubbly. I watch him eat caviar and wonder how he managed to pull this off so seamlessly. He finds his phone on the table and checks messages.

He's silent as I wait impatiently.

"What is it?" I finish my champagne, fearing the worst. "Please tell me Alena is okay."

"Kirill says she's fine. He saw members of the Russian mafia and the Irish at the airport." He chuckles. "They were confused at first, but when they saw our doubles get on the flight, they boarded too."

"What? You found doubles of us?" I remind myself to close my mouth. This is some serious spycraft.

"What did you think I was doing all week? This took a lot of time to set up and at a considerable expense, too."

"Where did you find them?" I relax, telling myself he knows what he's doing.

"Word of mouth. Many people in New York are in acting classes and willing to take a gig to build a resume." He drains his champagne and refills our glasses for the last time as the bottle empties.

"Wow, I never would have thought to trick our surveillance with body doubles."

He cocks his head and observes me. I must look a fright with my just-been-fucked hair. Self-consciously, I fluff it with my fingers then tuck my long bangs behind my ear.

"Leave it. You're perfect the way you are." His eyes focus on my face, then drift to my cleavage. "Why do you feel like you always have to compete for attention? No one holds a candle to you."

"I'm not used to attention," I murmur while staring at my plate.

"Well, that's got to change. You'll soon be part of a rich and powerful family whose members circulate in high society, attend galas, and donate to charities. When you attend those functions, you must hold your head high and with confidence." He chucks his phone onto the table. "Do you like the food?"

"Oh, yes, it's all delicious, thank you."

"I need to get some work done before we land." He stands, grabs his laptop, and disappears into the bedroom.

I clear the table, then make myself comfortable in front of the enormous TV monitor. I wish Alena were here and wonder if my phone will work. I connect to the plane's Wi-Fi and text her to see how she's doing.

Alena: *I'm fine. Just lolling around the house, waiting for this ordeal to be over.*

Me: *Any word on your future husband?*

Alena: *Not yet. The suspense is killing me. Oops, sorry.*

Me: *You're so funny. No harm done. I think we're in the clear for a while.*

Alena: *Yes, Kirill said the same. It's crazy that someone in the Russian mafia is following you. I don't get it.*

Me: *Me, either. I'm enjoying this private jet, though.*

Alena: *I bet you are.* She sends a winking emoji. *How's Dmitry?*

Me: *He appears to be horny and focused.*

Alena: *Sounds like you're hitting it off.*

Me: *Maybe. I'm reserving my opinion. I hear our wedding is in two weeks. Will you be there?*

Alena: *What a question. I better be your bridesmaid. People still do that, don't they?*

Me: *It doesn't matter. I'll be a bundle of nerves and can't do this without you, so do whatever you need to do to be there.*

Alena: *I'll do what I can. Gotta go but stay in touch.*

Me: *You, too.*

Now that I know the terrible people followed our body doubles, it confirms what Dmitry said about the stalker being after me, not Alena. I must have inherited my mother's suspicious mind because it's my instinct to distrust before I can trust. It's taken a few days, but I'm beginning to trust Dmitry and realize he knows what he's doing.

I grab the Hermes throw off the back of the couch, curl my legs under me, and settle in for a movie. Halfway through the movie, I stretch and yawn. The excitement, along with the food and the sex, has caught up with me, and I drift off without a care in the world.

I awake to the vibration of the plane hitting turbulence.

I sit up and, for a moment, forget where I am. I notice the overhead lights are dimmed to a relaxing color of blue. I look out the nearest window, and the sky is darker. I would like to know what time it is and count the five-hour time difference on my fingers. I look around for Dmitry.

"What is it?" His voice washes over me. I follow the direction of the sound and find him sitting in one of the four club chairs. He has it swiveled around, watching me.

My face is flush from the warmth of sleep and his intense gaze.

"I forgot where I was for a minute. Are there any new updates?"

"Not yet." His bad leg uncrosses from the good one, and he stands. "You need to drink water. Staying hydrated is important on these long trips."

He's right. My lips are dry.

He hands me a water bottle and says, "I've made lunch for you."

Of course, he did. The aroma of oven-roasted chicken with mango chutney is calling my name.

CHAPTER 24

DMITRY

I find myself in uncharted territory, watching Izzy sleep. She's curled up on the couch, and I don't have the heart to disturb her.

I spent the past few hours arranging for our pickup at the airport and emailing and texting Nikolay, Roman, and my mother regarding dinner. Anya is working with the wedding planner, so I emailed her a list of the flowers I think Izzy will like. I also emailed our jeweler and had our wedding bands made, as well as a pearl necklace and diamond earrings for her wedding day. Mom said the pearls are traditional. Izzy's wedding band will have an embedded tracking chip in case she goes missing.

I can't lose her. We've begun our journey together. To think she will ever leave me is one I refuse to entertain.

I also emailed her guard, Erik, a man our family has trusted for ten years. He's staying in the old carriage house that the previous owner had renovated into a huge apartment and game room.

It pays to be connected. A Russian oligarch originally owned the property. When he put it on the market, I got the first call and did a virtual walkthrough with the realtor. She said my future wife would love all the closet space. I bought it without stepping foot in it. Now the workers are tailoring things to my office preference. I also hired a new housekeeper to keep an eye on the house and be there in my absence. I also gave her instructions on the foods we like to eat.

Meanwhile, Kirill has men in Vegas trailing the goons following our actors. I'm feeling smug at how easy it was to outwit them. They are working under someone's direction. But whose? The mafia, just like the army, is all about following orders.

It's well known that the Russians use their media to manipulate their people and enemies. I'm beginning to wonder if the US media is stooping to the same propaganda and diversion tactics. We knew decades ago that the press would eventually cave to dogma. It only reinforces my suspicions regarding news stories about James Murphy.

If Izzy's mother loved and trusted him, I doubt he would sell her out. However, if he knew a secret and was tortured, I could see him giving that secret up.

I sit in one of the club chairs where I can watch Izzy sleep and work on my laptop at the same time. I search the dark web for any unpublished information about James Murphy. My computer has redundant firewalls and super secure servers, so it's untraceable and un-hackable. Still, it makes me nervous.

Social media is used to wag the dog, and instinct tells me James Murphy wouldn't steal from his own family. Maybe the investigation is a ruse by the government to extract information about his family. The feds might be trying to build a RICO case. But if that were true, we would've already heard about it because we all have a man on the inside.

Would Izzy's mother have trusted the Irish with her secret? Or did she take her secret to the grave? Nothing is adding up. I'm getting frustrated. I'd rather have this behind us before the wedding, but the plan I devised with my brothers will have to go into play. I pray we'll be able to handle the fallout. My gut tells me the men who want Izzy will come to the wedding, so we're making a long list of suspects and plan to flush them out.

Wedding, my wedding, the very concept seems strange. I never pictured myself married, but I am picturing her naked on our wedding day. My cock twitches at the prospect of getting her pregnant. I'm an insatiable, thoughtless bastard, but a bastard, nonetheless.

All I need is time to make Izzy fall in love with me so she never wants to leave her cage. I can't imagine going back to my life before her. That life was all about fighting and surviving. I served in the army, fought in a war, and by some miracle, made it home in one piece, then nearly got killed in a car accident. From now on, I will only fight my own wars, and this one is for us.

My brothers are setting up contingency plans and vetting men to work security for the wedding. It will be an extravagant and very public affair. Behind the scenes, we will be running a risky game plan.

This problem needs to be solved. I can't just shoot it like I would an idiot who fucks up in our organization.

I decide to do another search on Llea Sidova, the Russian don, Alexsei's wife. If she's worried about her son getting passed over when Alexsei dies, she will do whatever it takes to prevent that. At twenty, her son is too young to be a don. No one will take him seriously. Unless he is some sort of loose-cannon psycho that everyone fears or some genius at making alliances whom everyone respects, he'll be killed in no time. I don't see his mother putting him in that position, but you never know. There is always the chance that her desire for power is stronger than her maternal instincts. Now there's a viper you don't wanna turn your back on.

I pull up a picture of Llea Sidova again. There is something reptilian about her features. She strikes me as brutal and manipulative. I read some articles about her inner-city reading program, and she's very adept at orchestrating the narrative and the optics. Her sound bites are rehearsed and spot-on. It's all just too perfect. She's up to something. I need to keep my eye on her and those kids. Her husband is elusive, which is another reason to invite them to the wedding. Kirill will ensure they use the private jet and bring Alena and her parents.

Alena needs to be at the wedding as Izzy's maid of honor. Kirill will also attend. I've asked Nikolay to be my best man. Roman understands it has to be this way. If anything were to happen to Nikolay, I'd have to take over.

I don't know how one person does it all. It takes three of us, and even at that, we still have partners trying to fuck us over. One has to have balls but not be stupid. Short-term gains can result in long-term enemies. That's how, in this business, greed will get you killed.

I open another search window and bring up the documents on Maria's death. Just as before, the dates on the documents align with the death of Moretti's daughter, Mariana. The names aren't that much different.

I run my hand over my jaw and yawn. My eyes are heavy, and my mind is exhausted. I drift off to sleep, content for the first time in my life.

I wake when the engines whine, indicating we must be getting closer to our destination and descending. There's a bit of turbulence, and Izzy stirs.

She opens her eyes. Seeing me, she asks, "What time is it?"

"Time to get changed. We'll be landing soon."

"Oh." She yawns and pushes the throw off her lap. She stands and stretches before following me to the bedroom.

I pack my laptop feeling fairly confident I've prepared everyone in advance. I slip into a suit and dress shoes. It's time to resume the formal version of myself. The vacation is over.

Izzy is dressed in jeans and a Red Hot Chili Peppers t-shirt layered with a pullover sweater. I can picture her singing and dancing to the music at the concert. She won't be doing much of that anymore. Like it or not, she will go to the opera, the ballet, and the orchestra.

Izzy's in the bathroom packing up and comes out to brush her hair.

"Did you sleep?"

"A little bit."

I don't bother telling her I'm an insomniac. Or maybe I'm cured because when I'm next to her, I sleep just fine.

She dips back into the bathroom, grabs her toiletry bag, and tosses it into her luggage.

"Just leave the luggage on the bed. It will be handled. I made us a snack while you were in the bathroom."

She follows me to the table and helps herself to roast chicken, brie cheese, and sliced apples.

"What's the plan when we land?"

I like how she uses the word *we*.

"Well, you will assume the role of my fiancé, and I'll get back to work." It's better to leave out the other details for now.

CHAPTER 25

IZZY

e're in the limo that picked us up at the airport, and I wonder if it's armored. It doesn't matter. What does matter is that we're driving on the opposite side of the road. I'm nervous about crossing streets after Dmitry told me about all the Americans who get hit by cars yearly because they forget to look both ways before crossing. Good thing I will have a bodyguard to keep me safe, assuming traffic comes under the purview of his protection.

The air is cold, bitter cold. I'm in Dmitry's coat, but I still shiver. I discreetly sniff the lapels and breathe in the familiar scent of my fiancé.

I pull my phone out of my purse and text Alena.

Me: *We're here. It's late. I'm wired. What's happening at home?*

Alena: *Nothing to report. I got an invitation to your wedding. We're taking the jet with Alexsei. His family is coming too! Can*

Me: *Really? Is this wedding that important?*

Are the Volkovs that big? According to Alena, they've been in Russia since the collapse of the Soviet Union and have expanded significantly in recent years.

Alena: *If you want respect, it's a show of power and unity. That's why a mob hit at a wedding is so personal. Remember in The Godfather when Sonny gets married, and then he remarries?*

Me: *Oh gee, don't curse me. I'm doing this to stay alive. I'd rather elope.*

Alena: *Your wedding serves a purpose and sends a message. But there's no reason you can't enjoy all the glitz and glamour, woman!*

Me: *I suppose. I'll text you later.*

Alena: *Send me all the deets on your day.*

Dmitry is silent until I look his way. Then his stoic face turns to me.

"Are you concerned about something?" I ask. The thought of my big day being someone's last day weighs heavily on me. I pray that won't happen.

"Mm?" Dmitry looks distracted. He turns to me like I pulled him out of a trance.

"Why the long face? I thought you were happy to be home," I quip.

It's obvious Dmitry loves his family. I'm sure they've been through a heap of shit together. And his father dying so suddenly makes me wonder if that isn't pushing his *I want a baby* agenda. He hasn't said the words, but why else would he make me beg for him to fuck me, knowing a baby is a real possibility? I can't resist him. I don't even try. I have no problem begging because I'm addicted to his body and massive cock. I'm not ashamed to admit it. I have needs, and being with him makes the hole in my heart less empty.

I want family attachments, even if they're complicated and I don't understand what they're saying. Life has hardened me.

I was always the odd one out on holidays. Aunt Emma is much older and is a widow who never had children. She told me she helped my mom and treated her like a daughter, so raising me was like having a granddaughter. I wish I could get a message to her, but I can't have anyone else dying because of me. We're not that close, but she's the only family I have left.

"By the way, we have a housekeeper," Dmitry finally speaks.

"A housekeeper?" I'm shocked. "I don't need that. I can clean a house, Dmitry."

"I'm sure you can, but Volkovs don't clean houses."

"I wasn't born a Volkov."

Streetlights illuminate his face as we drive past them. I can see his eyes narrow, expressing his displeasure and putting me in my place.

"No, you weren't, but by association, you are one. Besides, the house is too large for one person to run. We have a chef, too."

"Most couples discuss things like this," I huff.

"We are not most couples," he says with a smug grin that ends the argument.

"This must be some house."

"I think you will like it." He goes back to staring out the window.

"How much longer do we have to drive?"

"We'll be there soon."

Within minutes we've turned off the main road and pulled up to a gatehouse. The driver rolls down his window and speaks to an armed guard. In less time than I can say open sesame, the gate magically opens, and we're driving through what looks like a compound. It's dark, but I can make out a massive four-car garage and outer buildings. We come around a bend, and I spot a two-story mansion painted a pale yellow Mediterranean color. Lit sconces adorn the front of the house. Spotlights in the yard shine on the walls. The walkways are illuminated with lights embedded in the pavers. A picture of this could easily be on the cover of a design magazine.

Our limo slowly circles to the back of the home and stops before a set of double doors. If they were open, I swear we could drive right inside. This door must be for deliveries, drivers, and hired help. Parked in the surrounding turnabout area are black SUVs and expensive sports cars. If the housekeeper is driving that Ferrari, I'm changing professions.

The driver jumps out and opens our doors. Dmitry speaks to him in Russian while he gets our bags from the trunk.

I hear the door to the house swing open. A tall man approaches.

"I'm Milan. Nice to meet you," he says, extending a heavily tattooed hand. Dressed all in back and looking like Lurch from the Addams Family, he's intimidating. I can see why Dmitry uses him for protection.

"Izzy." I take Milan's hand, and we shake. I make sure to keep my hand firm. I tell myself I have to fake it until I make it, even if it's an act. I cannot show fear, so I force a smile. Dmitry is his priority, but I need him on my side too. I'm sure there are no secrets between them because they're always together.

"Great." Dmitry claps his hands together as if the meeting is adjourned and walks toward the house with Milan by his side, speaking in Russian.

I look around but can see nothing in the darkness. The cold air tickles my nose. The men are way ahead of me. I run to catch up.

The first room we enter is the kitchen. It's warm and spacious and looks recently renovated, judging from the stainless-steel appliances. It must cost a fortune to power the huge refrigerator and freezer. Electricity is not cheap in Europe.

Rich mahogany cabinets and creamy-colored marble countertops give the place a homey feel. Copper bottom pots and skillets hang above the marble island. I could live in this kitchen. The walk-in pantry alone is big enough for a pull-out sofa.

Martha Stewart would be impressed. I still think she's a jailbird, but whatever. One can't live in New York City and not see the irony.

Milan pushes some buttons on the Italian coffee machine and pours a coffee for Dmitry. They will be up late talking over matters I'm excluded from, and it's okay. Less is more, right?

Dmitry puts down his coffee cup and approaches me.

"Take off your coat. Let me show you to our room so you can get settled. I'll give you the tour tomorrow."

"Okay." I hand him my coat, and he passes it to Milan. He takes my hand and walks me into another room and up a sweeping staircase to the second floor. We take the steps together. The walls are pristine, having been just painted. At the top of the stairs, I follow him down a wide corridor with flickering sconces lighting our way. The ambiance of the soft lighting is relaxing.

"Does anyone else live here?"

"No, Erik and Milan live in the carriage house on the property, and someone is always guarding the gate. I have the house under surveillance." He reaches out and opens an ornate wooden door.

"This way." We enter a large room with a king-size bed that dominates the room.

"Wow," I murmur. I take in the matching bedspread and covers that coordinate with the curtains on the windows.

"This way," he continues, walking into another room. It's a large bathroom with dual shower heads and a bench seat large enough for four people. It has a separate room for the toilet and bidet. We walk past the side-by-side sinks and into a closet as big as the bedroom. The walls are lined with shelves and drawers, too many to count.

Designer suits hang from a rack with plenty of room for more. I'm sure they're in my size. My eyes drift from the floor-to-ceiling mirror to the shoe rack and all the red-bottom shoes. He must like me in Louboutin shoes to have them here and in New York. The man has excellent taste and knows fashion.

One wall is lined with shelves filled with purses in every color. I recognize some of the bags like Prada, Gucci, and Louis Vuitton. At the top, where I can't reach, are vintage hat boxes and framed black and white images of Audrey Hepburn.

In the middle of the room sits a chaise lounge next to a marble-covered island. He opens one of the many drawers and says, "This is for jewelry."

"That's not necessary."

"Oh, it is. We'll get to that tomorrow. My closet is over there." He nods to the opposite side, and I see another closet similar to mine but full of dark suits and men's shoes. He's impeccable with his taste. "Do you have the credit card I gave you?"

"Yes, yes, of course."

"Good. You'll use it. Anya will take you around and help you find a wedding dress. Spare no expense. You will be the trendsetter in town."

I look back at the way we came.

"This is all connected?" I ask, feeling overwhelmed by the sheer size of our bedroom suite.

"Yes. So?" He waits as if my opinion is more important than all the other stuff he needs to get done.

"I love it." I cover my mouth and try to stifle a squeal of excitement. This is every fashionista's wet dream.

"Great. Then I expect you to get some sleep because I'm horny, and I'm going to fuck you when I get back." His eyes drill into me with a fierce desire that causes my ovaries to clench in anticipation.

"I'm going to take our play further, and you'll love it."

He takes three long strides, roughly pulls me into his arms, ravages my lips, and then releases me.

"That's a preview of what's to come."

He turns to leave. With my imagination running wild and my panties wet, I don't want him to go.

"Wait."

He stops at the door.

"Fuck me now."

With one eyebrow raised, he says, "Nice try, but I make the rules."

He leaves, much to my dismay. My heart is racing at the anticipation of having his cock buried in my pussy.

Damn it.

I throw my purse on the dresser and start yanking the drawers open, looking for sexy lingerie to wear. I'll show him.

I find a studded leather bra with matching undies. *Interesting.*

I also find a padded blindfold like people wear to sleep and wonder why it's not with the nighties.

I pin my hair into a messy bun and undress, throwing my clothes in the hamper. In the bathroom, I notice a basket full of scented soaps and bath bombs displayed next to a jacuzzi tub big enough to fit two people easily.

The man has thought of everything.

Almost.

I sniff all the soaps and select one that smells like cashmere, and head to the shower. After a long luxurious shower, I towel off and rub a lotion over my body. I have no problem getting into the leather bra, but it takes two attempts to get the matching panties on correctly.

I'm thirsty and hope to get downstairs and back without getting lost. The marble floors are cold, so I find a pair of slippers. I secure a silk robe around me and tie the sash.

I enter the hallway and retrace my steps down the corridor and staircase. In the kitchen, I find a glass in a cupboard and fill it with tap water. I guzzle it and turn to go back when I hear male voices. My curiosity leads me to a dimly lit room at the end of a long hallway.

I peek around the door and see that it's a library, and the only light is coming from a smoldering fire in the fireplace. Milan and another man are sitting with their backs to me. Dmitry is sitting on a black leather couch facing the door. His eyes meet mine, and he is not happy to see me. He says something in Russian and flies off the couch.

"What are you doing?"

"I got water in the kitchen and heard voices." My eyes beseech him not to make a scene.

He takes my arm roughly and pushes me up against the wall.

"You are mine. No one is to see your nakedness but me. Do you understand?"

"Yes," I mumble feebly. His aggressiveness makes me weak in the knees. I'm turned on, but also worried he might hit me. What did I get myself into?

"Upstairs, now." He barks his order.

I turn to go, but he grabs me by the neck to prevent me from leaving. I search his face to discern his mood.

He forces his knee between my legs. His mouth is on mine. I taste the scotch he's been drinking and smell the tobacco of a cigar. I inhale deeply as his lips crush mine with his need. His hand moves from my neck to my pussy, taking me by surprise.

I moan, wrapping my arms around his neck to keep from swooning.

He massages my clit, and I grind against his hand, trying to get more friction as my breathing turns raspy.

"You're mine, mine to love, mine to fuck," he hisses in my ear, giving it a nip.

He pushes the robe off my shoulders, leaving me exposed. The cool air hits my breasts, and I welcome it as I'm burning with desire.

"Say you're mine," he commands.

I turn my head, delaying my answer.

He thrusts his fingers into me, and I wince with pleasure.

"Say it, or you'll be sleeping alone tonight."

He kisses my neck. His lips reach my breasts strapped into the leather bra and on full display. He thumbs the leather back and rubs my nipple, causing my pussy to gush.

"What will it be, *Usha Moya*? Who do you belong to?" His anger has dissipated. He's making me beg. I hate myself for being weak.

"You." My voice is thready. My chest heaves. I yearn for him to grab me by the hair and ravage me, caveman style.

Our bodies convey what we don't put into words.

"That's more like it," he says, releasing me. "Now get upstairs."

I take to the stairs as if my life depends on it.

I run to our room, drop the silk robe on the floor, and crawl under the covers. My heart is pounding.

I look to the door, and there he is, watching me. He unbuttons his shirt, never taking his eyes off me. He walks into the room, kicks off his shoes, and disappears into the closet.

He returns, void of clothing, with a padded eye mask and what looks like a silk tie in his hands.

"You were quite the distraction. I had to make an excuse to leave my meeting."

He slips a strap off my shoulder and moves the lingerie to the side before he feasts on my nipple, taunting it and nipping, sending waves of pleasure coursing through my breasts.

My eyes widen.

He leans over me and grabs my wrists.

"What are you doing?"

"You'll like it. Relax." He binds my hands and ties them to the wrought iron headboard. He slips the mask over my head and covers my eyes.

I feel the mattress shift with his weight. The acrid smell of the tobacco, mixed with his musky cologne, tells me he's close—anticipation courses through my veins.

He cups my breast and kneads them. I move my legs together to stifle my need to have him between my thighs.

His tongue slips between the nipple and the leather bra, and he teases it, keeping my nipple erect.

He shifts his weight. I feel his lips on my belly, catching me by surprise. He drops kisses on one side, then the other.

I suck air into my lungs and stifle a moan.

I pull at the restraints, yearning to touch him, but they won't budge.

He chuckles and softly runs his fingers over my tummy and down my leg.

He kisses one breast and cups the other, playing with it as I press myself against him and use my legs to rub his hard cock. I want him in me. This game of torturing me with pleasure is…exotic.

I feel his engorged cock between my legs. I try to hump him, but he moves away, preventing contact.

He has total control.

My uterus contracts. I twist my hips under him, hungry for him to satisfy me, and yet he makes me wait.

I toss my head from side to side and bite my lower lip. This is torture, and yet it's exhilarating. I feel a need so primal that I want to rip the restraints, grab him, and fuck him until he's raw.

He takes the bra off and cups both breasts in his hands.

I moan.

"I take it you like this?"

"Fuck me, Dmitry, or I swear…"

His soft chuckle is the only sound in the room. He flicks my nipple before he grabs both of them, making them hard between his thumb and finger. He plays me like an instrument. I arch my back and lift my pelvis off the mattress.

"You swear to follow orders?"

"Yes," I moan. "Fuck me. Fuck me now."

With a flick of his wrist, he rips the leather panties covering my soft mound.

He slips his fingers inside me and moans.

"You're so wet for me," he murmurs. His cock is pressing against my thighs, causing my lower lips to quiver. My breathing is ragged through my open mouth. I'm so close to exploding.

The soft sound of silk slices the air with a flourish. My hands are free as the sash drops away. I rip the blindfold off my eyes and grab his hair, pulling his lips to mine.

He grabs my hands and holds them over my head as he enters me. I buckle under the pleasure. His cock taunts my smooth lips. I twist and buckle, not knowing whether to move or let him assume control.

He thrusts deeply, my clit hardens, and my body trembles as wave after wave of pleasure consumes me. I'm surfing an incredible wave as his cock strokes me until I'm spent. I wail when I come.

He releases my wrists and pumps me three more times before he lets out a loud moan, then releases his seed into me.

He holds me to him for a minute, then pulls out and slumps beside me.

I can't move. My arms and legs are fatigued to the point of no return.

"Are you happy now?" he asks as he lies on his back, staring at the ceiling.

"Yes."

"Good, let's get some sleep. Morning will be here in a few hours."

CHAPTER 26

DMITRY

I rise at the crack of dawn, shower, and dress casually in jeans and a sweater. I'm careful not to wake Izzy.

Leaving a note on her nightstand, I proceed downstairs to work on my laptop.

I turn some dials on the beast of a coffee machine and wait for the water to heat up. I sit on the barstool at the marble island and log on to the web.

Due to the time difference, Kirill isn't awake yet, so I read my emails. It turns out the actors I hired to pose as us in Vegas were found murdered in an alley behind the hotel.

"Fuck!" I yell, my voice echoing through the empty kitchen.

I sink my head into my hands, knowing my plan to save us killed two innocent people. I stand abruptly, almost knocking over the barstool. I feel like breaking something but not this fancy coffee machine. I take a deep breath and push the button to dispense coffee into my cup. It's too hot, but I sip it anyway. The irony of drinking a stimulant when I need to calm down is not lost on me.

Getting people killed is depressing, even for a man who's killed many.

A message has been sent.

Milan walks into the kitchen.

"What's wrong, Dmitry?"

I tell him what transpired, and he pulls up a barstool, sitting beside me.

"That's fucked up," he replies. "What do we do now?"

I rake my fingers through my hair.

"We continue as planned. We don't know who is behind this, but we know the Russians and Irish in New York want her." I stand and pace with my hands clasped behind my back.

"The decoys are dead. But you're on your turf now." He reminds me that I have a tactical advantage.

"Yes, until they find us. I doubt they'll figure it out overnight. I'll make sure Kirill has Alena on lockdown. She's the easiest way to get to Izzy."

"Right." Milan nods.

"I'll call Kirill on a burner phone, and I need you to finish with the security details for the wedding. We need to be prepared for anything."

"Sure thing."

I go back to pacing. "I'm missing something big."

"From what you've said, everything points to her being a Moretti. It makes sense. Moretti has a daughter who is unaccounted for, even if she supposedly died before Izzy was born. It's not a big stretch. People were paid off. It was easier back then, too. No cameras at intersections to capture the car accident. No digital footprints to erase either." He shrugs.

"Right. Is his daughter really dead? I ask myself that. It's possible her mother got caught in a web of lies. All it takes is one person to fold, and the house of cards falls," I say, refilling my cup.

"And the wedding plans?"

"Moving along. Izzy will coordinate with Anya on the final details. Invitations go out tomorrow, and everyone will know where we'll be on the wedding day, including our enemies."

"I know we're holding the event at the Fulham Palace with the Tudor Courtyard near the River Thames. A morning wedding, a simple ceremony. If all goes well, we'll use the terrace for a champagne brunch."

"That's too much ground to cover. Is it safe? We might want to change the venue at the last minute, book another place, perhaps. What if no one reveals their intentions?"

I rub the morning stubble on my chin. "That's a great idea. However, there will be so much going on that day that it's a perfect setup for someone to act. I don't see the event going to plan. The biggest concern is, can we protect Izzy when things go sideways?"

"Right, we have our work cut out for us," Milan murmurs as he helps himself to coffee.

Erik enters the kitchen and asks, "Where's the princess?"

"Sleeping."

"Who's sleeping?" All eyes turn to Izzy coming down the stairs. I turn to Milan and put a finger to my lips to indicate *keep quiet* about the information we shared. He's quick with subtle hints, and Izzy can't see me doing this.

"Obviously, not you." I push the button to steam milk, which makes a lot of noise, then turn to hand her a cappuccino as she joins us in the kitchen.

"Thank you."

"No problem," I reply as I casually sit down and close the lid of my laptop.

"Milan." She acknowledges my guard and turns to Erik. "I don't know you."

"No, ma'am. I'm Erik. I'll be your bodyguard."

Izzy surveys Erik. He's six-two and under two-hundred pounds. She nods her satisfaction and sits on the barstool beside me.

"What's happening today?"

"You'll go shopping with Anya, my brother's wife. She'll be by later today. You should become familiar with the house. Charlotte will be here in a few minutes."

"Who's Charlotte?"

"Our housekeeper."

"Oh," Izzy murmurs as she sips her drink. She's dressed in jeans and a long-sleeved dress shirt with gold buttons on the front. Her hair is in a messy bun, and I'd love to unravel it and make her come undone at the same time, but it will have to wait.

I'm pleased she's not insisting she does everything at the house. Frankly, it's too big, and we have too much to do.

"I have to see my brother. You stay with Erik." I give Izzy a warning with my eyes.

"Fine," she huffs.

I nod. "Good girl." I look at Erik, and he stands a bit taller. He's been trained by me. I know she'll be safe.

"We're off. I'll leave you to get settled." I kiss her full lips before grabbing my laptop and coat.

Milan drives while I sit in the back seat of the SUV. We're both silent, no doubt shocked by the turn of events in Vegas. Nikolay still needs to be told.

"What if your plan doesn't work? Have you figured out a contingency plan?"

"No, I'm not sure there is one. But this house is hidden under a shell company, so it'll be difficult to find. Did you double-check the security team on the perimeters?"

"Yes."

"Great, we'll see Nikolay, and then we have errands to prepare for the wedding."

I gaze out the window at the morning sun shining on the dew-covered greenery. The weather is still cold and won't warm up until June. We can't wait that long. Every day, these murders get closer to my love.

I call her my love when she's really my soul. She saved me from the depths of darkness, and I can't let anything happen to her. I made her a promise, and I made a promise to myself; whoever touches her dies.

"You could be right about Izzy. What if she is Moretti's grand-daughter? Who could her father be? How could Maria carry on an affair under her father's nose?"

"Girls, they find a way, just like boys who want to get laid. Get a friend to cover for you, and you stay off Daddy's radar?" he shrugs.

"I see your point. We need photo albums of her high school class and see if we can get a work history of her."

"That was a long time ago, boss."

"If you shake a tree, something will fall out. Please keep an eye on Alexsei's wife at the wedding. I don't trust her. He stays hidden, and I think she's the power behind the throne. He's Russian-American. Her family is from the old guard, and her parents were with the KGB. They're very cunning."

"No more than the current organization," he muses.

"Just the same, have someone shadow her during the wedding."

"Fine, consider it done."

We arrive at my brother's house, and their housekeeper lets us in.

"Do I hear my brother?" Nikolay greets us in the foyer. We hug and exchange greetings in our native language.

Anya joins us, dressed in a business suit. We hug, and I kiss her on both cheeks. "I have to rush out to school. I'll be at your house just before noon to take Izzy out. I can't wait to meet her." Her vibrant eyes light up when she's excited. I bet she's looking forward to having a sister-in-law to pal around with.

At the moment, I'm not sure where *home* will be. Russia would be too much of a culture shock for an American. I push Izzy but can't push so hard that she runs away. Baby steps are the best strategy.

"I'll text you her information and let her know. Take her somewhere nice for lunch and have a good time."

"I will, for sure," she replies. She gives her husband a kiss that would make a stranger blush, then grabs her coat and purse and disappears out the door with her guard.

"How's married life?" I ask, but I don't need to. My brother is glowing after that wet kiss.

Nikolay rolls his eyes, and his face breaks into a wide grin. He turns and heads to the kitchen. It wasn't that long ago that we sat in this very same kitchen planning Anya's rescue after her half-brother kidnapped her.

"You can't be serious. I died a thousand deaths until we found Anya and killed her psycho brother. Now it's you who has their hands full."

Nikolay slides into the kitchen nook and looks me over with wise, scrutinizing eyes.

"You look well, brother."

"Thanks." I can't stop from grinning.

"I can't wait to meet this woman who has you smitten."

"Mm. That's just between us."

He gives me an understanding nod.

"How's your arm healing?"

"Fine. You know me," I say with a shrug as I pour myself a coffee from the urn on the table.

"The girls will have fun today." Nikolay takes a swig of his coffee, and his housekeeper clears the table.

"Are you sure you wanna use Izzy and the wedding to bait the trap? What if Izzy is shot, kidnapped, or, worse, killed? I know what it's like to live in that fear, brother."

Our eyes meet. "I don't know any other way. We need to do this to flush out the enemy. They're not making any mistakes. They're not using technology, and even if they are, I can't track every phone. There are too many suspects."

He nods his head in agreement.

"I trust your instincts. I'm told the Russian contingency in New York City is looking into their tech man, Tito. More than twenty thousand has gone missing, and they suspect he has something to do with it."

"Kirill?" Nikolay asks about my best friend.

"He swears he has no idea whom Tito is working with or covering for. Izzy and I would be dead if Kirill were on their team. Trust me, I've considered it myself, but he checks out."

"Yeah, you and your trust issues and your rules." He leans back in the chair and drapes an arm over the back of it.

"Right. Well, Izzy has me breaking the rules."

"I bet." He chuckles. "Do you trust her?"

"I do, for the most part." I take a second to do a quick inventory and add, "I guess as much as I can."

How much do I trust her? Enough to want a child with her. I've never wanted to have a child with anyone before. If I'm taking on that level of commitment, it would be fucked up to do so without some degree of trust between us. I need to start trusting my future wife. Trust will bring us closer, but changing my ways is challenging.

"You look tired, Dmitry. Staying up at night?" he asks, a knowing grin spreading across his face.

"Of course." I chuckle. "She's a sexy woman and very accommodating. Who wouldn't want to stay up all night for that? I'd never wanted to live so badly until I met her. What can I say? I see a future with her."

"Yeah." He sits upright in his chair. "I understand. Don't wait until it's too late to say I love you. If you have it good now, wait for what happens after those words are spoken."

"We need to find the people behind these kidnapping attempts before they appear on your doorstep. Speaking of which, I have some sobering news. The actors who posed as us in Vegas were murdered in an alley."

"Mother fuckers!" Nikolay slams his fist on the table, sending our cups rattling.

"I know. I'm sick about it. I never dreamed it would come to this."

"Izzy has to be connected. No mafia would be going to this extreme otherwise." Nikolay runs a hand over his chin. Then he gives me an intense and severe look. "You're in danger." He shoves the morning paper to me. "Look what I found."

I pick up the paper that's folded to show only one article.

"James Murphy found dead," I read out loud. "Fuck! Just when I thought things couldn't get any worse." I groan.

"Right. Well, what do you think?"

"Murphy was involved with the Irish mafia and under federal investigation for a RICO case." I shrug. "The timing is concerning. He may have known who Izzy's father was and why she was so important to the Irish and the Russians. I can understand the Irish wanting her for leverage or to use as a bargaining chip if she's related to another mafia. The Italians are trying to coerce more money out of us; maybe someone wants to mend bridges while they're pissing off Alexsei Sidova. I've noticed he remains hidden while his wife is a public figure. I don't trust her. She's old school, from a KGB family."

"Interesting." Nikolay places his elbow on the table and rests his chin on his palm pensively.

"I think Izzy is part of the Moretti family. I just haven't figured out how she fits. The Don's daughter died before Izzy was born, and the paperwork matches."

"Documents can be faked."

"Right. I thought about that too. I would change my name, move away and never return. So, if Maria is Moretti's daughter, that means Izzy is his granddaughter, and the Irish might want to ally with them. They could squeeze the Russians that way. It would be a smart move on their part."

"Yes, but it doesn't explain why the Russians are looking for her. And how would they know the Morettis have a child they haven't seen in over twenty years?"

"If we knew that, we'd know who was behind everything. Tito has to know he's on our radar after we duped him with the Vegas trip."

"Fuck, yeah, and you're right, there has to be someone in the Sidova bratva who knows what the Irish are up to." Nikolay stands, and so do I. "I have to go to the office. We're opening a hotel in Japan. What a nightmare trying to compete with established hotels. We not only have to please the palettes of an international clientele but also impress them with the best sushi chefs, so I'm poaching our competitor's chefs."

I laugh. "Well played, brother, well played."

Caught up with the latest family business, we walk to the door.

"When are Roman and Mom coming?"

"Soon. Just do me a favor and make sure your bride isn't kidnapped before the main event." His words are spoken from experience.

"I'll do my best." I chuckle and hug him before joining Milan, who's been waiting in the car.

Izzy's past is littered with secrets. Even now, I'm keeping a few of them from her because I don't want her to worry. I doubt she'd see it that way when I tell her everything after we're wed. Until then, there's no reason to ruin the happiest time of her life. Yes, it's a forced marriage, but she's being a good sport. Then again, she's in a predicament, and I'm her only solution. When her enemies are revealed, and she's safe, I need to give her a reason to stay, like a baby, because I can't picture life without her.

"Milan, take me to the jewelers."

"Got it," he replies. I text Anya's phone number to Izzy and tell her to be ready before noon for her date. I'm glad Anya is taking her to the family's newly acquired boutique to help her pick a wedding dress.

My mother tells me the invitations have been sent. Should we change the venue at the last minute to ensure our safety? It would be a smart move. I could reserve a different venue under another name. I'm stressed about laying a trap and hope we don't get caught in it ourselves.

CHAPTER 27

IZZY

*D*mitry is gone when I get up, so I wander around the mansion, exploring. I've never been in a house this big. I smile, remembering the note he left, signed with words in Russian and his name. That he cared enough to leave me a note tugs at my heart, what it says is another mystery.

I find what must be the formal dining area that seats up to ten people. Good thing we have a chef if he's expecting me to entertain and feed that many guests at one time.

Then I find his office and can't resist intruding. What will this room tell me about him? The remnants of last night's cigars and their brandy dregs remain evidence he enjoys his time with the boys.

Long windows showcase a yard full of shade trees and a lawn big enough to host a soccer game. What a great yard for kids.

The office is decorated with dark wood and dark leather, very manly. The carpet is so dark you could kill someone in here and not worry about cleaning up the blood stains.

I'm tempted to climb the sizeable wooden ladder leading to the bookshelves out of my reach. I have one foot on the ladder when I hear Erik clear his throat.

I pause and turn my head to where he fills the doorway. I can see the bulge of a gun under his suit jacket, and I'm reminded that the threat is real and isn't over.

"I'll get that for you, ma'am."

"Please call me Izzy. Ma'am makes me feel old."

"Mr. Volkov won't like it."

"It's fine. I'm not one to stand on protocol."

Erik hastens to the ladder and holds it for me while I climb and run my fingers over the spines of ancient books bound in leather. I find the British classics by Charles Dickens, Jane Austen, and Emily Brontë, among others. There are books in Russian I do not recognize.

"Do you read in Russian, Erik?"

"Yes, I know both English and Russian. Do I need to translate?"

"I wish I knew what Dmitry says when he calls me Usha Moya. I'm probably not saying it correctly." I let myself down the ladder.

"It means *my soul*. It's a term of endearment."

My soul. Really? That's unexpected from a man who blows hot and cold.

"Wow," I murmur. Now I'm really confused. There are so many layers to this man.

"Do you like the house? He just bought it."

"Really? I love it. I mean, it's huge. Is it okay if I walk around?"

"Sure, I'll check in with the guard house and security staff. When you're done, I'm sure Charlotte would like to review menus with you and go over how you want the house to run."

"I don't know how to run a household. I've never had staff." I stand, feeling inadequate.

"Well." He straightens. "Dmitry would be happy if you took an interest, ma'am."

"Izzy, please," I implore him. "Leave my fiancé to me. We'll be together all the time; we may as well get to know each other. I'm going to keep exploring, and I'll meet you in the kitchen when I'm finished."

"And Mrs. Volkov will be here in two hours."

"Anya, correct?"

"Yes, I'll leave you to it."

Erik disappears, and I move on to more rooms. There's a media room, a rec room, and a formal living room. Upstairs is an informal living room with a huge flat-screen TV. I continue down a different corridor and find guest rooms with ensuites and private bathrooms. There's a huge common area for hanging out and playing board games.

When I think I've seen every inch of the place, I go upstairs to change and notice a room next to our bedrooms. I push the door open to find a turreted room with plush beige carpet and pale green walls. It's bright, with lots of natural light coming through the windows. I walk around touching white furniture like a dresser, cubbies, and bookshelves close to the floor. I open a door, thinking it's a closet. Instead, it's another room connected to this one, possibly for a nanny. Could this be a nursery?

My mind is overwhelmed with the possibility. How long has he been planning for a family, and did he know me before we met? Could he be manipulating the events behind our forced marriage?

I'm conflicted and find it too much of a stretch. He's done nothing to cause me to distrust him and his actions. He calls me his soul. Tears well in my eye. He wants a wife and a child. I'm wanted. If I can't find my family, I can have one with him.

I shut the door on the pristine room. It's personal, it has meaning to me, and now I know he wants a family. Would we live here? My mind is swimming with the possibility of being somewhere permanent.

I slip into our room, change into a warm outfit, and walk down the stairs to meet the staff. Me, with staff. It sounds so weird. I'm giddy and terrified at the same time.

Charlotte is a young woman with vibrant red hair and pale skin. She wears a beige uniform, a white apron, and sensible shoes.

"Charlotte." I extend my hand. We shake, and I find her hand warm and soft. Not what I expected from someone who cleans and tidies for a living.

"Ma'am."

"Oh, no. It's Izzy. I'm not formal," I insist.

"Izzy, I want to know what you like to eat. We can start with what time you want dinner served." Her face is open and honest, her voice friendly. I like her instantly.

"I have no idea." I cover my mouth with both hands. How can I be expected to make these decisions? "I'll talk to my husband. Let's start with seven o'clock and adjust if needed."

"Great. I need a list of food you'd like to eat this week. I do the shopping and will also pick up anything you want personally."

I let out a chuckle—so many decisions.

"I'll think about it. I do love a great rib roast, potatoes, and vegetables if that's possible?"

"Absolutely."

I hear a phone buzzing and look up to see Erik standing in the doorway.

"Anya is at the guardhouse. I'll meet her outside and start our car."

"Thank you."

He leaves, and a minute later, a young woman, whom I will come to know as Anya, enters like a breath of summer air.

She extends her hand and says, "You must be Izzy. I'm Anya."

Her honey-blond hair falls over her shoulders and curls perfectly to frame her face. She has a button nose and sapphire blue eyes. She's wearing an unbuttoned black wool coat, and she carries a handbag on her arm as she tugs off her leather gloves.

She gives me a short hug, and I wish I looked as stylish as her.

"I'm so happy to meet you. Do you know where we're going?"

"You're in good hands. We're having lunch, and I'm taking you to pick your wedding dress. Erik will drive us, and my guard will join us."

She doesn't look thrilled about being followed around, from her expression.

As we pull away in the SUV, it's the first time I see the house and the grounds in the daylight. Anya notices me craning my neck to take everything in.

"Quite the house, isn't it?"

"Amazing. I've never stayed in a place so nice. My best friend's place in New York is nice, but this is next level."

"Yeah, the bratva men tend to spoil their women. They would be content to live in a cave as long as they have their cigars and cognac. Not us. I'm taking you to lunch at Zima's, a Russian restaurant we own." She chuckles. I take it this is one of many restaurants they own. "You're getting married at Fulham Palace. It's a nice place, Tudor style, on the Thames. It's beautiful with old bricks and nice scenery. It's pricey and makes the right statement."

"Is that important?"

"Yes, you'll have a public wedding, tight security, and it will be beautiful. The invitations went out, so everyone will know the date. After lunch, I'll take you by our boutique, and you'll pick a wedding dress."

"It seems weird to hear you say that. I never intended to marry Dmitry."

"None of us ever intends to marry them, Izzy," she states matter-of-factly.

"Really?"

"For sure. There are arranged weddings, but for some of us, it's circumstances. My marriage was arranged. My family moved away, and he remained here. We were pledged by our fathers and didn't know it until they died."

"I'm so sorry, that's so sad."

"It comes with the territory. It's why we move about as safely as possible. Dmitry, he's quiet but smart. The men tend to brood, so don't push them. They have so much on their mind. Don't ask for details. They won't give them."

"That much I know. My BFF is Alena. You'll meet her at the wedding. She'll be my maid of honor. She's going to be married off, too."

"Ah, the Russian roommate."

"Yes, you heard?"

"Bits and pieces."

"I can tell Dmitry is crazy about you."

My heart leaps. Is he? Anya would know since they've known each other longer.

"How?" I quip.

"He's got a look about him. He even smiled today, which is unusual. Normally, he's not happy."

I'm not surprised. Any man who can stab another in the hand at a bar is used to brutal acts, not loving ones.

"What's their mother like?" I'm curious about his parentage and home life.

"His dad was a don who ruled with an iron fist, but he loved his sons. Nikolay and Dmitry went to boarding school, but Roman was the baby, and their mother, Natasha, couldn't bear for him to leave. She's tough, she's loving, and, at times, sentimental. She doesn't have that resting bitch face most bratva wives wear like a shield."

I chuckle. I like Anya, she has a sense of humor, and if she and Nikolay are in love, maybe there's hope for us.

"What do you know about us?"

"First, never trust anyone but the inner circle of the Bratva. I know you need protection, and this is the price you pay for it." She turns to me as the driver pulls up in front of the restaurant. Her serious face has my attention when she flatly says, "Dmitry will never let you go."

My stomach lurches. The truth is, I know she's right. He constantly reminds me that I'm his—his possession. I belong to him. And for that, I will be protected.

We get out and head towards the restaurant.

We're greeted at the door by the maître d' and escorted to a table near the window. When our waiter approaches, I ask Anya to order for us.

"Ivan, nice to see you. This is Isabella, Dmitry's fiancé."

He's a tall Russian with dark hair and dark brown eyes. His tattoos peek out from under his long sleeves and extend onto his hands. I bet his body is covered with them.

"Nice to meet you." He smiles, and I feel like it's forced.

"Hello," I reply to be polite.

Anya tells him to bring bottled water and food that sounds like Russian dishes.

When he leaves, I ask, "Do we know him?"

"He's one of ours. Most of the employees are from Russia. I'm so busy I don't get out much, and Nikolay and I come here often."

When the food comes, it's pretty good. I could get used to the beet soup. Anya fills me in on her studies. We swap information about ourselves, as girls do. After lunch, Milan and her guard take us to the family's store where I'm to try on wedding dresses.

The storefront is fancy, with white and gold lettering. It's the kind of place I would have walked past in New York because it screams exclusive and expensive.

We head inside, and our bodyguards take positions by the front and back doors. A store associate directs me to a fitting room where pre-selected dresses hang on a moveable rack. They're all exquisite.

"Take whatever you like. Our gift to you." Anya smiles at me.

"I can't accept…" But she prevents me from saying more by interrupting.

"The don wants to gift it to you. You should know better than to argue with him."

"Do you argue with him?"

"Occasionally, it's more about picking your battles. And, even then, we're the only ones who can make our men bend with our words. Their subordinates wouldn't dare question them."

"I get that, but this rushed wedding feels fake. I don't want to lie to everyone," I explain.

"Isabella, you're lucky to have a bratva man. He will protect you with his life if need be. And don't try to convince me that you don't love him. Even I can tell you're thinking about him. Plus, you've been texting him updates all afternoon. So, I don't think you're being honest with yourself."

She's right. I can't deny that I have feelings for Dmitry. My body yearns for him, and that's not all. My heart soars when he enters a room. I get wet when he looks at me, and I believe him when he says I'm his. He's destroyed the possibility of any other man replacing him.

"Ah, I see it in your face." Anya accuses me of having emotions for this ruthless man. "You can't hide the flush in your cheeks and the way your eyes light up at the mention of his name." Her eyes widen, as does her grin. "You love him," she says softly.

"Um." I'm at a loss for words. I thought it was just the porn star sex we're having that has me obsessed with him. The possibility of him loving me makes me giddy. "Really?"

"Oh, yeah, you may as well admit it. You're no good at lying, Izzy. Not to a woman who knows what love is with her husband. Does Dmitry know?"

"Oh, no," I reply, reaching for a wedding dress to try on.

"Well, good. Make him say it first."

"What if he never does?"

"Trust me, when a bratva man loves a woman, he practically brands her, and God help any man who looks at her a moment longer than necessary."

"Oh, yeah, I can see that. He's definitely all that," I murmur.

I strip down to my panties and try on the dress that grabs my attention. It's a mermaid gown of Chantilly lace handmade in France. I step into the dress and pull it up. My heart beats faster. The plunging neckline and fitted bodice push up my boobs and display my cleavage beautifully. The tight satin sash slims my waist. I twist to see the fishtail train. The deep V-back sexes it up. This is my dress.

Anya is waiting when I come out of the dressing room.

"I love it. Turn around," she says.

"Please, grab the phone out of my purse and video it. I have to send it to my girlfriend in New York."

Anya finds my phone and records me twirling in the dress.

"I love this dress," she exclaims. "It's incredible. The fit is perfect."

"I think so too."

"I'm told you are quite the fashion designer. I'm sure you would have taken the job with the ballet company if it wasn't for this sordid affair."

My mouth drops.

"What?" My voice is barely audible.

"Oh, you would never have been able to take that job anyway." She adjusts the train and takes more photos from different angles.

"You're talented. I'd never believe in a million years they'd pass you over. But their loss is our gain. I'd love for you to design a clothing line for us."

It's becoming painfully clear that when Dmitry is quiet, it's because he's withholding something. How dare he take away the job I wanted. The fun day that was going so well is now tarnished, and there isn't enough polish in the world to fix it.

"When did you hear this?"

"It was before you left New York. I don't know how that didn't cause a row, but I guess it's in the past." She puts my phone in my purse.

I storm off to the dressing room.

Have I been played? Why wouldn't he tell me? I bet he's hacked my email account and probably tracking my phone.

It's pointless to tell her I never got the email and blame Dmitry. She thinks we're a loving couple. She is a Volkov, and her loyalty will always be to her husband and his family. I'm just the outsider.

I let the store associate know I'm taking the dress, and she zips it into a long nylon bag. I say nothing in response to Anya's bombshell news, but she has to know it was a surprise.

Instead, we chat about the weather and traffic as we return to the house. The sisterly bond we were forming is sadly broken. There's no point lashing out at her. She's my source on the inside. Still, I've never felt so alone. I'm in a new country, and I'm not sure who to trust. Their bratva is a fucking secret society where the men rule, and the women follow blindly.

Not this woman, I tell myself.

I'm relieved when Anya leaves with her guard. Erik takes the dress upstairs to my room. Anger wells in my chest as I pace in the kitchen. A heavyset man wearing an apron is stirring something on the stove. He must be our chef, Jon. The smell of rosemary potatoes and beef makes me nauseous. Great, I'm so upset I'm sick.

"What's the matter, ma'am?" Charlotte asks as she makes dinner rolls.

"Nothing." I bristle. "I'll take care of it."

If marriage is nothing more than a glorified prison sentence, I need to show the warden who the boss is.

DMITRY

It's dark when I arrive at the house. The cold air settles in for the night as Milan and I enter the house. We shed our heavy clothing in the coat room. I texted Izzy earlier and didn't hear from her. Anya said they had a great time. I knew a day in the city would make my little bird happy.

I check my phone and see a message from Kirill. He tells me Alena's father claims there is an ongoing argument between Alexsei and his wife. They've had separate rooms for some time. This is interesting, trouble in paradise. Kirill will email me pictures from the private Catholic school and the Moretti children who attended it. I return the phone to my suit pocket.

I can smell prime rib cooking and drop by the kitchen. Oddly the staff is unusually quiet. I glance at the French chef, Jon, and nod. He gives me a quick nod back.

"Izzy?"

"Upstairs, Mr. Volkov," Charlotte wistfully replies, pointing up. She sets the table and busies herself, making the table perfect. I bound up the steps, two at a time.

Our bedroom door is closed.

I'm miffed. What kind of game is Izzy playing? She knew I was on my way.

I cautiously open the door to our bedroom and am immediately pelted with shoes flying at my head with precision and speed. I duck and deflect them with my hands and arms.

"How dare you!" she yells.

"What?"

I appear to be safe now as she's run out of shoes.

"You took away the job I wanted. How could you?"

"It was too dangerous for you to take. Besides, bratva wives don't work. I thought I made that clear." My voice is deep and author-itative.

"Clear? I'll tell you what is clear. You lied to me. You spied on me. It's the only way you would have known."

She's right. I am to blame.

Fuck.

"We were leaving. It's better to have a polite refusal saying you're out of the country and leaving your options open, isn't it?" I manip-ulate the situation.

"You never intended to stay in New York. You sabotaged my chance to have a life after this fake marriage is over!" she hollers loud enough for everyone downstairs to hear.

"Isabella. Enough!" I yell too, but with a *don't fuck with me* an edge to my voice. She freezes and looks at me like a startled deer. I need her to calm the fuck down and listen to me.

"You're being unreasonable. The Russian and Irish mafia in New York both have people hunting you. You would have been a sitting duck in New York, and you know it." My fists clench as I control the urge to punch a wall. Surely she will see my reasoning and be logical.

"Over what? No one can tell me what these men want from me. We have no idea when this will be over, and I'm so tired." Her voice fades away, demonstrating just how exhausting all this has been for her. I should've seen this coming. This is all new to her, and she's gone from a life of freedom to one in a gilded cage. She slumps onto the edge of the bed.

"I can't live in New York. I can't call my aunt and tell her what's going on. My only friend is thousands of miles away, and I have to live by rules I don't understand," she sobs. "I've lost everything meaningful in my life because of you." Tears run down her face. She wipes them with the back of her hand, smearing her eye makeup.

She has a point. This is what we do to our women. It saddens me to see her distraught. My heart aches, but my mind is focused on her safety. I can't cave to her demands. As much as I want to tell her what she wants to hear, I can't. I'm a bastard for keeping secrets, but I know what's best for her and what's best for us.

"Alena will be here for the wedding," I reply softly as I approach the bed. "Your aunt will be here as well. I've sent her encrypted messages introducing myself, and you'll find emails from her on your phone. I'm routing your emails through servers that can't be traced. You're free to talk to her and Alena about the wedding. The venue has been announced and is public knowledge."

"Why now? Couldn't you do this before?" She raises her head and sniffles, wiping her nose on her sleeve.

I grab a tissue from the nightstand and hand it to her. She dabs at her nose. I lean over her and place a kiss on her forehead. "I could only do so much at the time. Besides, I wanted you to spend time with me without the interference of others saying you don't know me well enough to get married. Your aunt has to believe we're in love. The entire world has to believe we're in love."

"And do you?" She sniffles, staring at her hands.

"Do I what?"

"Love me?" She lifts her head to meet my gaze. Looking into her eyes, my walls come down.

"I do love you, Isabella. Why else would I go to such lengths to keep you safe and give up my freedom?"

A tear slips from her eye. She quickly dabs it away.

"Tell me now if you don't love me, Isabella." My voice is raw. I'm exposed, but I have to know where she stands.

"I love you, too," she says. Her voice is soft as it fills my ears. I'm in disbelief but ecstatic.

I exhale. I didn't even realize I was holding my breath while I was waiting for her answer. I hope she knows we're not just fucking. I make love to her, and my heart is full of the promise of a new life with her beside me. She will keep me from slipping into the fray.

"Do you feel better?" I ask as I slip my arms around her and pull her into my chest.

"I guess." She lays her head on my shoulder. I brush her hair away from her face.

"Good. I want to make love to you. You drive me to distraction, but that's okay. You're my light on the darkest night, and I won't be denied," I whisper into her ear.

She's limp in my arms. Her blue-gray eyes are full of emotion as my lips descend upon her. I run my hand through her hair and pull her mouth into mine. We kiss and shed our clothing, throwing it about the room without thinking of anything but each other.

She lies on the bed, her breasts glistening under the soft light in the room. My cock is hard. I crawl onto the bed, slipping my fingers inside the woman I love. She's wet and spreads her legs for me.

I pull my fingers out and grab my cock, lining him up at her entrance. I lean over her, and she places a hand next to the bluebird I had tattooed on my chest today.

"Is that?" Her eyes search mine.

"It's for you, my love. You are my soul."

I enter her, and my world becomes a kaleidoscope. Images, feelings, and what the future will hold all merge together in my head. Her folds are slick, welcoming me. I balance myself on one arm as I lay over her and grab her firm ass cheek with the other. She's my woman. I'll be damned if I go a day without sinking my cock in her. I thrust into her. She moans under me. Her breathing comes quicker.

When our eyes meet, It's a meeting of souls. My heart may be black, but it's there for her taking. We're suspended in time as we share this special moment and meet each other halfway, letting our bodies do the talking.

She clutches at my biceps, and I feel her clit quicken as her head tilts back, and she screams my name when she comes. I thrust in her three more times, and my world explodes. I shudder under the intensity. It's as if I'd been choked out. All my blood flows to my head in a rush. I give myself a minute to recover before I fall beside her. She's given me the workout of a lifetime, and I'm satiated. For a man who has resumed his regimented days at the gym since we arrived, I should be embarrassed she kicked my ass. Instead, I smile and stare at the ceiling, enjoying the feel of her arm draped across my newly tatted chest.

"Before I forget, your wedding ring has an embedded microchip in case you're ever taken, and we need to track you. It will only be on my devices, but it's for your safety." I turn and find Izzy's body is relaxed. Her body is soft and warm. "With or without a microchip, I'll always find you, Isabella. You are mine, forever." She turns to face me and runs her fingers on the outskirts of the new tattoo.

"And you belong to me," she whispers.

CHAPTER 29

IZZY

By the time we made it downstairs for dinner, Charlotte had to reheat it. The beef was amazing. This sure beats cutting coupons and scrimping on buying things to make ends meet. The exquisite meal was outstanding. I have no clue how to cook prime rib, so I'm in awe of our chef, Jon. I never thought I would be one to let another person wait on me, but I'm getting used to it. I'm relieved I don't have to clean this house. I'd have no time for anything else without Charlotte's help.

We retire to our living room upstairs. I pour Dmitry a vodka, and I email my aunt, whom I know will be happy to hear from me. I explained a whirlwind love story and a trip to London. This way, all the pieces fit. Honestly, it's so unlike me because I'm a planner and don't give into whimsical and irrational behavior, but whatever.

Alena is sequestered with her parents, and the situation is grating on her nerves.

I encourage her and remain positive that Dmitry will flush out the men after me. I'm aware that my tapping on the phone keys echoes into the evening.

Dmitry is reading a book in Russian. It's so quiet here, unlike the city. I grab the remote and turn on the news. Alena asks how I'm doing and wants pictures of the house.

My eyes lazily drift to Dmitry.

"Oh, I forgot to tell you, Alena and Kirill are flying over with the don and his family."

"Really? I'm sure Kirill will be happy rubbing elbows with the man."

"Maybe."

"Is anything happening between Alena and Kirill?"

"She says they are such great friends she doesn't want to ruin it over a fuck."

Dmitry laughs so hard he coughs on his own saliva. He sends me a look of surprise at my frankness.

I shrug. "What do you want from me? I'm not a princess, I'm a New Yorker, and those are Alena's exact words."

"I'm sure." He smiles, and the news on TV is boring, so I flip to an old comedy show from America.

"Anya and I ate at Zima's today. It was very good."

"It better be. We spend a fortune on that restaurant," he mutters.

This is funny, as I know every business that handles cash is used to launder money. How can it cost them anything?

"Apparently, the bratva spends a lot of time there. The server, Ivan, knows of us and seemed overly friendly. I thought it was odd."

Dmitry flies off the couch, dumping his book. "What do you mean overly friendly? Did he touch you?" His eyes are a sea of daggers. I'd say he is pissed off.

"No," I quickly reply. "He just acted like he was inside the family instead of our waiter. Or am I missing something?"

"He'll be handled. He should know his place, and it's not mooning over my wife." His voice is stern. I'm afraid to move.

"Don't hurt him. I might be overreacting."

"You're observant. You knew you were being followed in New York. Trust your instincts. I'll have it looked into." He returns to his place on the couch. I decide it's men's business and pass his possessiveness off due to the stress he must be under for the wedding.

"So, how are you going to find the men after me?"

He closes his book. "I'm working on it. I need you to go about life as normal. I'm working behind the scenes. Also, I want you to trust your instincts. Anyone who might want to harm you will be at the wedding."

"You said I'd be safe once we came out, and it is official. I thought the MET appearance would be enough. What's going on?"

Then, it dawns on me. The wedding is a way to flush out our opposition.

"Wait, you're using me as bait?" I stand and toss my phone onto my seat.

He stands again and begins to pace.

"There will be a collection of dons, and one or more may want to see you and maybe grab you."

I raise an eyebrow at him. "The chip in the ring is your backup plan?"

"Kind of. I'm hoping we'll figure it out before then. We have tons of men working on the situation. We'll have men all over the venue."

"Fine." I sit and pick up, texting Alena.

"My mother will be coming to town. She's staying with Dmitry, and you'll meet Roman soon."

"Is it a good idea to have everyone at the wedding?"

"You have a point, but I can trust my brothers, and it would be noticeable if my mother were missing," he says as he reaches for his glass of vodka.

"Right, the family. Will I like your mother?"

"She can be reserved, but don't let it throw you. Do you like your dress?" He sets his glass on the coffee table and sits. I return to my seat and put my phone in my lap.

"Oh, yes. It was a gift from Anya and Nikolay. I hope it was all right to accept."

"Yes, it is. That's very nice. I'll be sure to thank him."

"Great." I yawn.

"I think it's time for bed. Tell Alena I said hello," he says, getting up. Then he waits for me.

I whip one last text to Alena and follow my husband-to-be to bed, and he cuddles me as I drift off.

Morning came too soon. I open my eyes. It's later than usual. I lean as if to get up. I'm so tired and feel like I have the flu.

Dmitry breezes into the room, back from the gym by the looks of his sweaty tracksuit and sneakers.

"Are you okay? I was worried about you." His eyes take me in.

"Feel my head. Is it warm?"

He approaches me and puts the back of his hand on my head.

"Normal. Should I get the family doctor for you?" He sits on the side of the bed. The mattress dips under his weight.

"The vet? No, thank you," I reply sardonically.

He chuckles. "Fine, it was a situation we didn't foresee that day."

"It seems like it was so long ago," I add wistfully.

"All the same, I think we should have you checked out."

"I'm fine. I'm sure." I move to get up, but my head is off balance. *Maybe my equilibrium is off.*

"Do you think someone drugged me?" I ask.

Dmitry's face turns white. He pulls his phone out, calls the guards to the room, and he mutters the doctor is on his way.

I lie back on the bed. Dmitry takes my hand. Milan and Erik are beside him.

"Has anyone been here? Anything unusual?" He's barking at them like a ferocious Rotty.

"No sir," Erik says.

"Nothing, Dmitry," Milan states.

"I'm feeling better. It's probably nothing." I brush it off, but he's not taking chances.

"You're staying here." He turns to the guards. "You two question the staff and report to me."

They leave the room, and panic isn't the look I want to see on his face. I've read stories of the Russians using poison on their targets, and they can reach anyone at any time.

"The doctor will be here in a minute. Did that kid Ivan put something in your food? When did you start to feel bad?"

"It was great food. I was fine."

An elderly man ushers in the room with an old black leather bag.

He listens to my heart, takes my temperature, and asks me to stand.

I throw the cover back and stand in my sheer nightgown. I use it because Dmitry likes seeing my breast through the thin, lacy fabric. I'm sure he likes me naked just as well, but it's drafty at night.

I stand fine, and he asks me to walk a few steps.

"Isabella, you are a young woman. You appear to be fine. Can I be so presumptuous as to ask what form of birth control you're on?"

Dmitry and I exchange a look. I immediately grab my boobs. Shit, they are larger and tender.

I use my palm and slap it to my forehead.

The doctor hands me a box. It's a pregnancy test.

Fuck. How could I be so naïve? My face turns a million shades of red I'm so embarrassed.

Dmitry is adding things in his head. A sly grin graces his severe but handsome face.

"Pee on the stick. You'll know in under three minutes," the doctor says as he zips his bag and stands, then turns to Dmitry.

I scamper into the bathroom. My heart is in my throat as I pee. How do I feel about this?

We've had enough sex to make it a new Olympic sport.

Then, I imagine a little version of Dmitry running around, and my chest grows heavy with a yearning for a family of my own. We love each other. I've been sidetracked by the circumstances of our weeks together and am still sitting as I watch the test turn positive. I check it twice and read the box a second time.

Do I say anything? How can I not?

We're in this together. Dmitry wanted it, and he's prepared, judging from the room at the end of the hall and the property around us that will be green in a few weeks' time. It's a perfect place to raise a family.

I'm embarrassed as I grab a house coat from my closet.

"Everything okay?" the doctor asks as he pushes his wired glasses up on the bridge of his nose. He's in his sixties and reminds me of the British show on vets in the English countryside that aired on the BBC years ago.

"Yes, fine," I reply demurely before thanking him for his time.

"If you are good here, I'll see myself out." He gives a glance to Dmitry and is gone.

We're alone.

I'm happy but scared and embarrassed. Everyone will know what we've been doing as soon as the baby bump shows.

"Well? I assume you're fine if you let the doctor go." I can tell he knows, or at the least, he thinks he does.

I let out a long sigh. "It looks like we're going to be parents." A tiny smirk escapes me.

"Great. We'll have to get the nursery ready and…"

"Wait. It's early, and it's definitely too early for all of that."

"Right."

"I don't want everyone to know before the wedding, and it's way too early to say anything," I warn him.

"Right. Okay, I'll let the staff know you're fine." He leaves and returns five minutes later.

"Let's eat breakfast together," he suggests. "What do you want?"

"Omelets. I'm going to get dressed," I reply as I duck into my closet, forcing myself to move due to how lethargic I feel.

I join Dmitry minutes later, and he's looking at his laptop at the table.

"What's up?"

"I had Kirill find old schoolbooks the Moretti children went to." He turns his screen to me as I sit beside him. "Do any of those girls look like your mother?"

"It's hard to say." I peer closer at the girls wearing plaid jumpers and wonder what their lives are like. "They all look picture perfect, don't they?"

"Looks are deceiving."

"Right." I recall Alena saying how the Italian Don is an abusive man.

"What is the plan for the wedding? I mean, do we expect someone to notice me?"

"I have to confess a few things," he starts the conversation as our filled plates slide under our noses. Orange juice and coffee are poured and placed exactly at one and ten o'clock on the table in front of my plate.

I place a napkin in my lap, and then I wonder how much longer I'll fit into all the expensive clothes I own.

Charlotte leaves, and Dmitry clears his voice.

"First of all, I don't want you to overreact. I know you'll be afraid, and I'm here for you."

"If this is your idea of a pep talk, you're failing miserably," I say as I rip a piece of toast off the crust and pop it into my mouth. I lift the fork and take a bite of the golden-brown omelet, and I'll be damned if having someone serve me food doesn't make everything taste better.

Dmitry takes a bite of the English bacon. He swallows.

"Dish," I say.

"Dish?" he inquires as his forehead raises, showing a tiny crease in his forehead.

"Tell me," I implore him.

"Oh, right. Okay, the actors in Vegas were found dead. So these men know we are somewhere else."

I swallow the food in my mouth and hope I don't choke.

"What? They were innocent. Why would someone do that?"

"It's to send a message to not fuck with them." His voice is lower than normal. I realize we don't want to broadcast this to the staff and, therefore, to anyone they talk to.

"What else?" I whisper.

"I know you'll be upset, but James has also passed."

"What?" My voice is sharp. This news is surreal and personal. I haven't seen him in all these years, and now, someone else, someone I knew as a child, has died. "Was it over me?"

He shrugs. "I think it would be naïve of us if we didn't know who you are. So, now we can assume the Irish know who you are, and somehow, a few members of the bratva know. That's my assumption."

"You kept this from me?" My voice is high-pitched. I tell myself to be calm for the baby. I figure it will arrive safely within the nine months of our wedding. My mother was Catholic, but we never went to church.

"Yes," he replies with a deep hiss. "I had to protect you, and I didn't want to tell you until you had to know."

"And you pick today for that?" I give him an unquestionable look of surprise and disdain.

"I can't help the fact it all ran amuck today. The baby, good news. The fact that we know what the others know is good. No?"

"You're right, but we don't know why they want you. Oh, by the way, did you notice anyone else in that picture from the school? Anyone look similar to your mother?"

"Not that I'm aware of. I mean, there were many Italian girls there. I never saw any pictures of my mother when she was young. I wonder if my mom and dad knew each other back then. I mean, she was so young to have a kid, y'know?"

He's pensive for a moment. "You have a good point. It makes sense your mother knew your father, but there's no trace to whom it might have been."

We're quiet for a moment, and I take the opportunity to eat more food.

"Izzy, are you mad at me?"

"For what?" I busy myself with pushing food around my plate before I load my fork again.

"The baby."

"Mm, the fact you kept my birth control from me and teased me into submission?"

"That."

"Yes, but I couldn't help myself. I'm addicted to you. So, here we are. Why were you so intent on having a child?"

"I wanted to make sure you didn't run from me." He finally eats some food and sips coffee.

"Where would I go?" I ask.

"You're tenacious. If you applied yourself to it long enough, you'd find a way." His matter-of-fact response makes me chuckle.

"Well, I'm preggers, so I guess your plan to keep me worked."

CHAPTER 30

DMITRY

"How do I look?" I'm wearing a beige pantsuit with matching heels. I look in the full-length mirror. I eye my stomach for a presence of a bump. I'm being ridiculous. It's way too soon for that. I fiddle with the diamond choker Dmitry gave me, and I slip the matching earrings into my ears.

The tattoo on his chest is healed. My heart melts when I glimpse it before he buttons his shirt.

The rehearsal dinner is tonight. It's only his family, Alena and Kirill.

"You're the most beautiful woman in the world, Izzy." He strokes my cheek with the back of his fingers, and my body tingles. I've been reading up on pregnancy, and the hormones make many women super horny.

I blush. I'm not used to being called beautiful all the time. Plus, I think he's biased.

"I hope your mother likes me."

"I'm sure she will."

He finishes with his shirt, and I help with his tie. He has a gold bar he adds to hold the collar in place, giving him a polished look. He's particular about his clothes, and his suits are tailored to fit him to a tee. It probably accounts for his excellent taste in jewelry. I bet he gets it from his mother, and I wonder if our baby will be like him.

I grab my clutch, and we walk down the steps. Erik waits for us, handing us a trench coat. Milan pulls up the car.

"Is it always so methodical?" I send Dmitry a knowing glance. I'm comfortable teasing him. The baby news opened up lines of communication, and we've grown closer. We were two people afraid to venture into love when we met, content with a hookup. Funny how life changes so quickly at times.

Now, we're a couple, a real couple who can speak their mind to each other and share our inner thoughts without being guarded. It's a significant change for both of us. I'm elated that I don't have to lie to his family. I've fallen in love with my beast.

Dmitry's dress shoes echo with my heels as we walk to the front door. He slides my arm through his and opens my car door, tucking me safely inside.

We arrive at 34 Mayfair, and I'm surprised to find we're eating in the trendiest restaurant in London as it's crowded. The entrance to the establishment is lined with tea tree roses that are beginning to bud.

"I hear movie stars come here," he whispers as men with top hats greet us at the door and take out coats. "We have a private room," he says and leads the way with our guards behind us.

"Are they going, too?"

"Sure, why not? They will be at the doors and escort you to the bathroom. We can't be too careful." He drops his voice. "Now more than ever."

I happen to agree.

I approach the sizeable, long table. I find Alena amid the sea of new faces. She jumps up and rushes to me.

"Oh, my God, it's so great to see you," she exclaims. She's dressed in a pricey dress and is wearing diamonds. Dmitry is greeting Kirill.

"You look amazing." She smiles and whispers, "I won't say a thing about y'know."

"I missed you so much." I squeeze her tight.

"I know. Are you excited?"

"Yes."

She moves politely to the side so I can greet Dmitry's family.

Anya is next. We hug. "You met Alena?"

"Yes, she's great. Are you ready for your big day?

"As ready as ever, I assume."

Kirill jets over to me and hugs me, then tells me Alena misses me, and they hope we return to New York City.

"I hope we do, too." I miss home and my best friend.

Anya leads me to her husband, and I notice he and Dmitry have the same nose.

"Welcome." He gives me a hearty hug. I move on to the man next to him. It must be his younger brother.

"Izzy, great to meet you." I put my hand out.

"You, too. I'm Roman." He shakes my hand, and I notice he's taller than his brother, with darker hair and a wider face.

Dmitry slides his hand around my waist, gives Roman his hand, and then pulls him into his chest in a half hug.

"Brother, how are you doing?" Dmitry questions Roman. "I hear you're holding down the fort in Russia.?

"I try." He gives his brother a nod.

Roman speaks to him in Russian, so I turn to the woman, who must be Natasha.

She's regal, with high cheekbones wearing a black evening dress with a high neckline. Her hair is in an updo, and she clasps my hand.

"So nice to meet you, Izzy."

"Thank you, Mrs. Volkov."

"Call me Natasha. Come, sit by me. I haven't seen Dmitry in over a month," she purrs.

"Natasha." I smile and follow her, taking a seat at the table.

Apprehension rises in my chest. I've wanted a family, but I'm overwhelmed by so many new faces. They've known each other forever, and I don't belong.

Alena comes towards me as the waiter gathers drink orders.

"Are you okay?"

"I'm not used to being in a room full of family. They're strangers."

"It will get easier. Just hang in there." She squeezes my hand to reassure me.

"Thanks."

"I hope you ordered a drink."

"I don't think one drink would hurt," I murmur.

A champagne bottle pops. I'm startled. My heart is in my throat.

Everyone is talking to each other, but I'm not Russian. I don't know what they are saying. I snag the flutes filled with the golden bubbly. Dmitry sits beside me and talks to his mother.

"What did you say?"

"Oh, sorry, we're getting caught up. She's been lonely, missing my father. I think the baby news would cheer her up."

"We can't say anything, especially since we don't know who's after us. Do you want the nefarious men after me to know this?"

I'm peeved that he would consider putting the baby in more danger.

"It's my mother, Isabella." His tone is cold. I wonder if his mother will take priority over me.

"I don't care. No," I reply, sending him a stern look that says this conversation is over.

"You will not embarrass me in front of my family. I make the decisions, and you will do as I say."

"Let's discuss this later. Your family sees us arguing, and they'll think badly of me." I survey the table to find Nikolay observing me. "I know they want you to marry a Russian. I see it in your brother's eyes. You're putting me in an impossible situation."

"They will get over it," he huffs. "Besides, he knows I love you. He adores his wife as well."

I'm miffed at his lack of empathy. But wait, he adores me?

"I'm not so sure," I reply, regarding his brother, who is the don. Don's scare the shit out of me.

"Izzy, is that a pet name?" Natasha interrupts us.

"It's a name I picked up. My real name is Isabella."

"That's so pretty. Anya tells me you will be the first to wear the designer gown you picked out."

"Really? I didn't know that," I politely reply.

"Oh, yes. The shop is for couture designs. We have connections in the fashion industry. So, I haven't heard any details. How did you two meet? I find it hard to believe Dmitry fell in love so quickly. He's not the type to settle down." She sips her champagne and gives Nikolay an eye.

This is not what I expected from his mother. Alena's words come back to me. The Russians won't accept the don's son, who was adopted. He's young and not Russian-born. It's obvious I'm Italian, and I don't belong, either.

I'm sick in the pit of my stomach. Why would the Russians be after me? Dmitry's family is friendly with the bratva in New York, and now I'm wondering if I've been duped. Is his family using me, and do they know more than me? Can I trust them? Do they have their own agenda? What if everyone here knows more than me?

Panic fills my chest. Who do I trust?

Alena.

I send her a nod to meet me at the door. I excuse myself telling Dmitry I'm going to the bathroom.

"What's the matter?" Alena whispers to me as we meet in the doorway of the private room.

"I'm wondering if I'm being set up. His family disapproves of me. His mother is asking me questions. I have a bad feeling they know more than they are telling me. Why would the bratva in New York be after me when Dmitry and Nikolay have relations with them? They probably have a mole to report back to them on what is going on in the Sidovo family."

We walk to the bathroom with a guard on our heels.

I push the door open and take a deep breath.

I check under the stalls, and by some miracle, the room is empty.

Alena takes a chair, meant for an attendant who isn't here, and wedges it under the door.

"I don't want to be here."

"You have to get married. You'll be on the run forever otherwise."

"Maybe it's better." I wring my hands.

"You can't raise a baby that way. You have no money. You won't be able to work. What spooked you?"

"The way his mother looked at Nikolay. It's like they are running an op. I know what you said about not being a Russian in the bratva. They look at outsiders with distrust. And I'm telling you, they don't trust me."

She lets out a heavy sigh. "I was hoping they would be different, but they are closer to the old guard and the old ways more than we are in America. Just hold your head high, and don't let it bother you. It will get better."

"I'm in a foreign country without access to my passport. I'm a hostage." My breathing is uneven. I feel like I'm going to hiccup but hyperventilate instead. Tears stream down my face. I try to focus on slowing my breath. I use a finger to wipe tears, but it's not enough. "He did this on purpose. He wanted a child. He did it to trap me." I'm numb with the realization that I've been manipulated. "I've been so naïve. Dmitry did this purposefully, knowing the day would come when I wanted to run. He knew I grew up without my parents and that I would never leave my baby."

There is banging on the door. Women's voices are heard in the hallway outside.

"Shit. I never thought about it." Her face falls. She's dumbfounded. "I was happy you fell in love for the first time. I never looked at the downside of this. It's my world. Not yours. I should have been a better friend and protected you." Her words are rushed as she grabs my hand in hers. When I peer into her eyes, I know we can do nothing.

Another bang on the door interrupts our moment.

"Just a second," she yells in frustration. "We've got time to work on this. We'll think of something. We always do."

I nod. "I don't know how we can get around Dmitry's trackers. He has my email and phone bugged."

"Fuck," she exclaims. "Between Kirill and Dmitry, we have our work cut out for us but don't give up hope. You have to throw them off. Play the game. We need to find out who wants you, and then we'll get you out."

She heads to the door.

I take toilet paper from a dispenser in a stall and dry my eyes. I take a few deep breaths and nod to Alena.

"Finally, the door opens." Alena jokes as the door swings wide, and women barge in, mumbling their annoyance.

Erik lurks outside the door and leans his head in, making sure we're both here.

I wash my hands, the water drowning our voices.

"We'll make a plan after the wedding. We can get burner phones," I suggest.

"I'll get one to you before I leave the wedding."

"Great." Now that I know where I stand, the panic recedes. I pull my shoulders back. I'm tougher than the bratva. I won't be broken.

IZZY

I don't allude to my displeasure with Dmitry. I smile graciously, keeping the conversation light. It's like a banquet of strangers. I find solace in the fact that Alena is here.

I order a steak. It reminds me of home amid a menu with quail and duck, none of which I find appealing. I'm not used to fine dining. The conversation swirls around the room like cigar smoke.

I circulate the room after dinner plates are taken away. Alena and I catch up on her life, and Kirill heads toward Dmitry.

"I can't wait to see you tomorrow. Did you bring your dress?" I sit in Kirill's seat.

"Yes, it's gorgeous, and it's pale blue. Anya insisted on paying for it."

"That's nice."

"You might have a friend in her," Alena suggests.

"Negligible."

"She's an attorney."

"She's married to the Don. I have to follow the rules," I murmur. Even if I don't know all the rules, I know not to piss Nikolay off.

"Okay, I'm meeting you at the Palace tomorrow." Then, she whispers, "You can do this."

"I know." It doesn't mean I'm happy about it.

Everyone lingers another hour. The ride home is quiet. Dmitry knows I'm not happy with him but says nothing. He speaks to Milan instead.

I'm emotionally drained when we arrive home. I have so many thoughts percolating in my head that I pray I'll fall asleep.

"Did you enjoy tonight?" Dmitry asks as he changes into loungewear.

"Very nice." I placate him. The food was excellent. "The ambiance was nice. Your family is on guard."

"Give them time. My mother is depressed. She lost the love of her life. They were together for over thirty years. It takes time to get over that. She'll adjust. Give my brothers the benefit of the doubt. I'm sure they will come around, too. We're not trusting. It comes with the territory."

As much as I want to believe him, I'm not sure it's in my best interest to do so.

"I'm tired. I need to sleep." I feign a yawn.

He kisses my lips. I want to hate him. Knowing I keep my suspicions to myself and it becomes more challenging when he slides his hand down my arm. He raises my hand and kisses the ring he gave me.

My breath catches in my throat. I will try to resist him.

"Goodnight," he murmurs against my hand. His warm breath stirs a familiar longing in me.

He slips out of the room. Exhausted, I fall asleep.

I have mixed dreams. I'm in danger. I'm running with a baby in my arms. I have to save my baby. I dart about, looking for someone to help.

I bolt upright. My eyes fly open. I'm awake and sitting in bed. I'm sweating. The room is dark and quiet. I remember where I am and tell myself I'm fine.

I search the bed for Dmitry, only to discover he never returned. I pick up my phone. It's two in the morning.

Will my nightmares return? Why was I running? Is it predicting my future, or is it my worst fears manifesting?

I fluff my pillow and lay my head on it. Pulling the covers tight, I know I need to feel protected. I need Dmitry. After last night, I decided I would become self-sufficient no matter what the circumstances are. The sooner I do, the better off I'll be.

* * *

"Aunt Emma," I exclaim as I dress at the palace. My aunt is a tall woman with gray hair. She is in her late sixties and beams at me, giving me a hug as soon as I enter the little room meant for the bride-to-be.

"How are you? I've missed you. I'm so glad you came." I hug her tightly before stepping back to take another view of her. She's wearing a light blue chiffon dress and matching shoes.

"I never dreamed you'd be marrying so young. I suppose once you moved to New York, it was only a matter of time." She laments that

I've grown up. "You're so pretty. Your mother would have loved to be here today."

"I know." I frown.

She takes me in. I'm wearing a Chanel suit with matching shoes. My hair is in an updo, courtesy of a glam squad that arrived at our home before sunrise. What is it with these early mornings? All I want to do is sleep and forget my suspicion that my husband is using me to get ahead in the bratva. Only I can't figure out why, exactly.

"She would be so proud of you, Isabella. You were the light of her life. I'm so happy to have met you both. How is Dmitry, and what happened in New York that you couldn't contact me?"

"I think it's a mistaken identity thing." I lie. "I'm sorry if I worried you. I'm sure everything will pass in time." I make light of my situation and hope I don't go to hell for lying, but I don't want her to worry. "I'm so happy you made it. It's all Dmitry's family here. Alena is here too. Did you see here?"

Alena morphs to my side. We hug.

"Alena, I love you so much," I whisper in her ear.

"I love you too. You look incredible."

"Do you remember my aunt?"

"Yes." She turns to Aunt Emma and hugs her. We took a few road trips to see her over the past few years. The three of us could watch our favorite movies together and make homemade pizzas for dinner.

"So, Auntie, do you remember my mother saying anything about who my father might have been?"

"Your mother was very guarded about her past. Have you learned something?"

I shrug. "I don't know if I'll ever find out. But Mom most likely changed her name. I have a feeling she was in trouble."

"She never liked answering questions. It was as if her past didn't exist. She was very protective of you."

"Did you know James Murphy? I remember they dated for some time." I'm being coy to see if she'll give me some tidbit of information.

"He was a nice man. I liked him. But I suspected he had things to hide as well. He had plenty of cash for a man his age."

"What do you mean?"

"He loved to spoil your mother. Which reminds me." She walks to a chair in the room and retrieves her purse. She pulls out a long rectangular box and hands it to me. "This is for you. They were your mother's. I'm sure you remember her wearing this on fancy date nights."

I open the box, and inside are Mom's pearl necklace and pendant earrings.

"Wow, I forgot about these."

"Well, you can't wear them every day. However, you wore them to prom."

I did. I remember going with a girlfriend from high school. I think I had anger over being alone in the world and held everyone at arm's length except Emma. I loved her with all my heart for taking care of me. She's sweet and rarely lifted her voice at me. She is the picture of patience. She never gets overly excited.

I take the pearls and look up at her.

"I'll put them on after you get into your dress."

"Thank you." I hand back the pearls and the box to her for safe-keeping.

"Well, it's time to get you in your dress," Alena interrupts.

"There she is," an excited voice greets me as a door opens, and Anya breezes in. She's in light blue as well and beaming. She's wearing a stunning necklace of sapphires around her exquisite neck. "I hope I'm not imposing, but I wanted to welcome you to the family and make sure you have everything you need."

"Thank you, Anya. The dress?" I glance around the old room with ornate gold fixtures, and an incredible chandelier hangs over our heads. I can't imagine how much it cost to rent this venue, but I know it's probably a fairy tale come true for women in England. It's as if we're royalty because we're standing here.

"It's behind the screen for you to change behind."

I nod and walk to the other side of the room. Alena is on my heels and follows me behind the screen. I begin to undress, and she hangs my outfit on hangers and onto the roller rack.

In the background, I hear Anya chatting with my aunt.

I step into the gown, and emotions course through me. Family and friends and men who want me dead are here. What a combination. I hope that after today it will all be over, and I won't have to look over my shoulder everywhere I go.

Alena zips my dress, and I turn around to see my reflection in the oval shape of a full-length mirror that sits on legs resembling the paws of a lion.

"You look amazing," Alena murmurs. "Dmitry will be out of his mind when he sees you."

"You think so?"

"I know so." She beams.

"Let's get your necklace." She grabs my hand, and we walk to the women in the room.

"It's an amazing dress." Aunt Emma claps her hands. "It suits you perfectly."

I'm sure she's wondering how we afforded this, but given the location of the wedding, I'm sure she understands I'm marrying a wealthy man.

She slips the necklace around my neck and fastens it.

A photographer approaches and poses us, snaps a picture, then continues to bark.

"Are you happy?" my aunt asks.

"Yes." The word leaves my lips before I realize I have spoken.

Am I happy? I was until I felt rejected by Dmitry's family. I have no clue where we'll be living after the wedding. I wonder if we'll stay in London. The house is too expensive for a second home, in my opinion. We have staff. God, I never dreamed I'd be getting married in a palace in my wildest dreams. Now if the secrets of my mother's past are brought to light, I'd be content.

Alena must have left my side because she slips a bouquet of white roses and lilacs into my hand. "Your bouquet."

"Did you pick these?" My eyes question her as I lift the bouquet to my nose and enjoy the scent of freshly-cut flowers.

The photographer has us pose together, *click, click.*

"No, Dmitry told Anya to get them. The chapel is beautiful. The banquet hall is stunning. The wedding planner is something else."

"I know. I'm sure Dmitry paid plenty for this."

"I'm sure he loves you. You should talk to him," she says in a low voice.

"You have a point. I don't know who to trust."

"It's time," Anya announces. "Follow me." Her heels click on the marble floors. Alena is beside me with a bouquet in her hand, and Aunt Emma has one as well. She's giving me away.

The photographer snaps away, and I flinch with the light.

We walk from our wing across pavers that open to the circular driveway in front of the palace. I'm sure horses and carriages used it back in the day. I'm in a surreal fairy tale reminiscent of a historical romance.

The overly large wooden doors to the chapel loom ahead of me. I grab the bouquet tighter. Everyone is inside the chapel.

Guards open the doors.

Anya makes her way to her seat next to an empty chair. Nikolay and Dmitry stand before the priest. I have no clue what faith I'm being married into. The chapel is filled with strangers. Trepidation fills my body. Are the terrible men here? What are they going to do? I rub my thumb over my engagement ring, making sure it's on my finger in case I'm snatched.

This should be a happy day. I wonder what my mother would have said to me today. I touch the pearls around my neck and tell myself she's here with me in spirit.

I stand in front of a full-length mirror, Alena and Anya at my sides.

"You look beautiful," Alena says. "Are you ready?"

I know my duty to the family, and at this moment, I relate to the

Royal family. I might not like the sacrifice I'm making, but it has to be made.

"I'm sure you miss your mom today, of all days. She loved you." Aunt Emma leans closer and whispers, "She'd want you to be safe."

Anya kisses my cheek. "You're all set. I'm sitting up front if you need anything."

"Thank you."

I watch Alena walk down the aisle. I hold my head high, everyone stands, but I keep my eyes on the altar. Dmitry eyes are vibrant as he takes me in. I know what he's thinking. I wonder what he has planned for our first night as husband and wife.

Music plays, and everyone stands. Aunt Emma slips her hand through my arm and escorts me down the aisle. She releases me to Dmitry, who takes my hand. Alena is to my left.

We stand facing each other and repeat our vows. It's a blur to me. A ring slips on my finger. My hand tingles from his touch. I hold his hand. It's warm and has shown me the most magnificent affection, but I can't shake the fact that he might have been acting this entire time. I slide the ring on his finger. We kiss, and I fake it for the crowd. I have a role to play.

Maybe today I'll break free from the past. We leave the chapel and walk into the reception area. Drinks are being served as silver trays by the palace's staff circulating like clouds on a summer day. I was told the help is full-time employees, but I noticed the waiter from Zima, Ivan. I wonder if he's here as part of Dmitry's team. It would be wise to have bratva men working undercover today.

People are rushing past us, shaking my hand and Dmitry's. I see the table for the bride and groom at the other end of the large hall filled with humungous windows.

Kirill appears. An older woman is with him.

"Dmitry, Izzy, I'd like you to meet Don Sidovo's wife, Llea."

"How nice to meet you," he replies. I take her hand, and it's her eyes that startle me. They don't match the fake smile on her face. Today is a banquet of who's who. The elusive Don must be at our wedding. Mm. I have no clue what he looks like.

Alena is to my right. I lean over, asking, "Where is the elusive Don?"

"Over there." She flicks her head toward the doorway we walked in through.

"Izzy, congratulations on your wedding day. I wish you all the happiness," Llea murmurs.

"Thank you," I reply.

I observe the women standing in front of me. She has the resting bitch face, and I don't believe the sincerity of her words. I casually look peripherally to observe her tall husband, who has left my side and is speaking to Nikolay.

"Excuse me," I murmur as I move across the room. Alena follows. "There is something about that woman. She asked too many questions about you on the plane."

"Really?" I stop, and Alena takes an extra step before she realizes I've paused. My eyes are on a tall figure. "Who is that?"

"That's Don Sidovo."

I don't know what was going through my head. I approach the man standing in a dark charcoal suit and touch his arm to get his attention.

Ivan pulls Nikolay aside.

Don Sidovo turns. Our eyes meet.

It's as if I'm staring into my own reflection. Goosebumps cover my body like a lotion. I open my mouth, but no words come out. The shape of our eyes and the color is identical. It can't be.

"You look just like…" he says, disbelief in his eyes.

"My mother?" I finish for him.

"Yes."

Tears well in my eyes. I gulp a breath as I throw my arms around his neck and close my eyes. My dad is alive! I put my cheek on his.

He is tall and robust. A man of stature and power. His hair is parted on the left, and areas of gray are peeking through his dark, thick hair. His arms wrap around me.

"Mariana Moretti," is the name whispered from his lips. "I thought she was killed. Where is she?"

I pull back from our hug. My eyes are misty, and the rest of the pictures will be ruined if I cry.

"Mariana? The daughter of Santino Moretti?" I ask.

"Yes." My heart breaks for a man still in love with my mother after all these years.

She must have changed her name to Maria. I'm trying to put together the pieces. She was killed in a car accident in New York City when I was very young."

His face falls. The shock and disbelief on his face is indescribable. "How can that be? She was so full of life. Maria died shortly after her father found out about us. I thought it was too coincidental not to be orchestrated. What happened?"

"I don't know. She told me my father was dead. I had no idea."

"How old are you?"

"Twenty-three," I reply as I pull my arms from his neck. I smooth my dress but never take my eyes off his. In my life, people disappear in a blink. "You're my father."

"You are my daughter." His voice is rings of pride and disbelief. "I never knew."

"What happened?" I want to know the details. How can this be?

"Walk with me," he says as we leave the event to go outside. He glances over his shoulder as if he's looking for someone. Is he worried? Why are we talking out here? He's a don. Why would he care who sees us?

The sun is brighter than I've ever seen it as my father slips his hand through my arm. The cloud over my life has been lifted. We pass the large water fountain and stop to talk, standing on the pavers.

"What happened?" I ask, anxious for details.

"She was so young, we were in love, but our families hated each other. She would sneak out of work at a coffee shop. When her father found out…." He closes his eyes briefly as if he's in pain. "I can only imagine. He's a bitter and mean man. I couldn't help her. His men would have killed me. My father sent me to Russia, afraid there would be a hit on me. I heard she was killed in a car accident."

"It must have been faked the first time."

He grabs my hand. It's as if he lost my mother a second time. "She was alive after the funeral her father held." His voice trails off. "That son-of-a-bitch. I'll kill him." His face contorts into anger. He grabs my hand, and his eyes soften. "I'm so sorry. I never knew. I wish I had. But Santino needs to pay for what he did to me. He took something from me that can't be replaced."

"We have to make up for lost time," I say. "Is starting a war worth it? I can't lose you again."

"We've been gone too long. Others will notice," he says, glancing nervously at the building. Who is he looking for?

"Someone is after me. In your organization and as well as the Irish," I blurt out.

"I heard rumors. I didn't know. I'm having people in my organization watched. You are the princess to unite the Italians and the Russians. The Irish won't like that, so if they get to you first..."

"They will form the alliance between you or the Italians to the detriment of the other." I finish his sentence. Judging by his anger, I'd say my bet is he will side with the Irish and take out the Italians as retribution.

"But why is someone in your organization looking for me?" I give him a quizzical glance, but we're interrupted by Ivan, who wants us to take pictures.

Ivan yells for us to gather by the fountain for a group shot. I search for Dmitry and see him walking toward me. I smile. I can't wait to tell him the news.

"It never stops, does it?" my father says.

"There are never enough pictures on an occasion like this." I smile as I glance at my father again.

I can't get enough of him. He's a stranger, but inside, it's as if I've known him forever. He takes my hand, giving it an affectionate squeeze. I pick up the corner of my dress to make it easier to walk over the uneven pavers, and when we are about to reach the water-fall, I hear a loud boom, and I'm thrown through the air. My ears are ringing.

My body hits the hard pavers. I cough. Someone is lying on top of me. I cough again. My body hurts. I'm covered in rocks and bricks.

I hear voices and sirens. Darkness takes over, but I want to stay awake. I fight, coming through as someone pulls me to them.

Dmitry.

What happened? My head hurts. I've ruined my dress. Rubble falls off me. Amid the smell of smoke, I make out a hint of musk and mint. I'm safe. My head is too tired to hold. I can't speak. I hear a man's angry shout, "Clear the way."

I slip into the darkness. I'm tired. So tired.

CHAPTE 32

DMITRY

𝓔rik alerted me to Izzy leaving the building with a man, and I assumed she was being kidnapped. I ran to the palace entrance and saw Ivan standing in the breezeway, a panicked expression on his face.

She mentioned he was here. What the fuck is going on?

I glanced at the fountain and observed a tall, distinguished man with my wife before the deafening sound of a bomb filled the air. I flinched, then looked to the fountain as bricks and mortar fly through the air. It's as if it's a highlight reel playing in slow motion. Alexsei and my wife are on the ground. He just shook my hand, and when our eyes met, I noticed his resemblance to my wife. I was pulled away for a second before all hell broke loose.

I yell for help as I run. It feels like I'm running in cement. She can't die. It can't be. We were so careful. I reach for her and discover Alexsei. He must have thrown his body over hers to protect her— my adrenaline surges. I pull him off her and lay him on his back. Nikolay is beside me and helps me dig at the rubble. My hands are bleeding when we reach her. I lift her into my arms.

"Let me help," Nikolay says as sirens blare in the distance.

"No, she'll be fine. Help her father," I shout as I carry her to the area where an ambulance is arriving. "Have the men round up Ivan from Zima and the don's wife."

My wife is still. I want to hear her voice. The medic wants to take her, but I refuse and put her on the gurney. I hold her lifeless hand. The men in uniforms want me to move away from her. I refuse.

My mother and Roman arrive. Roman pulls me away. I fight him.

"They need to do their job," he says. I know it's a reasonable statement, but she's mine to protect, and I failed her.

My heart is being carved out of my chest as I wait. It was a stupid fight last night. I was a bastard, arguing over something that was nothing, and I should have apologized to her. It's not in my nature to say I'm sorry for anything. We're the leaders of men. We take what we want and damn the consequences. I'm used to making problems disappear.

"Dmitry, we'll ride to the hospital with you," my mother says with concern.

"We've given her an IV, but we're taking her to the hospital," the paramedic says to me.

"I'm behind you," I reply without considering how I'm getting there.

Police are on the scene. Crime scene tape is being placed around the area.

"How is Alexsei?" I ask Roman. I'm responsible for this. It looks like we flushed out the villains, but at what cost?

"He's in the other vehicle. I assume he'll have more wounds as his suit jacket is ripped to hell. We'll check on him, too. Milan has the car waiting over here." He puts an arm around my shoulder and leads me to a vehicle.

I can't comprehend what went down. Ivan working at the wedding is suspicious. We had a traitor in our midst, and I never knew it. I don't miss details like this.

"She'll be okay. We'll make sure she has the best care," Mom says.

"You weren't even nice to her last night," I reply, angered that my wife's fate is unknown and my family disappointed me at the rehearsal dinner.

"I wasn't. I'm sorry. I was jealous. She's gorgeous and so in love with you. It made me resentful that your father isn't here to enjoy these beautiful moments with me. His death was pointless. I'm not proud of how I behaved. I'll make it up to you."

I turn to Nikolay. "You were exchanging looks with Mom. What was that about?" I won't tolerate my family treating Izzy like an outsider.

"I wanted Mom to be nice and give Izzy the family she never had. We're brothers. I'm not letting anything short of a betrayal come between us. I oversee everything, keeping men in line and making money. But my most important job is to keep the family together. I know you love her, Dmitry. I'd never come between you and your wife." He claps me on the back.

Did Izzy overreact? I saw the looks, and I'm sure Mom wasn't herself. She's not been the warm, nurturing mother she was before Dad died.

I put my elbows on my knees and sink my hands into them. Izzy and the baby have to make it. I can't think of any other outcome. I can't picture a future without her in it.

We arrive at the hospital. Nikolay jumps out of the vehicle with me. We wait in the emergency room. I pace.

"How long will this take?" I ask the nurse.

"As long as it takes. She's getting the best care. Please. Sit. It might be a while."

Nikolay hands me a coffee as if I need more stimulation. My heart is racing. My mind is reeling. Mom and Milan enter the waiting room.

"Any word yet?" Mom asks. Her face is pale, and I notice she's lost weight.

She's under duress, and now there is more. She was vigilant when my leg was injured. She sat with me every day that I remained in the hospital. I understand how this would give her flashbacks.

I go to my mom and hug her. "It will be okay. It has to be."

She pats my hand on her thin shoulder. "I'm sure she'll make it."

I wonder about the baby. It's so early. I'm relieved we didn't tell anyone, as it's unclear how much stress my mother can endure.

Roman, Alena, and Anya rush into the emergency room.

"Any news?" Roman asks anxiously.

"No," Nikolay replies in his baritone voice.

"Okay." Alena wrings her hands and begins to pace.

"We've rounded up Ivan. And we have men on Alexsei's wife. The bobbies are questioning her, but you know she'll cover her tracks," Roman says.

"She will be handled. Don't let her out of our enforcer's sight," I snarl. "Also, we need to have the Sidovo bratva haul in Tito. I'm sure he'll be averse to pain. I want to know what he knows."

"I'll make sure it's done," Nikolay replies as he walks outside to use his phone.

"He'll make sure justice is delivered," Roman says. "If I know him, he'll be happy to deliver the punishment."

"How did you know Alexsei was her father?" Alena asks.

"It all clicked when I saw him. I thought the Moretti girl's death was too convenient. But how did Maria die in an actual car accident years later? I hope we find out. I profiled Alexsei's wife. I ran her past history and figured she was an opportunist. Her son wouldn't inherit her husband's empire. She was desperate to make him the don, is what I think. Greed is usually the beginning of the end for those in crime. She wants to steal the throne from her husband."

"I can see that. She's flashy, bitchy, and a pathological liar. I flew with her, and she annoyed me. I felt like I knew Alexsei. I should have put it together." Alena stops pacing. "I should have warned her," she announces as our eyes meet.

"You had no way of knowing, Alena."

I don't need her blaming herself. She's Izzy's best friend and someone she trusts. I know how rare that is, as I only trust those who have proven trustworthy. It appears Izzy, and I are more alike than I thought a few hours ago.

"It's my job to protect her," I murmur and kick myself again for not being by her side when the bomb went off.

I hear the doors behind us swish. I turn and find a doctor with a white coat entering the waiting room. I rush to meet him.

Izzy is going to be okay. She has a concussion and is being moved upstairs to a private room.

"The baby is fine." He smiles.

I nod, filled with relief. I feel everyone's eyes on me. Nikolay's eyes meet mine, his eyebrows raised. Mom's eyes are tearing, and she brushes them away with her finger. Alena raises a hand to cover her mouth as she gasps in a sigh of relief.

"What?" I ask defensively. "We didn't want to say anything as it was too early." I gesture with my hands to demonstrate it was out of my control. "The doctor ruined the surprise," I add.

Nikolay and Roman chuckle in relief and discuss who will be the favorite uncle. I look to Mom. "Don't get sentimental on me," I say, but it's too late. Mom dabs at her eyes again, but her face quickly becomes a waterfall. She searches through her purse for a hand-kerchief.

I stalk off to find my wife.

* * *

When I find the room on the third floor, staff members are lifting my wife onto the hospital bed.

"She should come through any minute," the attendant states.

"Thank you."

I rush to Izzy's side. She's wearing a hospital gown, and her arm is hooked to intravenous fluids. She has sticky tabs on her chest, and the leads go to a heart monitor.

I grab her hand and sit by the bed. I sink my head into the blankets.

"I'm so sorry I argued with you. I'm sorry I didn't figure this out early. I should have been by your side when the bomb went off."

"It's okay. I was with my dad."

I jerk my head up, overjoyed. Izzy's face is pale. Her voice is weak.

Her lips look dry. But I'm elated she's awake and remembers what happened.

"What?" I ask.

"Dad threw his arms around me. He protected me."

"What did he say?" I stand and lean over the bed so I can hear her.

"He never knew I existed. I think his affair with my much younger mother and the fact her lover was Russian, who was off-limits, riled the Italians. It set into motion a deep-seated hatred by my family. Is he going to be okay? Please tell me he's going to be okay…" her voice trails as her lips quiver.

I realize how fragile she is and what a tragedy it would be for her to lose her father minutes after finding him.

"I'll call Nikolay. I'm sure he's checking on him."

She nods and drifts back to sleep. I hold my breath, afraid she might be in distress, and call the nurse. A woman in a white uniform comes to the room. Without a word, she checks her vitals and tells me she's sleeping, and she'll need a lot of it to recover from all the contusions on her body.

I hear voices in the hallway and the entire family piles in with helium balloons with *Get Well* stamped on them.

CHAPTER 33

IZZY

My eyes flutter open. White walls. I breathe faster.

Dmitry takes my hand. I search his face, and when he smiles, I know I'm safe.

Alena and Natasha murmur as they sit in chairs against the wall in my room.

"My dad?" I'm afraid to ask as the answer might mean I've lost another parent.

"He's banged up, but he's expected to pull through," he replies. "We'll take you to see him later. How do you feel?"

"Not bad, all things considered." I grapple with the bed and raise it so I can sit and see everyone. "How long do I have to stay here?"

"You might get out today."

"Is it safe now?"

"We have everyone rounded up. It appears James figured out whom you belonged to, but he only told a brother in the Irish mafia. However, they wanted to make a deal with the Italians, and…"

"I was the person to make that happen."

"Yes, as Moretti's granddaughter, you would make a suitable arranged marriage, which would have alienated the Russians."

"Wow, but the Russians?"

"Llea, Alexsei's wife, wanted her son to take over. She had a mole inside the Irish clan and ran her own game plan with Tito. He's the money and tech guy for the bratva. He was tracking the laptop I was given, remember? He was spying for her. He spied on everyone. He was happy to give up everything Llea did to find you. We think someone, maybe James, saw you in the city. It was a green light to set things in motion. James is the only one who knew you existed. He knew your name and where you lived. From there, you were trackable.

"I'm not sure if the Russians or the Irish obtained more information from him. We may never know. Llea was bitter as your father always loved your mother. I assume that's why the Moretti's *killed* your mother off years ago. It put to rest the need for anyone to look for her. You were her secret. When she ran away, she had enough money to change her name. She did a good job of disappearing as long as no one looked for her. James was her undoing. Without James, no one would have found you because no one knew you existed."

"That had to be so tough on Mom. No wonder she was lonely. She left behind her siblings and her parents. Maybe her dad mistreated her, too. There could have been pressure inside the home that made her decide to leave." I process this information, and it's surreal.

"What will happen to them? Llea and Tito?"

"Llea, you won't have to worry about it. I'm sure Alexsei's men will handle her. And you were right about Ivan. He placed the bomb, and his phone matched the messages on Llea's burner."

"So my dad was targeted as well. How did he not know?" I look to my husband for answers.

Dmitry is quiet. He shrugs his shoulders. "I don't know, my love. All I know is that you and our baby are healthy. I'm sorry about the argument."

"Thank you." Maybe my beast has another side to him that isn't so beastly after all.

"What day is it?" I ask.

"The day after our wedding, why?"

"I wanted to know how long I was out," I reply. "Is the baby okay?"

"Yes." Dmitry pours water for me and lifts it to my lips.

I sip.

Natasha walks to my bed.

"I'm so sorry you didn't think I liked you at the rehearsal dinner. The fact is, I miss my husband. I wish he were here." She pauses, then takes my hand into hers. "Your wedding reminded me of when I was your age. Welcome to the family. And I can't wait to see this love child."

I quickly glance at Dmitry. "The doctor spilled the beans. They apparently gave you a pregnancy test due to medications or something." He chuckles. I know he's really not all that sorry. But he is beaming with pride.

"Alena, are you okay?" My friend comes to my bed.

"I'm great. You gave us a scare, but the worst is over," she breathes. "Now I can escape house arrest." She smiles, and I wonder how long she will stay in London.

"I hope we'll be able to spend some time together before you head home."

"I'd like that. Your house is large enough for one more," she teases me.

"You saw our house?"

"Well, I saw pictures of it. What about a honeymoon? I never asked you if you were taking one. I mean." Her eyes dart around the walls and to the bed. "This isn't a honeymoon."

"I don't …"

"Yes, I planned a week in Bali. I thought you'd like to see another country."

"Bali? That's incredible."

"Wow, lucky girl," Alena says. She squeezes my hand. "I'm so happy everything worked out."

"Me too."

Natasha and Alena head out for lunch, and Dmitry gets me out of bed. I walk out of my room, and there are bobbies standing guard.

"What's that for?"

"Someone tried to kill you and your father," he whispers. "I'm not sure they'll ever figure it out." We head down the hall to my father's room, which is also guarded.

I'm nervous about seeing my dad. Machines are beeping. He appears to be sleeping. I walk ahead of Dmitry and take my father's hand. Dmitry puts his hand on my shoulder.

"Dad, it's me."

The handsome man in the bed wakes. He blinks a few times.

"Izzy, it's you. It's real."

"Yes. It's me. How are you?"

"Much better now. It wasn't a dream? You're my daughter?" His eyes gain a sparkle at the realization.

"Yes. How are you feeling?"

"I'll be fine. Don't worry about me." He's distinguished with gray hair around his temples. His high cheekbones make him look younger, as I know he's in his early fifties.

"I'm going to worry about you." My eyes are misty. "I was told my father was dead years ago. I can't lose you again."

A chair scrapes as it crosses the floor. Dmitry slides it under me.

"Tell me about it. My wife tried to kill me, and she knew about you. I had someone tracking her devices. I knew she didn't love me, but she's maligned men against me for power. She was after a jewel. I didn't know what it was."

"I'm sorry. We've lost so much time already. I want to get to know you."

He moves his head in disbelief. I'm sure that was a bitter pill to swallow. Betrayal of a spouse is brutal at best. For them, it was fatal. I'm sure we'll never see Llea again.

"You're still the don, and business is going as usual," Dmitry interjects.

"Terrible thing being a don. It takes up the years I have left, and for what? I have two children who are spoiled and live entitled lives of luxury I pay for. I wasn't a good father. I spoiled them and my wife."

"I don't know anything about being spoiled. Mom and I got by. We didn't have luxuries."

"I see you were raised with old-world values. You take pride in paying your way. You have spunk, just like your mother. I admired that about her."

"It wasn't easy for her, but she provided for us." I agree.

"She hated her father. He forbid us to marry. Our families were enemies. When he found out about me, he beat your mother. I found it strange that she was killed in a car accident. I've always had her in my heart." He uses his other hand and places it on his chest. "What was your life like?" he asks. He sits taller in the bed, and his eyes go over my face, committing it to memory. "You're so much like her. You look like her, you know. You have her gentle demeanor, but when you're pushed, you'll push back."

"Maybe. Dmitry is a good provider. And we have a great home for the baby."

"What baby?"

"Ours, it's very early, but his family knows, so you should know too."

"Well, that's incredible. I never thought about being a grandfather, but I like the idea. I'd like for us to get to know each other."

"We will," I reply, wondering why he's talking like this. "We are, aren't we? We've seen each other twice in as many days." I remain positive he'll pull through. He has to.

His chuckles make a hearty sound. "True. However, I'm thinking of something more permanent."

"What are you saying? We can travel between New York and England." I glance at Dmitry. "Can't we?"

"Sure, any time you want to go," he replies.

"I've missed out on your entire life. I don't want to miss out on anything. I want Dmitry to be the new don so that I can retire."

I open my mouth and turn to my husband, raising my hands and silently asking *what do I say to that?*

Dmitry shrugs.

"Dad, I don't understand. You can't bring an outsider into your bratva, can you?"

"I'm the leader. I can do whatever I want."

Mm. I'm stumped.

"I want to get to know you. I can help Dmitry adjust. His reputation precedes him. He's worthy of such a position. I didn't extend an invitation to meet while he was in New York due to the danger around me. But your man has been to war and is savvy with people. That's what you need to be a don. You have to know what makes other people tick."

I'm wondering what my husband has done to gain the favor of my father.

When I listen to Dad's voice, his words come from a place of profound love. I understand why the Moretti's had to kill off my mother's memory with a fake death. My father would have searched for her forever. The Moretti family isn't built on love. It's built on lies and the destruction of others. In fact, the Moretti's didn't come to our wedding, even though they were invited.

"The Moretti's don't protect their own," I murmur.

Now, I no longer wonder why my mother left. She never felt the unconditional love of her parents. No one stood up for her. After she left, everyone moved on with their lives. My grandfather, Santino, wanted this and orchestrated everything to make it impossible for my mother to return to New York City and, more importantly, to keep her away from my father. His plan kept them separated forever.

"He's a vile man. I have the proof I need to go to war, but I can't do that to you. The Moretti's are your blood, too."

"I don't care to see them. I refuse."

"I want you both back in New York City. I'll return as don and put things in order. I'll take Dmitry under my wing so he can take over."

"That's not necessary, Dad."

"I know. It's what I want. I haven't traveled. I haven't enjoyed life. I want to enjoy the time I have left while I can do what I want."

"What about your son?" I ask. I don't want my husband in danger.

"My son is too young. I'll give him something else to run. He's not cut out for our business." He waves his hand through the air as though it's nothing. I've never met his son. His kids didn't attend the wedding. I'm sure their mother made them stay home, knowing what she was going to do with the bomb.

I glance up to find Dmitry speechless.

"Two bratva's merging. We can expand," Dmitry speaks as he paces.

"That's what we need, new blood, new energy." Dad looks at me, "You'll be the Principessa you were destined to be, Isabella."

"I don't need that. I just want you in my life."

"You have that. You might tire of having me around, but I'll never leave you."

A tear slips from my eye. My dad loves me. Damn, these pregnancy hormones. At last, I finally know what happened in my mother's young life. I find closure and peace. She must be looking over me because out of the chaos, I've found my father and a new family with my husband.

Dmitry leaves us to talk. After an hour, a nurse says I must leave as my dad needs rest.

I kiss his cheek and return to my room. I'm discharged from the hospital, and I'm relieved. I want to go home. Erik and Milan shower me with hugs and well wishes. I've survived my first day as a bratva bride, and I have so much to celebrate. Dmitry helps me into the car.

The mansion never looked more inviting than today. I can't wait to take a real shower and get into something less fancy. My wedding dress might not recover from the incident.

"What do we do with that offer?" I ask my husband.

Charlotte brings Dmitry a vodka. The smell of dinner being cooked by our chef makes me hungry. We settle in the downstairs living room. It's as if nothing happened after our wedding, yet our entire life has changed again.

"What do you want?" Dmitry sips his vodka. "I know you want a relationship with your father, and it's tough to do it over the long distance."

"True, but your family is here."

"My family is wherever they need to be. You're my family."

I nod.

"One brother is in Russia and is here. We could be the anchor in New York City."

"Are you comfortable with that?"

"Maybe I can give fashion designing a whirl."

Dmitry settles back in his chair. He lifts the shot of vodka. "Maybe." Then he gives me a brutally wicked smile. It dawns on me that we never consummated our marriage.

"I love you, Isabella." He crosses the room and kneels in front of me. "You are my sun and the moon. I would travel anywhere to make you happy."

"Did you know who my father was?"

"I had no clue, but I didn't like what I saw of his wife. The Moretti's? Yes, I think we all can agree on you being Sicilian. Your father could have been anyone. I didn't want to trust you. It was odd that you never knew more. Trust goes against my rules."

"You and the rules," I mock him. "You didn't trust me?"

"I thought there might be more to your story, but as time passed, I learned I have to trust someone. And with that, I realized I should start with the woman I love."

"Smart man, I agree." I lie back on the couch and observe my husband.

He walks across the room, takes my hand, and kisses it. "I love you more than you know."

"I am beginning to get that," I reply demurely.

Dinner is announced.

"Keep it warm, Charlotte," my husband says as he sweeps me into his arms.

I hope you've enjoyed Brutal Promise. Please leave a review!

Continue reading in Sinful Promise
Or https://geni.us/SinfulPromise1
This is the final interconnected standalone in the series. This is
Roman's love story with a HEA.

King's Promise

Brutal Promise

Sinful Promise

Borrelli Mafia Series

Nanny for the Bodyguard (prequel at my shop)

Mafia King: Matteo

Vengeance and Vows

Scandalous Vows

Dangerous Vows

The Black Card Society

The Billionaire's Hookup (novella)

The Dark Billionaire

Mafia Reader/fan group

https://www.facebook.com/groups/478242870016630/?ref+share

Maine Megaladons Football Series

Faking it with the Football Star

The Player's Obsession

Scoring with the Coach's Daughter

Maine Maulers Series Hockey Series

Maine Maulers Hockey Series

Rookie in Love (now in audio)

Jagged Ice

Hotter than Puck

Benched by the Nanny

Puck in the Oven

Pucking the Team Captain

Pucking with the Goalie

Pucked Over by Cupid

Zoe Beth Geller's Hockey Pond

Facebook fan group

https://www.faceboook.com/groups/1414368522250349/?ref=share

Sin Bin Hockey Series (College Series)

Tyler: Hooked (Free prequel to the series)

The Sin Bin Hockey Series

Jackson: Against the Boards

Alan: Between the Pipes

Erik: Fire and Ice

Blayze: Slap Shot

Paavo: The Defender

Spencer: Penalty Box

Isak: Coach

Kaden: Game Time

Liam: The Enforcer

Jake: Roughing

The Sin Bin Hockey Series Box Sets

The Sin Bin Hockey Series Box Set Books 1-4

The Sin Bin Hockey Series Box Set Books 5-7

The Sin Bin Hockey Series Box Set Books 8-10

Zoe Beth Geller's Hockey Pond Reader/Fan Group

ABOUT THE AUTHOR

Zoe Beth Geller, a captivator of hearts and a master of suspense, crafting mafia romances filled with unexpected plot twists and thrilling surprises. Her literary journey doesn't stop there; she also delves into the vibrant world of sports, creating enthralling hockey and football romances that never fail to score a touchdown or shoot a hat trick with her readers. A proud resident of Southwest Florida, Zoe cherishes the sun-kissed life alongside her loving family. When she isn't weaving romantic tales, Zoe revels in family get-togethers, enjoying the playful company of her two cherished labs, and indulging in a well-brewed espresso. Each story she writes is a passport to adventure.

ZBG Dark Mafia Romances
https://www.facebook.com/groups/478242870016630/?ref+share

SIGN UP FOR MY NEWSLETTER!
https://geni.us/MafiaNewslettersignup

Follow me on TT at zoebethgellerauthor10

shopzoebethgeller.com